Fiona's Guardians

Dan Klefstad

Burton Mayers Books

~ CONTENTS ~

Part 4: Una Striga Vitae

Bonus Content

ACKNOWLEDGMENTS

Thanks to all the readers who encouraged me to write a sequel to Fiona's Guardians. I will have good news soon! Special thanks to Susan for her love and patience

A MESSAGE FROM FIONA

Hello mortal. I'm touched by your interest in those who work for me and those who used to. A handful truly deserve to be remembered in a book that never goes out of print. Their loyalty and talent are the reason I've existed for two and a half centuries. A few, however, earned the painful and premature deaths detailed in these pages. For me, loyalty comes first and must be constant. That's not to say a partnership with me can't end in mutual agreement. It just never happened before. Still, I may allow my current guardian to retire. After serving longer than any other, he might well live his remaining years in a manner of his choosing. This would create an opportunity for another to earn his substantial salary and benefits. But a warning is in order: The work is as relentless and unsparing as my hunger, and everyone I employed has murdered at least once on my behalf. Not that this is the preferred option. There are other, less extreme ways to obtain blood for me, and Daniel built a robust network that can be handed off to a successor. He's in the car now, looking at his watch, wondering when we can go home to his decanter of scotch. From what I see, nothing in your cabinet would satisfy him so, rest assured, I won't leave with any of your bottles.

I see you've been reading job postings. Do not ask if I offer a retirement plan. In truth, I've never understood the concept. Each evening I awake knowing I'm the chief executive for extending my life, so ceasing work would amount to suicide. But this is what Daniel wants, and I owe him for that time he saved me from dying. It's in the book.

My favorite chapters feature Agripina, the one who created me. Driven by hunger, she brought me to the edge of death but changed her mind when I started turning blue. She claimed she saw something worth preserving: a simple, unselfish nature that disappeared when she opened a vein for me. Since that moment, the only feeling I've known, besides adoration for her, is a craving that never ceases. That is, until the instant I tasted regret – the perpetual pain of guilt -- at not being with her when our enemies reappeared. They're in here, too. And so is my revenge.

Go ahead, indulge your curiosity. When you finish reading, I'll visit again and make myself visible. You'll find me sitting in that chair over there, and we can talk about your future.

Until then,
F.

~ PART ONE ~
A HUMAN GUARDIAN SPEAKS

TWO MONKS WALK INTO A DINER

A man with a shaved head makes the sign of the cross over his breakfast. "Bless this food, Heavenly Father, to give us strength. Bless our waitress who shares the name of the Virgin Mary. May she receive the tips she deserves to afford the operation she needs. And bless this coffee so we have the energy and focus to exterminate your enemies. Amen." Brother Raymond is just about to eat when his dining companion interrupts:

"Vivat Mors Strigae." This slightly older man sits opposite reading a tablet. He looks up. "That's our new 'amen.'"

The junior monk considers this. "It sounds rather awkward to my ear, Father Abbot. 'Vivat' meaning 'long live' followed by 'Mors' meaning 'death.'"

The abbot shrugs. "It's too late to change the name of our order. And there's no changing Latin."

"Indeed." Brother Raymond raises his eyebrows. "How are the crosswords today?"

"I'm looking at job postings."

"You've been our abbot for six months. Already weary?"

"I'm doing research. You wouldn't believe how many odd ones are out there." The abbot scrolls down. "Brother Raymond, while I'm doing this, would you look for wooden bullets?"

"Sorry?"

"Bullets. Made of wood. Whoever's got them, I want them."

Raymond considers the idea. "It's an intriguing variation."

"I thought so."

"There is some history to this." Raymond pauses to swallow coffee. "The Germans and Japanese practiced with wooden slugs toward the end of World War Two. But they used smaller charges to prevent the bullets from disintegrating. I'm afraid less power would mean reduced speed and penetration."

"Some hardwoods will stand up to a full charge. From Africa,

Australia..." The abbot squints at the nearby window. "Would you ask Mary to lower the shade?" While Raymond waves and points to the window, the abbot scrolls down again. "How many recruits do we have?"

Raymond grins. "One hundred as of Friday."

"A fifth of what we need." The abbot shakes his head. "We're paying for wages, office space, and equipment every day, and yet..." He pauses as Mary pulls the shade down to the sill. When she leaves, he whispers: "No combat. The cardinal wants to see progress."

"Don't blame me." Raymond aims his fork at the abbot. "You haven't provided arms for training."

"I'm not giving arms to men we haven't indoctrinated." The abbot glares, the fork retreats, and his finger points back. "You fill the ranks as instructed, then I'll provide the weapons." He returns to his tablet. "Besides, armed or not, I won't send a mere hundred recruits against ten strigae. I might as well order them to walk off a cliff."

"I thought we confirmed four."

"Meet Number Five." The abbot taps the screen and turns it toward Raymond. It shows a blue image of a man's face, fine-featured but hard

-- like a sadist with a title. "28 degrees, like the rest of them." He lets it fall into Raymond's hand. "We spotted him last night in Chicago."

Raymond enlarges the image. "Any evidence they're reproducing?"

"Not   yet."

"What about bodies?"

The abbot spears a sausage link. "None that would draw our attention." He bites off half and chews loudly.

Raymond slowly nods. "That bolsters your theory about humans supplying them, so they don't have to kill."

"And attract attention." The abbot wipes his mouth with a napkin. "I'll check with hospitals and blood banks to see if they're missing any bags. Get me 400 more by next week."

"Recruits? How do you propose I do that?" Raymond frowns as he returns the tablet.

"Go on Facebook and Twitter. Say righteous men need help fighting evil."

"We'll get nerds and wackos."

"People become nerds and wackos when they have nothing to believe in. You and I will inspire them." The abbot finishes his coffee. "Our quarry is also hiring, just so you know. I emailed one of their ads to you." He slides out of the booth. "Write like them and you might get somewhere."

After the abbot leaves, Raymond picks up his phone:

Wanted: a strong will and flexible morals. Unusually high compensation for following directions, never asking questions, but also improvising when necessary to complete assigned tasks. No vacations, but lodging and meals provided, plus healthcare. Loyalty and secrecy a must. Successful candidate most likely to be an orphan who dislikes speaking to strangers.

DEAR APPLICANT

Congratulations. Out of hundreds of candidates, you stood out for your "unwavering persistence to get the job done" and "antipathy toward vacations and family obligations." Well played. No doubt you will deserve the eight-figure salary and opulent benefits that come with this job. But I must warn you: The more you read, the more my employer will consider you a threat if you decline our offer. If you have no intentions of taking the job, delete this message now before reading further.

-
-
-
-
-
-
-

This is your final warning: Turn back if you'd rather not devote every day of your prime years to an employer who demands utter secrecy and loyalty. Take a moment to reflect on which is more important: a career that allows for family and vacations or a mogul's retirement. The job does occasionally allow time for recreation. Right now, I'm enjoying a 1948 Graham's port – a gift from my employer and one of the last such bottles in the world. I also have enough money to retire on my own Greek island. I hope you land in a similar place when your time comes. To get there, though, you'll have to do more than drag your soul through the mud. Your hands will forever bear the stains of someone else's suffering, though I'm pretty sure no one else will notice.

If you've read to this point, the job is yours. So, Dear Trainee, it's time to meet the boss who will give final approval. Wear a suit and tie next Thursday just before midnight. Be courteous but reserved, and always assume your thoughts are on display because they will be. With this in mind, do not even contemplate the words "That's impossible" or "That goes against my beliefs." Should these or similar phrases emerge, everything will end. Abruptly.

I'd also advise you not to stare at her eyes, mouth, or any part of her body. If all goes well, I'll train you for two weeks. If you're wondering whether there's a title for our profession, it's "guardian" or "caretaker."

Another important word you need to be aware of, but never say, is the Latin noun for our employer and her associates: striga. I'm saying it here, once, for instructional purposes. Uttering this could expose your employer to those familiar with ancient languages. Moreover, it's an insult equal to the worst human slurs. Say it and expect a cruel death.

There is one more word you must never give voice to, one that will become obvious as I fill in more details about the job, the one you'll protect, and me.

My first employer – not even a century old – was actually my neighbor. It's 1986, my sophomore year at college. I haven't met him yet but see his "roommate" every night returning with a plastic cooler. Around 1:00 a.m., he walks by as I fold laundry downstairs. He never speaks but nods politely. Then one night, covered in blood, he asks when I'll finish using the last available washer. "Someone tried to rob me, but I fought him off. The blood is his," he smiles. "I'm Ramon."

Each night after, Ramon says, "Hi" as he walks by. Until the night before my final exams. As usual, I study downstairs while doing my girlfriend's laundry; she works the night shift at the hospital. But I hate studying so I welcome the distraction when, an hour before dawn, a stranger enters the room. Wearing a tight vest and tie, he gazes at the period stain on one of Sarah's panties. Then he hands me a cream-colored envelope that feels old. Inside is $300 plus a note and key. "Ramon's dead. I need you to contact his family. Last name Valenzuela."

I look up. "Why don't you do it?"

He looks out the window. "If you don't know

the difference between Camus and Sartre by now, you never will. Am I right?"

"That depends. Are you a philosopher or dressed like one for Halloween?"

He looks like he's about to rip my head off. Then he takes a deep breath and walks out. "You're low on iron. Buy some red meat."

I open the note:

Daniel,

Tell the funeral home to pick up Ramon tomorrow. You, and only you, will let them in. After they leave, lock the door behind you. I'll collect the key tomorrow night. For this, I'll pay an additional five hundred. I might even offer full-time work so you can stop pretending to be a student.

Søren Fillenius.

~

The apartment is filled with dark furniture and portraits of nobles. I pull back heavy curtains and tie them to boar's tusks jutting from the wall. The books on the shelf are leather-bound with gold titles. Most are about the onetime rulers of Carpathian Mountain kingdoms.

A knock on the door. I realize I don't know which room is Ramon's, but then I see one of the bedrooms has a lock that bolts from the inside. The opposite door opens easily, and I show the men in. Ramon lies on the bed, arms folded. The nightstand has black-and-white photos of his family.

~

"Next time, make sure you draw the curtains when you leave." Søren hands me the promised money.

"Does that mean I'm hired?"

"Once you take this job, there's no quitting."

"What is the job?"

"You clean the house, buy blood for me, and get two thousand dollars a month."

"Are you a vam…"

"Don't." A long fingernail stops just short of my face. "That word is forbidden."

I wait for the curved claw to withdraw. "Where do I buy this blood?"

"Hospitals mainly. Some are at least an hour away, so you'll take my car. There's a pick-up schedule on the refrigerator." Søren waves a bejeweled hand toward Ramon's room. "You'll sleep there."

"I sleep with my girlfriend."

"Sarah's fucking a gynecologist." He chuckles. "Believe me, you can't compete."

"How do you know?"

He frowns at me. I shift my weight to the other foot. "Standard week?"

"Pardon?"

"What days do I have off?"

"Ha!" He leans closer. "I'll tell you when I get a day off."

~

Søren owns an '81 Honda Accord which, at 250,000 miles, is nearing its end. While good on gas, it's far less glamorous than James Mason's '63 Cadillac in *Salem's Lot*. For me, Mason is the archetypal caretaker with his bowler hat, silver tipped cane, and three-piece suit. He and his...employer...Kurt Barlow, buy and sell antiques, moving their shop to whatever hunting ground seems most promising:

Barlow & Straker Fine Antiques – Opening Soon

It gives me chills every time I remember it. Not that I completely enjoyed the movie because Straker dies while defending Barlow's lair. Sorry for the spoiler. In fact, every guardian portrayed in similar films dies violently. I think about each of them as I drive east to Chicago or north to Rockford. Søren never buys locally.

"Where's Clarence?" I ask a stranger at Northwestern Memorial.

"Family emergency. I'm filling in."

His lab coat has no ID. Clarence is supposed to page me when problems occur. "Who are you?"

"He said you'd be upset." The stranger takes a case from the refrigerator and opens it. "Ten bags of O negative. That'll be 15 hundred."

10

"No," I straighten. "I said ten bags of A positive for one thousand."

"Fuck." He looks at the bags. "She gets O negative."

"Who?"

"Never mind. Come back tomorrow."

FIONA

"There's been a mix-up," I announce as I enter the apartment.

"I know," a woman replies. As the door opens, I see her relaxing while Søren empties his decanter into her glass.

Søren tilts it higher to get the last drops. "You'll have to go out again. Call our man at Rockford Memorial."

"He's tired, look at him." Fiona extends her hand as she approaches. I never shook Søren's so I'm surprised by her icy fingers. She holds on as I try to withdraw. Finally, I relax and look at her: black hair and eyes, red lips, purple gown with a long slit, smooth thigh, black pearls resting above the palest breasts I've ever seen. "It's okay. I'll get coffee on the road."

~

I can't stop thinking about her which is how I miss the classic signs of a dead alternator. The headlights slowly dim before they and the dials go black. Exhausted, standing on the shoulder halfway to Rockford, I'm ready to chuck it in:

"Fuck you, Søren! If you want blood, fly out here and drain me. Here." I tear open my collar and shout at the stars. "PUT ME OUT OF MY FUCKING MISERY." A honk reminds me that I strayed into the road. I walk, zombie-like, toward the Amoco station a mile back. This truck stop is busy for a Monday with dozens of rigs parked in front.

"What'll it be Honey?"

I stare at a menu, trying to look normal. "Just coffee."

"Cream?"

"Sure."

"I thought you might be here." Fiona gathers her gown, exposing lace underwear as she slides in next to me. I look to see if anyone else saw her come in. Everyone ignores her, even the waitress who reaches across her to deliver my coffee. Suddenly I'm hyper-aware: Here's the most beautiful woman east of Hollywood, dressed to the nines, and no one is looking at her. My eyes are still scanning when I finally speak. "It's not fair if only one of us is visible."

"You can see me. You can also see my driver who sabotaged tonight's order."

"Where?"

"Aston Martin. Center window."

I see a hulking sports coupe with the steering wheel on the wrong side and a shadow behind it. I put a dollar on the table. "I'll speak to your driver."

"It's too late for talk." Fiona hands me a foot-long scabbard covered with jewels. I slide out a blade shaped like a boomerang. When I slide it back, Fiona is gone.

~

"Who the fuck are you?" The woman gets out on the right-hand side. "And what are you doing with my Gurkha knife?" She looks into the window. "Where's Fiona?"

"Fiona says you deliberately screwed up tonight's order. She's done with you."

"Done with me?" She takes out a revolver and taps it against her chest. "You know what I did? I got cancer. That's why she's getting rid of me.

"No Tanya," Fiona steps through the door. "You're trying to starve me."

"Wow, you're losing weight already." Tanya aims the gun. "Time to lose some more." A second later, the gun falls to the ground with a hand attached to it. Tanya looks at her bloody stump. "What the fffffuck?"

I swing again, cutting through her neck. As her headless body collapses, I stare at the blade, trying to comprehend. Fiona opens the left-side door. "Put her in the trunk and let's go."

~

"Watch your speed."

I look at the dial. "It's in kilometers."

"88 and keep it there." Fiona glances at the trunk and sniffs.

I hold up a flask. "I collected some."

"She had cancer."

"You mean, you don't..."

"You wouldn't eat meat from a diseased cow, would you?"

"I'm not sure I'd know." I shift into third. "I'm not sure I know anything anymore."

Fiona is staring at the giant orange ball hanging low over the surrounding farmland. "Harvest moon." She sighs. "Not much of a harvest tonight. That was some fancy knife work."

"That was a real sharp blade."

"It's yours."

"This too?" I hold up the revolver.

"No. Open it."

I release the cylinder and see it's fully loaded. Fiona removes a bullet with her long nails. "Look." She turns on a light and holds it in front of me.

"Is that wood?"

"Yep." She tosses it in back.

"Does that...work?"

"I'm not going to find out. We have to ditch the car."

"Really? This must've been expensive."

"Everything in my world is expensive -- and disposable." She points ahead. "Pull off there."

I ease off the highway while Fiona punches the cigarette lighter. We stop behind an abandoned barn and she turns her back to me. "Unzip." I do as she says, exposing a crocheted bustier that looks centuries old.

"Undo me."

It takes a few minutes to loosen the laces. She pulls the garment away from her as she exits the car. Then she rolls it tight, crushing it with her fingers, and stuffs it in the fuel port. I use the cigarette lighter. As the material ignites, I glance at her large breasts with dead-white nipples.

"Not what you expected, huh?"

I look away. "Sorry."

"I meant me owning an Aston Martin."

~

Fiona's home has soft colors, curved furniture, and silk pillows. But the floor plan is the same as Søren's: two bedrooms, one bath, small kitchen, large living room – all on the second floor. She stands at the edge of the hallway, wearing a pink silk robe with a long-necked bird on one side. Her head rests on the wall.

I rise from the couch. "Do all of you own apartments?"

"We can't maintain a yard and exterior." She walks unsteadily toward the couch, accepting my outstretched hand. I sit next to her and notice wrinkles near her eyes and mouth. "How can I help?"

"You know the answer, Daniel."

"Name the supplier and I'll get it."

"They're not available, thanks to Tanya. We have to move."

"Where?"

"First I need to eat. Now."

"There's a hospital in town."

"Too risky."

I pause. "Does it have to be human?"

She scolds me with a look. Chastened, I look at my right arm. "I could spare a pint. Maybe two."

"I need ten."

"I could...find a homeless person."

She nods. "Park down the street when you're ready." Her voice is brittle. "I'll come down."

~

A woman looks up as I enter the tent village under the bridge. "Ten dollars will feed me and my baby. Can you spare it?"

I step closer. She looks like a road-tested rocker, but the well-defined tattoos suggest she might still be in her 30s. As she scratches bruised and scabby forearms, I focus on the ink crucifix between her right thumb and forefinger. "Where's your baby?"

"Sleeping. All it takes is twenty to feed a family."

I point to her jacket. "Those Navy pins, are they yours?"

"Fuck that supposed to mean? Of course they're mine."

I point to a patch on her shoulder. "Corpsman?"

Scratching her arms again. "USS Virginia. CGN-38."

"See any action?"

"October 23rd, 1983."

"Huh?"

"October 23rd, 1983. Lebanon."

A demolished building leaps from my memory. "The bombing of the Marine barracks." I pause. "You went ashore for the wounded?"

Scratching furiously now.

"I was just curious."

"YEAH I WENT ASHORE." She folds her arms tightly. "Tried to save one life and lost three."

"Hmm."

"Guy with rebar in his throat was a goner. Shoulda gave him morphine and moved on."

"Hmm."

"DO YOU HAVE TWENTY-FIVE OR DON'T YOU?"

I crouch down. "I'll give you fifty if you take a ride with me."

Her eyes narrow. "Where?"

"Not far."

"You're not a serial killer are you?"

I smile. "Do I look like a serial killer?"

She glances away. "What do you want?"

"What any man desires but can't get at home."

She notes the absence of a wedding ring and I can see her struggle. I offer her my other hand, but she bats it away. "Well, good night." I start walking back.

"Fine. But no rough shit.

SEX, DEATH & DENTISTRY

The stolen car is in a secluded lot. As we approach, a battle rages in my mind:

"Killing her is a mercy because she's a hopeless addict."

"She can still get clean. She can learn to live in an apartment -- with her baby."

"And where was that baby? She's lying to get more sympathy."

"Killing a veteran – a homeless veteran – is unforgiveable. No jury would side with you."

"If you don't kill her Fiona could die."

"This woman gave everything for your freedom. You owe her. Let her live."

"IF YOU DON'T KILL HER FIONA WILL DIE."

"STOP IT!" I put my hands to my ears.

"You're freaking me out." She stands a few paces behind me, uncertain, a slender silhouette against the setting sun.

I manage a smile as I open the door. "What's your name again?"

"I didn't say. What's yours?"

~

The previous month, I read about human dentistry to see if we're that different from vampires. Not much, it turns out. If you start with the upper jaw, the first tooth right of center is the right maxillary central incisor, followed by the right maxillary lateral incisor, followed by the right maxillary cuspid, or canine (right fang in vampires). Then the right maxillary 1st and 2nd bicuspids.

When she takes me in her mouth, I can tell which ones are missing. She hums a tune which I find comforting as I pull the twine slowly from my right sleeve. With my left hand, I wind the string above her head. I stop when it's about three feet long.

She stops too. "Is this going anywhere? I haven't got all night."

"Look at me."

"I am but there ain't much to look at here."

"Look up here."

Earlier, under the bridge, her eyes were cold and hard as flint. They're softer now as she puts on a pout. "What's a matter, baby?"

My left hand swoops twice around her neck before I pull the rope tight. She gasps as one hand scratches my face and the other scrapes the door. I turn to protect my eyes as she kicks toward the passenger door, feet straining to reach the window. The twine digs deeper and deeper and I think her skin might break. The rope does instead.

She spills out onto the ground, coughing. Then she tries to scream, only croaks. As she stumbles away, I start the car and put it in reverse. Two seconds later I feel the impact. When I get out I see her crawling on her elbows, dragging her useless legs. "Son of a bitch," she wheezes. "You sick motherfucking son of a bitch."

I stop next to her. "I'm sorry."

She spits on my shoe but I'm focused on something she said. "Were you telling the truth about the baby?"

She's still now, elbows in the gravel. "That's something you'll never know."

I sigh. As I wrap a fresh length of twine around her neck, she starts to whisper:

"The Lord is my shepherd; I shall not want. He maketh me to lie down in green pastures: he leadeth me beside the still waters. He restoreth my soul: he leadeth me in the paths of righteousness for his name's sake. Yea, though I walk through the valley of the shadow of death, I will fear no evil: for thou art with me; thy rod and thy staff they comfort me. Thou preparest a table before me in the presence of mine enemies: thou anointest my head with oil; my cup runneth over. Surely goodness and mercy shall follow me all the days of my life: and I will dwell in the house of the Lord forever."

I wait to be sure she's finished. Then I step on her back and pull the twine tight.

~

The adrenaline shakes my body as I drive back with Fiona's dinner. I'm also starving. I swear, if an animal crossed my path I'd chase it down and eat it with my Gurkha. When I imagine this, I realize this feeling – the thrill of the kill – is what Fiona has missed since the dawn of modern policing. You probably haven't felt it yet. When you do, you'll have a window into her dreams as she lay still during the day: the panicked breathing, the breaking skin, the gush of hot blood.

Your job, Dear Trainee, is to keep those longings in her past with a donated supply that never ends. If there's a break in the chain, you'll be the predator. The guilt is not impossible to overcome, at least I hope so. Perhaps the Ionian Sea will wash away the blood of my victims. Maybe the sun will blind others to the monster among them. And hopefully the wine will make me forget. This vision kept me going through all my years of service. You'd do well to find your own and cling to it.

I wish you well.

D.

WOLF GETS AN INTERVIEW

I fantasize about her every morning in the shower. I wait until after dawn when I know she's home, asleep. Where does she go at night? Eyes closed, I replay the image of her long bare back. Then I pull her close, hike up her dress and take her from behind. Grabbing her hips, I pull hard and watch her head bob and hair fly – enjoying total control. But it never lasts more than a few seconds before her head turns, her mouth opens, and the whole thing unravels. It's not what you think. Better start at the beginning, which is a month ago.

My fantasies involve girl "friends" who gained 35 pounds since freshman year. Not me. I have high metabolism and low liquidity, which means I'm starving on my daily ration of ramen. The State of Illinois failed to fund tuition grants again and, midway through my third year, the university stopped fronting cash. Reserves are dry, they said. Well, so are mine. I upload my resume to a handful of job sites, but it's not long before everyone says "No thanks" because I lack a degree. The only hit comes from someone named Daniel. No last name, no company logo, just Daniel and a Gmail. I send a simple question: What kind of job is this anyway?

There's just one objective: to serve our employer.

Our employer? Will you be my supervisor?

I'll retire after I train you. Until you're ready to take over, I remain in service.

In service? Where are you, Downton Abbey? :)

Daniel cuts to the chase: The salary has eight figures. Then, an ultimatum:

The more you read, the more my employer will consider you a threat if you decline our offer. If you have no intentions of taking the job, delete this message now before reading further.

This is followed by several empty spaces:

This is your final warning: Turn back if you'd rather not devote every day of your prime years to one employer who demands utter secrecy and loyalty. Take a moment to reflect on which is more important -- a career that allows for family and vacations, or a mogul's retirement.

As an aside, he says he's drinking some vintage wine given by "our employer," one of the last of its kind in the world. But I'm focused on those eight figures which I only half believe until he says $10 million.

"OK." My fingers move quickly. "I'm in." Seconds go by that seem like minutes. Then:

Our employer is displeased that you don't own a suit. Borrow one, plus silk neckwear, and learn to tie an Eldredge knot. Your wing tips are fine but need polishing. Get a haircut and tell your barber you want a shave. Under no circumstances are you to shave yourself. The next cut beneath your Adam's apple could be your last. She's smiling as she says this, but I wouldn't call it a joke. See you next Thursday just before midnight, upstairs at the Blarney Pub.

~

It sure seemed like blarney, but how would a prankster know what's in my closet, or that I shave badly? Maybe a hacker peered through my laptop or phone, which makes me wonder if I'm interviewing with the CIA or Russian trolls. Whoever it is probably doesn't live in a small college town so I'm feeling important as I enter the pub and climb to the second floor.

Daniel told me about the black fedora but not the dangling sleeve. "I like a man who arrives early." He extends his left hand, confidently waiting for me to approach.

I forgot what real shoes sound like; the room echoes with wood heels hitting old planks. Daniel's hand is warm and dry. He indicates his head toward a wooden table with two empty chairs.

"I told the house to leave us alone but we can have a drink later." His smile disappears as he asks for my phone. I take it out but keep it at my side. Daniel's eyes remain locked on mine. "You didn't tell anyone where you were going tonight, as I instructed?"

I straighten. "I'd rather not answer."

"How's that?"

"For all I know this could be an ambush. Not answering is the only protection I have."

Daniel's eyes narrow. "Listen carefully. You won't leave this room unless we're satisfied with your answer. Are you armed?"

We're satisfied? I look around. "I have two to your one, so yeah. Better armed than you."

Laughter erupts from my right. I turn and see a woman in a slender black dress, hand over her mouth, sitting in one of the chairs. She lets me glance at her plunging neckline before looking dead at me. "He didn't tell anyone."

Daniel gives a slight bow in her direction. "This is Fiona." Then he grabs my phone and walks toward the door. "Meet me downstairs."

An empty chair beckons but I hesitate, sensing something I've never felt before. Vibration isn't the word -- nothing emanates from her. Instead, I'm like a chunk of debris floating toward a black hole. My steps ring in my ears as I near the table and pull the chair; the scraping legs sound like a child being murdered. I consider offering my hand but her nails are shaped like hawks' beaks.

I clear my throat as I sit. "I appreciate you taking the time to discuss this opportunity, but I'm...disturbed... that you've been spying on me."

Dimples form as her lips curl upward.

"Do you work for the feds?"

She shakes her head.

"Police?"

She frowns, examining her nails, and I wonder if this suddenly bored woman will rip my face off.

"Are you in business?"

"I'm in the business," she rises, "of surviving." As her dress glides toward the unmanned bar, I stare at her exposed back. The dress pools around her feet which I can't see; the floorboards are silent beneath her.

Returning, she sets down a glass and reaches between her breasts. Out comes a small flask which she empties into a glass. She swirls a liquid that's way thicker than wine, sniffs, and swallows.

Then her mouth briefly opens, exposing stalactites on either side of her tongue.

BANG. The chair hits the floor. "Who…What are you?"

She offers me the half-filled glass. I sniff. Horrified, I let it fall but hear no crash. It's in her hand again, singing softly as her finger circles the rim. "This." Her eyes burn like hot coals as her lips envelop the blood-soaked digit.

"Is it…human?"

Bored again, looking at her nails.

I'm tingling as my blood pounds against my face. "Are you a –
"

"That's not an Eldredge knot."

My hand reaches for my throat but I'm distracted by her accent, which isn't American and not quite English. I'm sweating, trying to avoid staring, but my eyes settle on her breasts again. She snaps her fingers -- forcing me to look up. For several seconds, her nails scrape against each other as she dares me to say or do the wrong thing.

I find my voice. "Will I have to kill anyone?"

"Not if you do your job right."

"Will I bring victims to you?"

Her eyes aim briefly at the door. "Go talk to Daniel."

I glance at the door. When I turn back, she's gone.

~

"Each order is the same." Daniel slides a fifty toward the bartender and waves off the change. "O negative. She needs ten pints every night." He swallows some scotch. "I have people at hospitals and blood banks in Chicago, Rockford, Madison, even St. Louis."

"That's five hours away." I down my bourbon in one swallow. Throat burning, I push the glass back to the bartender who refills it.

"St. Louis is the backup for when hang-ups occur."

"Hang-ups."

"The supply gets interrupted some times. All it takes is one train crash or explosion and our bags get sent to the ER. Other times," he shrugs, "someone forgets."

I grab my fresh drink. "And how do we pay for all this bloo --"

"The product?" Daniel's voice drowns me out, and he scolds me with a look. "You invest her money." Then he swirls the dark, heavy liquid under his nose before sipping. "Lately we're staying away from tech stocks. New administration, playing it safe. We're in toothpaste, deodorant – stuff people use every day."

"So they smell good if we experience a 'hang-up.'"

"Very funny."

"Tell me: How often will I...disappear people?"

"You won't have to if you're..."

"Doing my job – she said that already." I search his eyes, looking for a glint of humanity. "How many times did you have to kill for her?"

He turns away. Frustrated, I down the rest of my drink.

"Slow down, that's expensive." Daniel sniffs his. "This is a lonely job, one where you're constantly on duty. Good liquor is the only reward we have time for."

Ignoring him, I catch the bartender's attention. "Hey. Do you believe in vampires?"

Daniel eyes me carefully as the barkeep counters: "I got a wife, two kids, two car payments, student loans, and a cat with panic disorder. The whole world's sucking me dry."

"Well, have I got an opportunity for you."

Daniel slaps an extra fifty on the counter, grabs my collar, and hauls me away.

"Wow, pretty good for one arm." My mouth feels like it's stuffed with marbles. Outside, Daniel shoves me against the bricks, my shirt balled in his fist. "The answer is four. Want to be Number Five?"

"Why not?" I stare back, eyes watering. "She scares the fuck out of me."

"Finally, you're showing some brains." He lets me go. "But it's too late to back out. Walk away and she'll find you."

"Maybe it's for the better." Head reeling from

alcohol, I remember a trope from vampire movies. "Can she make me?"

"What?"

"Can she make me like her?"

"I guess, but what's the point?" He takes out two cigars and hands them to me along with a clipper. The labels say Habana Cuba. "Cut the rounded ends."

As I do this, his left hand dips again into his pocket. Out comes a vintage Zippo which he uses to light mine first. "I was your age when I started working for her." After lighting his, he exhales a cloud above his head. "I won't sugarcoat it. I have no family, no friends, and a lot of bad memories. But it's almost over. I did 35 years. You might get away with 30."

I cough. "You make it sound like prison."

"More a tour of duty."

I pick a tobacco shred off my lip. "When...how do you feed her?"

Daniel inhales deeply and exhales over his shoulder. "I'll explain everything tomorrow."

"There will be a tomorrow, huh?"

"Long as you show up."

I take another puff and feel myself getting used to the smoke, which is earthy and smooth. I relax and let it sink deep inside before blowing it out. "Where does she go?"

"What?"

"After you feed her. Where does she go?"

Daniel looks at me for a few seconds. "It's none of my business."

"Aren't you curious? I mean, does she have to be back by sunrise? And do you wait up for her?"

"Why are you focused on her going out?"

"Because I'll be pissed if I drive a hundred miles, risking arrest for stealing blood from people who need it, and she's out there killing someone for a snack or whatever."

He silently takes another puff.

"You've wondered about that, haven't you?"

Daniel takes the cigar out of his mouth and inspects the glowing tip. "I suppose she just hangs out with the others."

"How many others are there?"

"You'll find out soon enough."

Frustrated again, I latch on to another topic. "She's a hunter -- I could sense that right away. Why wouldn't she and 'the others' kill some poor bastard just because it's fun?"

"It is not fun."

I exhale more smoke. "Finally, you're sounding like a human. I don't want a job that makes me feel dead inside."

"When you get that feeling, and you will often," Daniel looks toward the second-floor window, "think about the money you're saving for the day you can retire."

I step forward, trying to glimpse his eyes. "How do you know she'll let you go? You know too much. So do I."

"I promised to keep my mouth shut, and she said I could go after you're up to speed." He smiles a little. "She's not a monster, you know." Then he walks away. "Meet me here tomorrow, same time."

"Wait, I have more questions."

"Forget them." He turns, smoke obscuring his face. "From now on, you'll get no more answers. They are the answer."

~

Back in my apartment, I need another shower. Taking off my suit, I feel something in the jacket. It's an envelope addressed to "Mr. Wolford Perry." Opening it, I find this strange name under my photo on an Illinois driver's license, U.S. Passport, and other documents – even a Michigan concealed-carry permit. There's also a card, lightly perfumed:

Dear Wolf,

I like your style, but Man-Behind isn't for me.
However, I'll get behind any man who keeps me "in the red."
See you tomorrow…

F.

JASMINE & HEMOGLOBIN

Brother Raymond and another bald man watch as Old One-Arm drags The Kid out of the bar. The other monk rises, intending to pursue, but Raymond puts a hand on his shoulder. "Brother Leo's outside. He'll follow them."

Brother Xavier sits back down and glances toward the bar. "The Kid said something about vampires."

"You'd think he saw one by the look on his face." Raymond's eyes go to the ceiling. "Up there."

"You ever see one?"

"Not in the flesh."

Xavier balls one hand and smacks it into the other. "What I wouldn't give to have our weapons now."

"Be patient, Brother, they'll arrive soon." Raymond scans the crowd with a thermal imager. "No evidence of a striga here."

"Well if it does show," Xavier takes out his rosary and kisses the crucifix, "this will protect us."

"That only makes them angry."

"You sure about that?"

"I read accounts from the last war in 1900." Raymond looks up again. "Anyway, if the striga's not down here, among its prey, then it moved on. It should be safe."

The two walk upstairs and enter a room occupied only by a table and two chairs, one upright, one on its side. Xavier steps in and sniffs. "Jasmine, orange blossom...ambergris? Now I know what the Angel of Death smells like."

Raymond walks toward the center, stops, and 360s with the scanner. Satisfied, he pockets the device. Then he picks up a small stemmed glass from the table. Holding it to the light, he sees dark red liquid pooled at the bottom. He hands it to Xavier who raises his eyebrows. "That human?"

"There may be enough for a sample." Raymond uncaps a small

bottle and holds it between them: "Pour it in." Xavier carefully drains the remaining drops. When finished, Raymond seals the cap and shakes the solution. Then he unwraps a plastic card, half an inch thick, and sets it on the table. Opening the bottle again, Raymond sticks a dropper inside, draws up the liquid, and fills a small well below an indicator strip. "Now we wait."

"For how long?"

"The *Benedictio Armorum* should be enough." Raymond nods. "Go ahead and recite."

"But we don't have any weapons."

"Let us pray..."

Xavier folds his hands in front of him, crucifix dangling from the rosary. "May the blessing of almighty God -- Father, Son, and Holy Ghost -- descend upon these weapons and upon whomever wears them, for those who wear them in the defense of justice: You, O God, who live and reign forever and ever."

"Amen, and...We're getting something." Raymond points at the indicator strip. "See how those lines turned red? Human hemoglobin."

Xavier leans in. "How was this procured?"

"I don't know." Raymond glances toward the door. "But we're definitely marking this place."

"Too bad the Devil got her first." Xavier's nose tilts up again. "That perfume is intoxicating."

Raymond stomps his heel. "A distraction." His voice practically drips with venom. "Impure thoughts jeopardize more than your vow of celibacy. They're a threat to every brother who thinks you have their back."

"Don't worry, I'll shoot to kill." Xavier stares back. "Just make sure I have the right bullets."

"You'll have them soon enough." Raymond puts the wine glass in a bag along with the indicator strip. Then his phone beeps. He stares briefly at it before looking at Xavier. "We have an address."

SOLSTICE (1998)

"Daniel -- is it finally gone?" She sounds annoyed behind the barely-opened bedroom door.

"Let me check." I walk into the kitchen where President Clinton is saying, "I did not have sexual relations with that woman..." I turn off the TV with one hand and peel back the curtain with the other. The last rays of light retreat over the horizon. I wait a few seconds more. "Yes, it's safe."

"You have no idea how lucky you are, surviving under the moon *and* sun." Fiona enters the kitchen, anxiously tying the silk robe which clings to her skin. "At least the nights will get longer now."

"The sun can kill me too if I spend too much time in it." I fill a crystal glass with Ruby – her name for it -- and set it on the table. "Ultraviolet rays cause skin cancer. Which reminds me: I'll need a few hours off tomorrow to see my doctor. I have a mole I'm worried about."

"Where?"

"On my back."

"Let me see." Fiona seems genuinely concerned.

"It's nothing. You must be starving."

"If you're worried, I need to be worried. Take off your shirt."

"I'm not worried." I set the decanter on the table, unbutton, and expose my upper body. She moves behind me and places a long, curved nail on the bumpy blemish; the rest of my skin gets goose flesh.

"How long have you had this?"

"As long as I can remember, but it changed recently."

She leans closer and sniffs. I also inhale, detecting yesterday's perfume in her hair – plus a whiff of flesh in the early stages of decay; she needs to drink now. The odor hangs in the air after she walks to the table and picks up her glass. "It's nothing to worry about, but I can cut it out for you."

29

"Thanks, I'll have my doctor do it."

"Suit yourself." She sips the O negative I bought yesterday. "Does he have hospital rights? We could use another source."

"She."

"Oh." She takes another sip. "What does she look like?"

"Brown skin, black hair. She's Indian."

"Is she Mohican?"

Fiona once told me *The Last of the Mohicans* was her favorite book. She still keeps the first edition next to her bed, plus a pen in case the author is around to sign it. For a while, a rumor circulated that James Fenimore Cooper was turned into an "immortal" but that story died a century ago.

"No, from India."

"Oh. I've never been." Her brow wrinkles. "Maybe before but I can't remember. Is she pretty?"

"I guess. Why do you ask?"

"Well," she takes another sip and I can see her skin regain its luminescence. "A man needs a woman now and then. Right?"

"She's married."

"And?" Her lips curl into a smile, briefly exposing her canines. Out of habit, she covers them. "When's the last time you were...carnal with someone?" Her eyes sparkle as she says this.

"I don't know."

"Really? That's terrible. I can give you a night off if you need it. Just remember: If your doctor takes you to bed, be especially pleasing. We need people who know people."

"I'll keep that in mind."

She looks at the clock and hands me the empty glass. "I'd better get dressed."

"That's right. The Solstice Ball."

"YES." Fiona twirls around the kitchen, arms holding an imaginary partner. "The return of the darkness."

"Will Søren be there?"

"Count Fillenius is on the guest list. Why do you ask?"

"No reason."

Her face fills my vision; our noses almost touch as her eyes search mine. "He'll only stay for the day if that's what you're concerned about."

"I'm more concerned about the way he treats you."

"What do you mean?"

"I…" The words stall inside. I want to tell her she doesn't have to share the O Neg and a room with a guest who acts like he owns the place. Every time he's here I struggle to conceal my hatred for the way he lords over her – and me. I turn on the faucet and rinse the glass.

"You know I can hear your thoughts."

Both my hands land on the counter. "Then you know it upsets me when he drinks half our supply and doesn't pay for it. You'd think a count could afford to reciprocate."

"Whose supply?" I half turn and see breasts bulging over crossed arms, eyes burning through me. It's the silence that hurts the most though; her words are the only clue as to what's in her head. She remains in the kitchen just long enough to rub that in before leaving. Finally, before entering her room: "Just make sure there's enough Ruby for both of us."

~

My alarm goes off at 5:00. Fiona never asks me to check that she's home by dawn but I do it anyway. Her door, across from mine, bolts from the inside and I never test it to respect her privacy. To be honest, I'm afraid to discover she sleeps with her eyes open; I saw that in a movie once. Before I go to bed, I leave a small stemmed glass on the kitchen table for a night cap. If it's empty when I rise then I know she's safe, although sometimes she takes the glass to her room. But this morning it's there and it's full. The calendar says sunrise is at 5:15 and full daylight is at 5:34. I grab my keys and prepare for a search I only imagined. Then I hear a giggle from her bedroom, followed by another voice that sounds like Søren's. My sudden relief is spoiled by a feeling that goes beyond anger. Only after I return to my room and lay flat do I realize how disappointed I am.

She could do better. Why doesn't she?

~

31

"I'll bring it to her." Søren stands in the kitchen, bejeweled hand open, waiting for the O neg. Ben Franklin once joked that guests, like fish, begin to smell after three days. Søren's been here for nearly a week. I gaze in his general direction, trying not to look at the window shade. At 5:21 the sun might be high enough to set him ablaze. The only thing keeping me from tugging the cord and letting it fly is Fiona; she'd never forgive me. I don't care that Søren can hear this.

He straightens as I hand him the glass. "She'd have to turn you in, you know. The trial would be swift and you'd suffer the worst pain imaginable. Then, just before you die, they'd make Fiona cut off your genitals and stuff them in your mouth. We both know she's too sensitive for that." He stares without blinking as he sips from her glass.

I fill the sink with soapy water, resigned to washing extra glassware when I should be out scoring more O neg.

"I'd have had you drawn and quartered if you left with anyone else. You know that, don't you?"

I shrug. "At the time I really didn't care."

Søren seems hurt. "Why? Was I such a bad master?"

"I'm still figuring out what you're good at."

"Here's one." Icy fingers twist my face toward his. "Fiona considers me an ideal companion – something you could never be." I attempt to look away but he squeezes harder. "You should also know this: Fiona wants you to return to me if she dies so show some respect."

Fiona never mentioned anything about this. She's only two centuries old. I assumed she'd be fine as long as I set my alarm each night before dawn. My voice cracks: "Fiona expects to die before you do?"

"Anything can happen." The much-younger Søren lets me go. "We immortals suffer when the sun is in Cancer."

"Cancer."

"The Crab. Its claws remain open for twenty-eight days – waiting for us to be in the wrong place at the wrong time. Fiona is more likely to die now than any time throughout the year."

I ignore the fact that Søren is just as vulnerable. "Why not move to Australia during the summer?"

Søren is briefly rattled. "You see, remarks like that make me fear for Fiona under your care. Do you know what it would take to move her, and me, across the globe?"

"I said nothing about you."

Søren's gaze is as cold as outer space. "She will hear about this."

~

"You really need to be nicer to him." Fiona sits at the kitchen table, leaning her head on one hand. "He has feelings, you know." She glares at me but then giggles, covering her fangs. "God, he bruises so easily – like a hemophiliac."

"Søren says I'm to return to him as part of your...estate plan. Is that true?"

"Well, I did steal you from him. There's a law against that."

"He wouldn't press charges."

"True. He needs me -- or rather this home as an occasional place to land."

"Where is he?"

"Oh, you didn't know? He's on his way to Australia." She laughs suddenly. "The other day he said, 'Did you know it's winter down there?' Can you believe it? He didn't know!"

I look down at the table for a few seconds. "But I'm to return to him in the event..."

She shrugs. "I promised, apparently, and..."

"Guardians are second-class citizens."

"Look at you, reading *my* mind."

My mouth twists as I taste a truth that's only been implied. "Does this mean I can never retire?"

"Oh I wouldn't say that." Her head straightens. "But I'll need you for as long as possible."

WOLF AT FIONA'S CASTLE

"Why O negative? Why not O positive or something?" I watch Daniel pour the red liquid from a decanter into a stemmed glass.

"The taste, I guess." Daniel shrugs. "Pure aesthetics, like the crystal we use: Waterford instead of Baccarat."

"My grandma had a set of Waterford." I watch Daniel set the decanter on a cart covered with a white cloth. Next comes the filled glass. "Is she Irish?"

"I think she was born there but I don't really know."

The last 24 hours have broken open my entire world. I met my first vampire and got my first job working for one. But Daniel's response is too much, as my raised voice indicates. "You said you worked 35 years for Fiona. How come you know so little about her?"

He frowns. "Our conversations focus on the day to day. What stocks are hot? Should we invest in bonds or gold? How's her supply? Did that new connection deliver as instructed? We don't have time for personal stuff."

"But you would if she stayed around instead of going out."

"That's her business. Our role is clear: do your job, don't ask questions, collect your pay. Like any other job."

"Except the money." I still can't believe the paycheck Daniel promised next Friday. He said I'd earn even more when "fully operational."

"Indeed." Using his one hand, Daniel tries to slide the tray to the cart but stops when blood nearly spills onto the white cloth. He sighs. "You do it." I grab the tray with both hands and set it gently on the cart; the O neg wobbles just a little. "Follow me." Daniel pushes the cart to her bedroom door and knocks three times.

A bolt clicks, the door opens, and Fiona stands wearing a silk robe, rose-colored, with a long black bird down one side. A faint odor of death invades my nostrils; I didn't smell this when I met her last night. She steps aside as Daniel wheels the table to the center of the room. I pause at the threshold, looking for guidance, but they have their backs to me. Finally, I step in.

Fiona spritzes perfume on her wrists and between her breasts. Her eyes re-direct my attention to Daniel who reaches into his pocket and sets a handful of notes next to the decanter.

"These are items for her attention. They include updates on our supply, finances, and recommended investments. Fiona will let us know if she requires anything more." He turns to her. "Anything before we go?"

"No." She sets down the perfume and begins combing her hair. Daniel's head bows a little before he walks to the door. I start to follow, then turn and point to the glassware. "That's Lismore, isn't it? The pattern. My grandmother had a set. It belonged to her mother."

Fiona looks at me and gives a slight nod. I press further. "She put her stemware on a silver tray with a lace – oh, what do you call it – doily made in Ireland. She was from Waterford. Worshipped at Trinity Cathedral."

Fiona just stares back; I feel a tap on my shoulder. "Let's go."

~

"She doesn't say much, does she?" I watch Daniel count the bags in the refrigerator.

"God dammit, we're short for tomorrow."

"I see nine."

"She needs ten. Every night." He shuts the door. "I need you to go out and bring back eleven pints." He scratches the order on a notepad. "Take the Prius. Punch Northwestern Memorial in the GPS. Your contact is Marcos." He tears off a sheet and hands it to me. "I'll call ahead but I'm writing his number at the bottom. Text with the code when you arrive."

"What code?"

"PUNT in all caps. That's our signal for when we're short." He opens a drawer, takes out a wad of cash, and starts laying $100 bills on the counter. When he gets to $6,000 he scoops these into an envelope which he hands to me. "Get going."

"What will you do?"

"I have to sell stocks. That's a whole different level of training we'll get to next week." He points to the key rack. I grab the remote tagged "Prius" and head for the garage.

"And don't mention the silver tray again. We never use silver."

~

No silver. What about mirrors? I forget whether Fiona's room had one. I can picture lots of perfume bottles, combs and brushes – plus an unmade bed with purple sheets that looked like silk. There was also a large painting of a crumbling castle in a foreboding landscape covering a space where the window should've been.

All this foreground memory competes with an undertow of attraction and revulsion; the silk stretched over her nipples, the whiff of decaying flesh quickly followed by a spritz of mountain flowers. My brain is stuck in a zone that gets progressively murkier as I approach her food source.

PUNT

The reply takes a few minutes: *RM 404 Patient Jorge Garcia*

~

In 404, Nurse Marcos takes a blood pressure reading while a TV shows a *Breaking News* graphic followed by the headline *Special Counsel Charges Three Former Trump Campaign Officials*.

Marcos tells me to follow him. We go to a room at the end of the hall with one comatose patient hooked to an iron lung. Marcos lowers his voice. "What's your name?"

"Wolf."

"Wolf?"

"Short for Wolford. Wolford -- "

"No last names. And you work with Daniel?"

"Yes."

"Tell me something about him."

"Just one arm. Left."

"Something else."

"He is…completely without humor."

Marcos smiles. "He wasn't always that way. You want eleven pints of O negative?"

"Yes."

"That'll be eight thousand."

"Wait, it was supposed to be six thousand."

"The price went up."

"Did you tell Daniel the price went up?"

"That's not how this works. You should never assume anything."

My face gets hot, my breathing slows, and my voice starts to shake. "I am not leaving without those bags."

Marcos crosses his arms, biceps bulging beneath his scrubs. "And I'm not letting them go for under eight."

"Fine." My hands go up and I walk by him. Then I grab my pocket knife, run to the other side of the patient, grab the cord for the iron lung, and wrap it around the blade. "Eleven bags of O neg. Now."

Marcos, seeing I got the drop on him, acts normal. "Go ahead, cut it. You'll have swarms of people here in a second."

"Have you ever been a patient? This guy will die before anyone responds -- and you'll get the blame."

"All right, stay cool." Marcos takes out his phone. "I'll have someone meet you by your car."

"No. He comes here with the bags in a cooler-"

"Of course they're in a fucking cooler."

"Here. Now." I point the blade at him. "You don't leave this room, and you don't make any moves I don't like." Then I point to a chair. "Have a seat."

~

Marcos and I watch a CNA named Cathy open a cooler and show me the eleven bags.

"Hold one up so I can see the label." She glances at Marcos, but he offers nothing so she complies. "Okay, close it and set it over here." I take a deep breath. "Cathy, I want you to know something. My employer understood that today's order would be $6,000 but Marcos upped it to eight at the last minute. He didn't tell you that, did he?"

She looks at him again, but Marcos just glares at me.

I glare back. "This asshole tried to cut you out of that extra two grand." I toss her the envelope. "There's six. Keep it all if you want."

"Motherfucker!" Marcos leaps up and hurls himself at me. An alarm sounds as both ends of the cord fall to the floor.

~

"Well done, Wolf." Daniel stacks the bags in the refrigerator. "I'm disappointed about Marcos, though. He'd been reliable for years." He takes an ice pack out of the freezer. "Here."

I wince as I put it against my bruised cheekbone. "Cathy sure was pissed. She pepper-sprayed him."

Daniel smiles. "I already reached out to her." He opens a decanter and pours two generous glasses of scotch. "She'll get us twenty bags by Monday for a reasonable price." He caps the decanter and looks at his watch. "Fiona should be home by now."

"I am." Both of us turn as she enters the kitchen wearing a peasant-style dress – full length, low cut, showing off the palest breasts I've ever seen. She stops in front of Daniel, her back to me, one hand motioning toward her face. He bends a little to inspect her and nods. She turns and locks eyes with me. "You've been wanting to speak with me. Come to my room."

~

"May I pour you a glass?"

"No need. Sit down." Fiona points to a chair by the vanity – which has no mirror – before stepping behind a three-panel screen with Japanese artwork. I hear her unzip before noting: "That's quite a shiner."

"Yeah." I chuckle. "You should see the other guy."

"Marcos." She growls the name. "Oh, I saw him. God, it's so hard to find a human you can depend on -- present company excluded. Why would he risk a solid business partnership for two thousand dollars?" She steps out clad only in silk and I have to turn away.

"Look at me."

My eyes land where I think hers will be.

"Daniel will drive you back to Chicago. There's a park. He'll need you to dig the grave."

"Wow. Okay." I feel a lump in my throat. "When do we leave?"

"In a few minutes. After your drink."

Don't rush this moment, I think to myself. You might not get an audience like this again. I tilt the glass and swirl the dark liquid in my mouth before swallowing. Then I hold it up to the light. "Lismore again."

"Which brings us to your earlier question about my glassware."

"Waterford versus Baccarat -- you heard that?"

"I hear everything." She sits on the edge of her bed, grabs a pillow, and squeezes it against her, staring at a crystal vase. "I was born in County Waterford in 1750. My human name is Fiona Mairéad Fitzgerald. I became...what I am...when I was seventeen."

"And how did you become...what you are?"

She glowers. "You want me to explain the birds and bees of my kind?"

"Does it involve an exchange of blood?"

A pause. "Yes."

"And were you...did you...?"

"You're wondering if I was a virgin. Why is that important?"

"W-what I wanted to ask is: if you had children."

"You mean, besides siring someone?"

"Does 'siring' mean what I think it means?"

"Mm-hmm."

"Then yes."

"What's this obsession with my supposed motherhood?" Her eyes widen. "Ah, your parents died when you were very little. When your grandparents died, you went into foster care." She nods. "You miss having a family." She gives a rare, gentle smile. "You understand, there's no way we're related."

"Are you sure? My grandmother and great-grandmother came from Waterford."

"Half of America has Irish ancestry."

"But this seems unusually close. Your DNA might match mine."

"DNA?"

I stand. "We could go online, or even get tested to see if we're family."

"Wolf." Her hand goes up. "The only bloodline I have comes from my sire. My human blood was replaced. And you're forgetting something: I never said I had a child."

"Well...did you?"

For the first time, her gaze becomes uncertain. She looks away.

"There must be a reason for all this crystal." I look around her room. "You have Waterford everywhere."

"I left very quickly after my transformation." She pauses. "I have no idea what, or who, I left behind."

"You mean..."

"ENOUGH." She stands, eyes flaming red. Long canines appear and she turns and covers her mouth. After several long seconds, she speaks calmly: "I'm giving a little of my time because I'm grateful for the work you did today, and that you will finish tonight. But inquiries about my human past are off limits." She turns to look at me, eyes normal again. "Is that clear?"

I indicate my head toward the door. "Did he ever ask you this?"

She uncovers her mouth. "He's wise enough not to."

Chastened, I nod toward the gothic ruin covering the window. "Waterford Castle?"

"Yes."

"Ever think of going back there?"

"Go." She tosses the pillow against the headboard.

I take my drink toward the door. Before I grab the handle, I half turn. "I'm sorry, Fiona."

"Bury him deep and leave no evidence. From now on, it's all about the job. Understood?"

PRE-ATTACK

"Hold on, Father Abbot, let me put you on speaker." Brother Raymond hits a button. "Can you hear me?"

"Loud and clear. What's the plan?"

Raymond pushes the phone back toward the center of the table. "Our target lives in a town home, protected by two guardians. Tomorrow, they'll take possession of a new refrigerator which is scheduled to be delivered between ten and noon."

"Did they ask for the old one to be hauled away?"

"No, which tells us her network of blood thieves is expanding."

"'Her', Brother Raymond?"

"Sorry. Its."

"Okay, delivery is after ten. When does your team arrive?"

"We knock on the door at nine forty-five."

"And by 'we' you mean?"

"Brothers Xavier and Leo, plus novices Nguyen, Byrne, Mbutu and Garcia."

"Okay, six gunmen against two. Where will you be?"

"Driving the truck with the winch. I'll wait down the street and pull up after Brother Leo confirms his team is through the rear door."

"Have you identified the room where our target is sleeping?"

"Upper floor, northwest side."

"All right, walk me through it."

"Brother Xavier is primary through the front. I'll have him explain."

Xavier leans toward the phone. "Father Abbot, I will carry a fake tracking scanner built around a customized gun. When the door opens, I'll hit the guard with a half-inch bullet which will expand to one inch on impact. Death will be instant, and the bullet will remain in the body so as not to threaten our team behind the house. Novices Nguyen and Byrne will follow me in."

"And the other guardian?"

"Before he can react, Brother Leo will enter the rear door with novices Garcia and Mbutu. They will eliminate the remaining threat and proceed upstairs, opening all curtains and shades leading to the target's room. My team will wait downstairs for Brother Raymond."

Raymond leans in. "I will pull up on the lawn and Brother Xavier will grab the winch end. Once he's back inside, I'll radio Brother Leo's team to break into the striga's room. They will attach the winch to the target, alert me when they've done so, and help guide the striga down the stairs and into daylight."

"It'll make a spectacular sight for the neighbors." A pause. *"Shoot video. I'll want to show it to the cardinal."*

HAUPTSTURMFÜHRER FILLENIUS (1944)

The Russians knew they had no chance; we surrounded them. They also knew we'd have no mercy, but they surrendered anyway. They gave up their weapons and helmets, hoping for cigarettes which we no longer had. Were they buying time? Somewhere across the drifting snow, their swine kin prepared another attack but we didn't know when or how many. So we tried beating the details out, smashing their fingers and noses with rifles. After burning precious calories, we huddled in our so-called "winter outfits" and stamped our feet to get the blood moving. Then we tried to strip their coats which covered neck to ankle with thick, coarse wool. I know very little Russian but it was clear we'd have to shoot them first. Happy to oblige, I ordered my last surviving officer to line them up and empty our German guns on them. The captured ones work better when frozen, and we'd need those for the next assault.

A corporal limps toward me and salutes. "Herr Hauptsturmführer, shall we aim for the head? The coats would be intact then."

"If you want pig brains on your collar, that's your business." I yank the magazine from my pistol and count the remaining ice-covered rounds. "I'll take the three on the right."

Up to now, I thought Der Führer might introduce a Super Weapon that would the stop the Red Army from entering Germany. But when half our guns failed to perform a simple mass execution, I knew it was over. The war would go on for another fifteen months but this moment in Estonia is where the end began – for Germany and these mongrel fucks who surrendered everything but their coats. At least their weapons worked; my men were thrilled. I, however, counted every one of the eleven bullets they spent.

"Hauptsturmführer Fillenius!" Major Haas motions from a staff car that must've arrived while we were firing. I walk quickly and salute, expecting a reprimand for wasting ammunition.

Haas ignores the bodies. "I'm going to Tallinn to prepare defenses there. Need I remind you of Der Führer's directive?"

"Stand and fight. No retreat, no surrender."

His driver, a lieutenant, salutes. "We know you'll give your all for the Fatherland."

I ignore him. "Can you send some food, cigarettes, bandages – anything?"

"I'll assess the situation and let you know." Haas motions to his driver who shifts into First. "Don't let us down, Søren."

His use of my Christian name is another sign that the "thousand-year Reich" will last little more than a decade. I salute once more as he drives toward the final sunset I expect to see. I try to savor it but someone yells *"Deckung!"* and I jump into the nearest trench.

~

I've seen men hallucinate before they die, so I'm not surprised by the woman wearing a low-cut peasant-style dress. This moonlit vision is a welcome distraction from the gurgling in my throat and lungs. A sucking chest wound gets priority in any triage, but there's no one left to plug the holes. Suffocating, I try to relax and enjoy this little film about an underdressed brunette walking toward me through white and crimson snow.

"You don't look Russian," I wheeze. "Estonian?"

She gathers the long fabric as she kneels, and I see blue veins in her large white breasts. Long fingernails like shell splinters descend toward me, and I wonder if she'll gouge my eyes out. I close them as she brushes aside a stray forelock.

"Please." My eyes reopen. "Just stay with me."

"What a pity." She says in English. "You look like an angel." Her fingers brush snow off a patch on my uniform. "SS Nordland." Then she frowns and grabs a handful of hair, lifting my face toward hers. "I could have used those prisoners you killed."

I focus on her accent which is different from that of my language tutor in Copenhagen. "American?"

Her grip tightens. "You wasted them!"

Wasted? What did that mean? This was more than a war. It was

44

a crusade against Slavs and other sub-humans, and Jewish bolshevism – a crusade I joined four years ago to help the Nazis take over my native Denmark. The fact that the Aryans failed means nothing matters anymore – *nichts*. Nearly defeated, I spend one of my remaining breaths on a question. "What do you want?"

"What do you want, Søren?"

Definitely a dream; even my dog tags use an initial for my first name. But I consider her words. "Leave the war. Leave this fucking continent."

Her eyes narrow as if preparing to divulge a secret. "I'm going to America."

"Take me with you."

Her face nears mine, eyes glowing red, and her lips part, revealing two long canines. "You're a monster," she hisses. "Only a fellow hunter can go with me."

"I ...Who...What are you?"

Her mouth closes but her glowing eyes remain fixed on mine. Of all the things I expected to see while dying, I never imagined a seductive hellish creature calling me a monster. What does that make her? My frozen lips barely move: "Vampyr?"

She scowls. For a moment, she appears uncertain about what to do. Finally: "You're useless now, nearly bloodless, but I can change you." Her face is so close our noses almost touch. "First, I'm going to give you something I never had: a choice."

"Make me one of you."

"You haven't heard the terms."

"I don't want to die."

"If I save you, the sun will be your mortal enemy. And your thirst will never end."

"Please..." I cough a final time as my lungs collapse.

Both her hands support my neck as she moves behind me. Then she rests my head in her lap and holds her right hand above my face. A nail slices her wrist and my head turns away as blood rains down.

"Open." Her fingers squeeze my jaw. The drops cover my face as I struggle for my last breath.

"Be still."

~

When I awake, I hear a heart beating and know immediately who it belongs to. I sit up and hear his panicked breathing, but pause to take in the surroundings of a command bunker I visited once, now abandoned. Fiona relaxes in the Field Marshal's former wing chair, sipping from a glass of red liquid that I already know – I can smell it. And I want it.

"You can relax." Fiona swallows. "It's safe here."

"Safe for whom?" He yells from across the room. "Hauptsturmführer Fillenius! Untie me and arrest this woman!"

"Sturmbannführer Haas," I rise, noting the major's civilian clothes. "Where did you go after you left our position?"

"To Tallinn – like I told you!"

"He's lying." Fiona examines her nails. "I found him at the Loksa Shipyard, arranging passage to neutral territory. He and his lieutenant – who's delicious, by the way -- had Swedish passports."

I glare at him sitting in a wooden chair, arms and legs bound. "Stand and fight, you said." Then I see the passports on a nearby table, plus a dozen gold coins. "My men were killed – all of them – covering your rear."

"Oh, I think Lieutenant Becker covered his rear just fine, wouldn't you say Major?" Fiona smiles as she takes another sip.

"Søren, listen." Haas fixes his eyes on me. "She kidnapped us in Tallinn, planted that stuff on us, and killed Fritzi."

"Don't call me 'Søren' – I do not consort with cowards!"

Haas's face wrinkles with disgust as he looks at Fiona. "Then, like an animal, she bit his neck and drank his blood."

I inhale deeply, suddenly aware that my teeth are longer. Haas's skin reveals a spider web of throbbing vessels, but I know which one to attack first. I glance at Fiona. "Can I take him now?"

Fiona looks amused as she leans back in the Field Marshal's chair. "Permission granted, Hauptsturmführer."

~

The Stockholm Palace looks stunning at night, yellow lights reflecting off the sandstone exterior. But the fact that a King lives there -- plus the surrounding architecture, music, and fashions -- reminds me that we're still in Europe. I look at Fiona's hands which rest on the wrought iron balcony, and place my right on her left. "I hear the war will be over soon."

"Yes."

"It should be safe to travel, no?"

"It's never safe." She looks at me. "The first leg, to England, is a small risk. We could take two or three passengers, but we'd have to share them. The second leg, though..." She looks at the night sky. "That would be seven or eight – again, shared – so we'd still be starving. If we're alive when we get to New York, the police will know something's wrong and board the ship. All they need is a little luck and they'll find our trunk."

"Why not have separate trunks?"

"That doubles the chances they'll find one. If they discover you or me, they'll keep looking."

"Remind me. Why are we doing this?"

She points west. "Because that's where we'll get dinner every night." She waves toward the city. "They just had two devastating wars, and God knows if the Russians are finished marching. There aren't enough people to hide behind while we make the others disappear."

I gaze at the rising moon and imagine how it looks from New York, Boston, or Chicago. Then I lift my glass. "To America. May we thrive among her teeming multitudes."

"To whoever controls the universe," Fiona raises hers. "May she still need us enough to grant safe passage."

WOLF LEARNS OF MORS STRIGAE

"The Council will have a special meeting." Fiona, arms crossed, sounds tense as she stares at the floor. Usually, after rising, she says "Good evening" as she enters the kitchen. Tonight, her eyes look red and puffy as if she's been crying.

"When?" Daniel looks up from his laptop. I, the server, stand ready to pour her breakfast.

"December 21st."

"Next Friday?" Daniel lowers his reading glasses. "That's the Solstice Ball."

"It's cancelled." She walks toward me, silk clinging to her body, hand outstretched for the O negative. December 21st also marks one year since I started working for Fiona. Since then -- since our conversation about Waterford -- she's done nothing to even hint that we share some connection. Most times, she talks with Daniel, and nearly all those conversations are about finances.

"How's our cash flow?"

"We're getting good dividends." Daniel looks at her. "What's wrong?"

Fiona turns her attention to me. "Wolf, you'll wait at table throughout the conference." Back to Daniel: "You'll supervise. Three shifts of four footmen."

Daniel glances at his empty right sleeve. "That beats holding a decanter for several hours. Wolf, how'd you like to serve the Council leader?" I'm about to answer when Fiona interjects:

"What can we sell today?"

"Banking stocks. Or gold, if it's that serious."

Investing is the part of the job Daniel loves and I hate. He spends most of his time researching corporate earnings and all that. I just like scoring O neg, which gets me out of the house. It also allows me to see what my former friends are posting on Facebook. Speaking of which, my phone is buzzing with notifications...

"Gold."

Daniel nods and puts down his glasses. "What's so urgent that would replace a Solstice Ball with a conference?"

"Guys."

Fiona shakes her head. "I don't even know where to begin." She takes a long drink from her glass.

"GUYS."

Daniel shoots me an angry look. "You'd better not be posting anything."

"You got to see this." I scroll through an article. "A group of masked men dragged a woman out of her home in broad daylight and set her on fire. This was in Michigan. They hooked her to a truck winch and say they didn't use gasoline or anything – just the sun. They're claiming she was a vampire."

"WOLF." Daniel stands, admonishing me for saying that word.

"Sorry – sorry Fiona – but you need to see this." I turn the phone to show a woman screaming as she burns. Then a hooded figure steps in front of the smoldering ashes:

"We are Mors Strigae, sworn enemies of creatures like this. Vampires are everywhere – feeding on your neighbors, draining the economy, and corrupting the moral fabric of society. Join us in our crusade to destroy every one of them. And their human helpers!"

Daniel's face drains of color. "Who are these people?"

"Her name was Agripina and they are FUCKING MONSTERS!" She hurls the empty glass across the room; the crystal explodes into hundreds of pieces that ricochet off the walls. My ears ring as we wait for her to recover. Finally: "Wolf, please fill another glass for me."

While I pour, she turns to Daniel. "They're monks who were supposed to have disappeared at the turn of the century – the last century. I need you to dig up information about them and present your findings to the Council." She nods as I hand her a fresh glass. "We know everything up to 1900. Just give us their recent activities." Then she takes the glass back to her room and slams the door.

~

I've been assigned to Miklós, the family's oldest. At 800 years, he is also the thirstiest. He motions for another refill, and I immediately step forward with the decanter. Standing at his right, I pour A negative – his favorite – into a gold goblet. Once it's filled, I step back to the wall while Miklós raises a withered hand. "The Council will come to order." Ten faces turn toward him, each seated clockwise from their leader according to age. The fourth seat is empty. We're in a candlelit room inside a Greystone home on Chicago's North Side.

Miklós dabs a black napkin to his lips before speaking: "Konstantin will make arrangements for Agripina's memorial service, which will be next Wednesday." Konstantin, second oldest, sits stone-faced while the others glance at the empty seat. Miklós pauses before continuing. "Our lives are no longer secret. What we need to do tonight is agree on a plan to address the immediate threat." He nods toward the third in line. "Ferdinand will devise a plan for how we'll live once this crisis is over." His grey hooded eyes scan the group. "What I need are suggestions for our immediate response."

Søren Fillenius, seated on the other side of Miklós, leans forward. "We need to find the group's leader and kidnap him. Then we'll ransack his mind until we learn who his lieutenants are. We'll repeat the process all the way down to the rank and file."

Konstantin dismisses this with a wave. "Their minds are filled with one thing, and one thing only: God. If you want to listen to them pray ad nauseum, be our guest."

"Then we'll torture them." Søren taps his chest. "I'll get them to talk."

"Torture doesn't work," Konstantin fires back. "They'll lie to stop the pain."

Ferdinand chimes in. "They're fanatics, Søren. They'll happily accept martyrdom over divulging information."

Søren shrugs. "Then I shall oblige them."

Ferdinand raises his voice. "You'll do nothing until we agree on concerted action."

Fiona stands. "We know how they're locating us."

All turn to the now fourth-oldest. "My senior guardian has been studying this group and has important information to share. Daniel." Fiona points to her chair.

A rumble emerges as Daniel takes her seat and sets an open laptop on the table. Fiona looks at Miklós. "I'm lending him my chair so he can address you directly and answer your questions."

Daniel bows his head: "Members of the Council, please accept my condolences."

Miklós regards this mortal for a few seconds. "Proceed."

Daniel adjusts his glasses. "Last year, Mors Strigae established their headquarters about a hundred miles southeast of here."

Another rumble, followed by hissing. Miklós crushes his goblet with his fingers and smashes it down like a gavel. "The S word is forbidden in every use of speech – including proper nouns. This is your final reminder."

"Forgive me." Daniel inclines his head again. "Two years ago, they bought a ranch near the junction of Interstates 80 and 39 to set up a training camp. They also went on a spending spree." He checks the screen. "132 pickup trucks, all with winches. Dozens of axes and large hammers, crowbars and chains. Plus guns and ammunition."

Ferdinand growls: "Everything they would need to break in and drag an immortal into the daylight."

Søren quickly follows: "And kill any humans who interfere."

Konstantin addresses Daniel. "You haven't explained yet how they found Agripina. Do so now."

"Drones." Daniel turns his laptop to show a thermal image of a residential street at night. The camera zooms in from above, recording a passing cyclist at 98 degrees Fahrenheit. Seconds later, a blueish figure exits a nearby home. The camera tracks it, recording a temperature of 28 degrees. A gasp erupts around the table while someone asks: "Is that Agripina – the one they murdered?"

"I think it is!"

"ORDER." Miklós admonishes the group before returning to Daniel. "Where did they get the money for the ranch and equipment?"

"I'm still trying to find the source, but I have more urgent news to share." Daniel indicates his head toward me. "My associate drove down to the ranch this week to fly our own drone over the property. Over two days, he saw no signs of

activity – no people, no trucks."

Miklós seems puzzled. "Do you believe they abandoned the place?"

"After training and arming themselves, they don't need it anymore." Daniel looks around the table. "Right now they're probably doing thermal scans in every American city."

The Council silently absorbs the news while Søren turns to Fiona. "Does your senior guardian know if the ranch is for sale?"

"He's in my seat. You'll need to ask him."

Søren turns to Daniel. "Well?"

"Since you asked, yes." Daniel stares unblinking at his former employer. "It went on the market this morning. Interested?"

"Yes." Søren looks around the room. "I think we should all buy it."

Miklós turns. "Why?"

"It's the last place they'll look," Søren suppresses a smile, but it's clear he's pleased with himself. "Plus, there's safety in numbers."

"If I may add," Daniel closes his laptop, "the listing agent may lead us to the owner who, in turn, may lead us to the group's financial backers."

Miklós frowns. "Gathering in one place for any period is risky."

Ferdinand leans forward. "Remaining separated, though, could allow the monks to pick us off," he glances at Agripina's seat, "one by one."

Konstantin turns to Miklós. "It wouldn't hurt to inquire about the property."

"I agree," Søren chimes in.

Fiona places a hand on her guardian's shoulder. "I nominate Daniel to be our agent."

"Well," Miklós looks around the table, "we have to do something. Those in favor?"

~

Daniel's bedroom is spare: a bed, desk, and computer. No pictures or artwork. I hand him a glass of scotch while Fiona lounges on the bed, contemplating his suitcase. Once again, my eyes struggle to remain far from her breasts which nearly spill out of the gaping robe. She looks at Daniel. "How long have we been together?"

"35 years."

"In all that time, we've been apart only once. You lost your arm, remember?"

He smiles grimly. "Don't worry, I intend to keep the other."

She sits upright and pulls the silk around her. "How long will you be gone?"

Daniel swallows some whiskey and thinks. "A week. Two, maybe." He nods in my direction. "Wolf has the pickup schedule, plus a list of backup providers. You'll be in good hands."

I try to reassure her. "We have 20 pints in the chiller. That's a two-day supply." Fiona ignores me.

Daniel sets down his glass and locks eyes with her. "While I'm gone," he speaks in measured tones, "I think it would be best if you stay out of sight. By that, I mean, in the house."

Woah. More than once, Daniel told me never to question Fiona about her nightly sorties, so I expect a sharp rebuke. Her expression, though, resembles that of a girl gazing at a protective father. "I understand."

She doesn't get up as he lifts his suitcase. I step aside as he exits the room. In the kitchen, Daniel sets down the case. "Still have that pistol I gave you?"

I nod.

He reaches above the cupboards. A second later he hands me a short version of an M16 rifle with two curved magazines taped to each other. "This is fully automatic. Each mag has 30 rounds. Press the release." I pull out one magazine, turn it over, and insert the other. He points. "Pull that to lock and load, and that's the safety. Now look at me." Daniel's always been serious but this time his gaze thickens my blood. "Don't wait for them to enter the house. Start firing the minute you see them."

Seconds later, he's out the door. I'm still holding the weapon when Fiona enters the kitchen. She glances at the gun, then looks at me expectantly. I set it on the counter, pour a glass of O neg, and watch her take it to the living room. She turns on the TV but angrily turns it off when that video plays again. I sit on a nearby chair and notice a deck of cards on the coffee table. Daniel likes to play Solitaire, which I find boring, but I know a game two can play.

"Want to play Slapjack? My grandmother taught me this." Fiona looks at my hands as I shuffle the deck and divide it in two. "Keep your cards face down, but we'll each draw one at a time off the top. When you see a Jack, slap it. If you hit it first, you get the discard pile. The goal is to win all the cards." I draw a King which starts the center pile, and look at her. "Your move."

She does nothing except swallow O neg.

I reach over and draw her top card, a Queen, which I toss on top of the King. Then I draw a Five.

She stares at me. I draw from her stack again and toss a Ten on the center pile. Next, I draw a Jack and slap it.

She looks at my hand, then at my face. Her eyes burn fiercely. I dare not breathe as she sets the empty glass on the table and rises. "I'm going out."

~ PART TWO ~
AD RURSUS CONVENTUM NOSTRUM

FIONA'S FAREWELL

Der Vampyr. El vampiro. Un vampire. Il vampiro.

In every language where the noun "vampire" has a gender, it is male. Latin languages allow you to convert the noun to female – *la vampira* – but conversion does not equal default.

Most of the names you know also are male: Count Dracula, Count Orlock, Barlow, Louis and Lestat. By contrast, two of the best known non-males -- Claudia and Eli -- are or present as young girls. And adult females like me, how do we come into being? We are *sired*. Even if the creator's name is Agripina.

On this moonless night, I ignore the falling object ahead of me – just a meteor? – and focus on a vision that seems almost within reach: red hair, emerald eyes, skin the color and translucence of parchment. I want to remember how she looked when I met her 250 years ago. But as my fingers extend toward her face, she disappears. Heartbroken, I stop in the middle of the street and gaze at her only memento, a bee frozen in amber.

"Your transformation present." Agripina watched as my hand opened to reveal the entombed insect. I stared open-mouthed at this moment captured centuries before my human birth. "Look how it traps the sunlight," I said, holding it near a candle. "Like the bee landed on a spoonful of honey in the middle of the afternoon." I leaned forward to kiss her lips which felt normal, not icy like the first time. Then I stood still as her arms reached around my neck to fasten the chain. The amulet fell gently against my heart. Then she rested her forehead against mine. "It's good to have a reminder of life under the sun." She frowned. "My creator gave me nothing."

Miklós. I don't care that he neglected to commemorate her new life. But I'll never forgive his failure to stop her annihilation, even after I warned him Mors Strigae would return. "Those monks are fanatics," I once declared to the Council. "Men like that will never stop trying to exterminate us." Miklós bristled. What did I, a female, know of this ancient order that he, a hero, didn't? After all, we annihilated Mors Strigae during the last war. Secret Vatican records call it the Battle of the Catacomb, but it was a simple ruse that took advantage of the monks' poor leadership. It still irks me that Miklós took credit for this "victory," thanking Konstantin and Ferdinand for their help, while ignoring those who fought most of the skirmishes: me and Agripina. Flush with victory, the males decreed we should move to the New World, where most humans hadn't heard of our kind; they would be easy prey. But before they left, I shared a concern with Ferdinand about new techniques police were using:

"They can determine how long a body has been dead."

He shrugged. "And?"

"That means they know when someone dies at night."

"And?"

"They have chemicals that reveal drops of blood. They could follow the trail to our homes and use that evidence to obtain a search warrant."

"Fiona, what's your solution?"

"This." I slap a newspaper on the table. The headline read: *Blood Bank Opens, Issues Call for Donations.*

He looked up. "Are you suggesting that we stop hunting humans?"

"I suggest we start hiring them."

"To what – give blood?"

"No. Steal it."

My idea was simple. We'd hire people who handled donated blood. They'd steal just enough for our needs, an amount that wouldn't be noticed so long as people kept donating. Ferdinand laughed and ordered me to leave his home. Then he took my idea to Miklós and Konstantin, convinced them it might work, and took credit when it did.

When I finally arrived in America, decades later, I learned we had reverted to an ancient way of living: individual households, spread hours apart like islands, each responsible for their own blood supply. I saw two problems. First, the oldest immortals had the wealth to maintain networks that rarely failed. Those younger and poorer, by contrast, struggled. They often had to take humans to avoid starving, which triggered investigations. Living on a single property, I argued, allowed for centralized management so everyone would get what they need – without police interference. A single property also addressed my other concern: defense. When Mors Strigae returned, as they always did, we'd need an armed retinue to protect us during the day. Gathering our guardians into one force would accomplish this. When I raised this at a meeting, the elders smugly replied the monks were "dead as the Dodo." Without urgency, they saw no reason to change. We continued living as islands.

Want to visit my island? Beware. It's a steaming volcano in my image that's ready to blow now that Agripina is gone. For too long, males of my kind waged war, legislated peace, and kept power for themselves. Then, perverting my idea, they grew lazy on donated blood and devolved from hunters to gentrified parasites.

Meanwhile, Mors Strigae introduced drones with thermal scanners – something for which we had no defense. They located Agripina at night, when she was too powerful to confront, and waited for when she was asleep.

If you've seen that video, as millions have, you'll guess my kind is on a path toward extinction. Perhaps you'll approve. But Agripina did not deserve her fate, and you should at least know why.

"Never take children." She pointed at the upper windows of a thatched farmhouse. I didn't need to look up; I heard their little lungs breathing in and out, and my stomach growled.

"If your choice is between a child and hunger, go home hungry." She pointed toward another room where someone peed into a chamber pot; the odor was doubly pungent. "The same goes for women with child."

"That doesn't leave us many choices."

"Sure it does. There." She pointed toward another house a mile away. "A man who beats his wife and cheats his neighbors. He's our first meal tonight. The world will be better for it."

"I didn't realize we had to be so... ethical."

"Humans need ethics, we don't." Agripina placed her hands on my shoulders. "All you need to remember is this: God put us here to feed on humans, but we can be smart about it. Take mature victims and you won't run out of food. Select undesirables like Mr. Wife Beater and nobody will miss them. And no one will come looking for the killer."

Just last year, Agripina teased me about my human appearance when we first met: the smell of horse sweat on my body, the straw in my hair, freckles on my cheeks. She discovered me in a barn one night, singing to the animals. She wanted me right then but waited.

"Such a lovely voice. Such a beautiful girl." She smiled wistfully. "I climbed into your bed while you were sleeping. Do you remember that?"

I confessed I didn't.

"Probably for the better." She took each of my hands and kissed them. "I think neither of us knew it would end with you being my eternal companion."

Then she asked if I still had that bee in amber. My face melts as I remember unbuttoning my blouse to show her. Blood clouds my vision, overflows, and rains down my face to the pavement, followed by the amulet which bounces away from my feet.

Orphan is too simple a word. It addresses abandonment, but not the loss of someone who remembers you from your previous life, a life you can't remember without her help. If there is a noun for this condition it better be feminine. Should one of the elders say, "Sorry for the loss of your sire," I will attack without concern for the consequences. I could kill Ferdinand -- he's only a century older. But Konstantin is powerful; he'd destroy me before I reached Miklós. Is it worth holding back a little longer? Perhaps it's best not to appear too mournful and wait for the right moment to strike. There, Agripina, how's that for philosophy?

I hear a strange sound. I stop and see a disk with four propellers stuck in a tree. Is this the meteor-like thing I saw earlier? It buzzes intermittently, like a dying cicada. I pull it down and see two propellers are damaged, as if it collided with a larger object.

Turning it over, I find a lens staring at me. A blinking light tells me it still works.

~

"Father Abbot, you need to see this." Brother Leo nods toward a screen with a stuttering image. "The unit is damaged but still transmitting."

The Abbot leans in. "What am I looking at?"

"It's blue, 28 degrees." Leo points. "We have a hit!"

"Yes, but where?"

"This one went down an hour west of Chicago."

"Zoom out – I need an ID."

Leo adjusts the frame, revealing her face. The abbot gives a long, low whistle. "The Devil keeps tempting us, Brother. She's more beautiful than the last." He checks his tablet, swiping through the images. "This appears to be a new one."

"Attention, Mors Strigae. This is Fiona, addressing you for the first time since your defeat at the catacomb."

The abbot raises his eyebrows. "Are you recording this?"

"Yes, Father Abbot."

"Miklós, Konstantin, and Ferdinand send their greetings. They, and I, eagerly anticipate the rematch you're no doubt hoping for. Think you'll fare better this time?"

"Coordinates, Brother – where is she?"

"I'm re-directing two more, hoping to tri-angulate."

"Meet us next Tuesday in Chicago on North Astor Street. A large Greystone, quite a bit different from the catacomb where your order suffered its worst humiliation. Ad rursus conventum nostrum."

The screen goes blank.

PRAISE THE LORD
AND PASS THE WOODEN BULLETS

An iPhone screen goes live, and Wolf's face pops into view:

"Hey, Daniel, remember me? I'm the guy who's blowing up your phone but you haven't answered so I'm putting out an SOS, hoping you'll find this message in the event that something, I don't know, happens to me." He takes a deep breath. "Sorry for the drama, but things are crazy unpredictable around here. Fiona's been gone for two days, which you'd know if you read my messages. Then yesterday, another vampire -- who claims he's a friend of Fiona's -- moved in. His name is Søren and said you knew him. I don't know what your history is with this guy, but he looks like a motherfucking sadist. Very different from Fiona who, yeah, can be bitchy sometimes, but not a stone-cold killer. I think Søren knows Fiona disappeared, but he isn't saying anything. He only speaks when ordering pints from Fiona's stash and, frankly, I'm not comfortable delivering it to him." Wolf looks off camera and whispers. "He went out a little while ago, and I'm pretty sure one of our neighbors is gonna die." A short laugh. "Hunters gotta hunt, right? At least I'm not on the menu – yet." Back to the camera. "So that's my report. One vampire disappears, and other moves in. Like cats, except cats are cute. Well, Fiona's more than cute. Smokin' hot, actually." He shakes his head. "I don't know how you can work for her and not constantly be thinking about fucking her. Maybe you do. Whatever the case, I'm worried. What if she doesn't come back? I mean, yeah, I don't want anything to happen to her but, honestly, I felt protected when she was around. Like I'm part of her team. Anyway, if I die before you get back, Søren is your number one suspect. Okay?"

The screen goes dark.

~

Shortly after recording the video, I'm counting the remaining bags of O negative when – finally – Daniel calls. I pick it up. "Fiona's gone. Søren's here. Something's up."

Søren grabs the phone, crushes it, and tosses it in the trash while his other hand yanks a bag from my hand, slices it open, and fills a glass. He barely turns his head as he enters the living room: "Bring me another in five minutes!"

I exhale slowly through clenched teeth. Vampire law stipulates that guardians must serve any immortal who visits – even those we detest.

"Don't say 'vampire."

I forgot: They can hear our thoughts. Just focus on the work…

"Good boy. And order some A positive for me."

I'm about to pour a second pint from Fiona's supply when Daniel opens the door. He pauses in the hallway, staring at the intruder, before walking out of view. I follow with two glasses, one filled with scotch, the other with O neg.

"A lot happened since you went away." Søren nods toward the opposite chair framing the cold fireplace. "Have a seat."

Daniel sets his suitcase on the floor, noticing Søren's empty glass. "I hope you left some for Fiona." He looks around. "Where is she?"

"She's…unavailable."

Daniel marches up to Søren and stares down eagle-eyed. "Where is Fiona?"

"A little more respect, mortal," Søren glares back. "Or I'll rearrange what's left of your body so your ass becomes your face and vice-versa."

"But you won't." Daniel plants his hand on his hip. "You're here, which means you need my help."

"Well," Søren's eyebrows lift, "you are perceptive. Fiona always said you were her best guardian."

"WHERE IS SHE?"

"HAVE A SEAT."

I set Daniel's whiskey next to the empty chair, hoping that will defuse the standoff. Daniel picks up the glass but remains on his feet.

"She's under house arrest," Søren accepts his drink without

looking at me. "They arrested her yesterday."

"Who arrested her?"

"Ferdinand and Konstantin. She's staying with Miklós now, but incommunicado. I'm not allowed to speak with her, and she's my sire."

Daniel nearly chokes on his drink. "What?"

"Oh you didn't know?" Søren waves dismissively. "Doesn't matter. The important thing is we need Miklós to delay the trial."

"Tri – what the fuck is she on trial for?"

Søren's gaze is so intense that I start shivering. "She gave the monks the address of our meeting home. Of course, they torched the place."

Daniel's face drains of color. "Why would she do that?"

"They also killed three guardians. They, at least, are replaceable."

"You wouldn't say that if you had one."

Søren's eyes narrow. "I seem to recall having one who left suddenly in the 1980s." He waves again. "But enough history. The elders want to know what else she told the monks."

Daniel recovers from his shock. "And you think I know something."

Søren looks at him for a few seconds. "I had hoped you would, but it's clear you don't." He takes another sip, then dabs his lips with a black napkin embroidered with a gold F. "Perhaps we should talk about your trip to the ranch. Did the owner accept our offer?"

"You're asking about real estate? What are you doing to free Fiona?"

Søren looks at his glass. "I'm working on that."

"Doesn't look like it to me. What about you, Wolf?"

"Nope." I shake my head. "Someone sent him on an errand."

"Sure looks like it." Daniel turns back to Søren.

"Who sent you?"

Søren grins innocently. "I'm following up on my brilliant idea to buy the ranch after our enemies abandoned it. You're our agent – give me a report."

"'Our agent'." Daniel sets his drink on the table. "The elders sent you."

Søren purses his lips. "My position…is difficult." He uses the napkin to buff the large ruby on his right hand. "I'm the junior member of the Council. Miklós, Konstantin, and Ferdinand – they call the shots. I could be arrested too, if I disobey."

"So you're proving your loyalty to them." Daniel leans forward. "How about doing the same for Fiona?"

Woah, Daniel, let's not poke the vampire; I hold my breath. Søren inhales deeply as his hands grip the arms of the chair. Then, eyes closed, he rises. His body shakes and I think he might actually reach down Daniel's throat and pull out his guts. When his eyes reopen, they are blood-red. "Don't question my feelings for her again."

I step between them. "What do you want from us?"

Søren keeps his eyes on Daniel. "I want you to proceed with the purchase and keep me posted as you prepare to close."

"So you're all moving there." Daniel thinks aloud. "And Fiona? She'll be held there before her trial, right?"

Søren hesitates. "That would be a reasonable assumption."

"I know that, but is it correct?"

I speak up again: "What if the monks return to the ranch and Fiona's locked up? She'd be a sitting duck."

Søren finally looks at me. "You have a better idea?" When met with silence, he starts pacing. "We need to come up with a plan. Both of you -- start thinking."

Daniel's eyes follow Søren. "If we agree to help, I want you to guarantee our safety."

"Even if I wanted to – and that would be a stretch -- it's out of my hands." Søren glances at me as he passes by. "I've been ordered to dispatch you both when you're no longer useful."

"Fiona would never forgive you."

"There you are correct." Søren stops. "So you two are safe as long as Fiona's alive. And I'm safe as long as I feed your information to the elders. Are we on the same page? Good. Now let's begin again: What's the owner's name and did he accept our offer?"

~

Father Abbot clips Fiona's image to a wire, flips a switch, and watches it retreat toward the back wall. Her large eyes and low-cut dress were captured by a thermal camera. But instead of yellow waves, Fiona's below-freezing body shows up in blue. What would her voluptuous breasts feel like if he got the chance? Would his hands go numb? The abbot turns off the pulley and watches her face and neckline halt above a line reading 50 FEET. His groin tingles as his thumb strokes the crucifix on his pistol grip. "You are indeed a temptation, my dear." He takes a deep breath. "I release the spirit of Jehu against Jezebel and her cohorts. I command Jezebel to be thrown down and eaten by the hounds of heaven." Then he raises the gun and fires once, which is all the time he'd have in an actual encounter. The practice round misses her heart. If this were real, she'd be drinking from his jugular.

Someone taps his shoulder. Startled, Father Abbot lifts one ear cover. "Brother Raymond, you have a light footstep – sure you're not a vampire?"

Raymond offers the thinnest of smiles. "I heard from the buyer. His bid is two million."

"For a 500-acre ranch?" The abbot stares at the gun. "That's lower than I expected."

"We need the money."

Father Abbot shakes his head. "We should wait for a higher bid."

"That could be months, and we're at war."

The abbot's eyes brighten. "If I hit her heart, we reject the offer."

"And if you miss, we accept?" Brother Raymond considers this. "The Lord has unexpected ways of revealing the true path."

"Indeed. Cover your ears." Father Abbot aims again, fires, and slowly lowers the pistol.

Raymond squints toward the target, then lowers his head. "I'll tell the buyer we welcome their offer."

"Thy Will be done." The abbot sighs. "Did you bring the bullets I ordered?"

Brother Raymond places a 50-round box on the table. "Australian Buloke, as you requested."

Father Abbot sets his pistol on the table and removes his yellow glasses. Then he grasps a round between thumb and forefinger, holding it to the light. The tan micro-grain wood is smooth as silk. "Allocasuarina luehmannii."

Raymond folds his hands in front of him. "Furniture oak is a lot cheaper. A hundred boxes of this will bust our budget."

"Only the hardest hardwood will do, Brother." The abbot grins. "This will penetrate a standard door, plus two guardians, and still stop a vampire's heart. More efficient than a sharpened stick, eh?" He elbows his lieutenant. "Besides, we just sold a ranch. We can afford these now."

Raymond frowns. "My latest sums included a higher price for the property. We were already short before this new expense."

"The Lord will find a way, Brother – He always does." Father Abbot stuffs the bullet into the chamber and Brother Raymond again covers his ears.

"And when the Lord God shall deliver them before thee," the abbot raises the pistol, "thou shalt smite them, and utterly destroy them; thou shalt make no covenant with them…" He fires. "…nor show mercy unto them."

The bullet leaves a hole in the center of Fiona's heart. "Hallelujah!" Father Abbot beams while Brother Raymond clasps his hands in prayer: "Now I know that the Lord gives victory to his chosen king; he answers him from holy heaven and by his power gives him great victories."

"Amen."

"Vivat Mors Strigae."

Both men are silent while the abbot holsters his gun. "Find any more vampires?"

"No." Raymond indicates his head toward the target. "And no further sign of the one who betrayed her foul kin."

"Females, Brother," Father Abbot loops a scarf around his neck, "they always have an agenda. Probably wanted to bump off her rivals."

"That's why our enemies will perish." Raymond gives a sidelong glance as they near the exit. "They lack discipline and act in isolation."

"And they only eat one thing – amazing they don't die of boredom." The abbot dons dark sunglasses. "Want Mexican today? Or Thai?"

Raymond holds the door for his boss. "I found a sushi place you might like."

Father Abbot strolls into the sunshine. "And Jesus said, 'Follow Me, and I will make you fishers of men.'"

Raymond watches him for a few seconds before continuing toward their SUV.

~

"The agent for the ranch is one of the higher-ranking monks, Brother Raymond." Daniel looks up from his notepad. "I believe he's second in command to the abbot."

Søren keeps his eyes on Daniel while I fill his glass. "What's your sense of this Raymond?"

"He's cautious." Daniel swallows more whiskey. "I detected ill-will toward the abbot who will make the final decision. We might be able to exploit that."

"Yes but how?" Søren takes a quick swallow. "We need a specific wedge to drive between them."

Daniel nods once. "Brother Raymond seems disciplined, and committed to his cause. But during our meeting, he became impatient with the abbot who didn't return his texts. One of those conveyed our offer."

"What does that tell you?"

"Either the abbot is unreachable or he's indecisive. Either one suggests he shouldn't be the leader."

"That's the gap we're looking for." Søren points. "There's nothing more dangerous than a subordinate who thinks he's the better commander."

"What are you proposing?"

"We wait." Søren smiles. "You made the offer. If they accept, the elders will proceed with the move. If, however, Raymond is ready to usurp the abbot, then we can take advantage of the chaos that causes." He turns to me. "We might even be able to place one of our own in their group."

A NOVICE NAMED WOLF

Diary of Brother Raymond Keane
Mors Strigae training camp, Arizona.

Our struggling novitiate finally had a good week. Wolf Perry's knowledge of scripture is, to be charitable, limited. But he's well-informed about vampires which makes him uniquely qualified to succeed in our order. For instance, he knows exactly how long between meals before they start to decay. He knows the type of dwelling they prefer and how they prevent sunlight from getting in. He even told me that vampires prefer different blood types – a revelation. It's almost as if he were raised by these evil creatures, which of course is nonsense; vampires are incapable of nurturing. Nonetheless, Novice Perry is vague when asked for details about his experience. All this makes me wonder about his reasons for joining us. Is he after glory? The thrill of combat? Revenge? I'll circle back after I assess his abilities. Tomorrow, if it pleases God, I'll focus his next lesson on scripture central to our mission.

~

"Novice Perry: All who die in God's grace, even if not purified, are assured of eternal salvation. But after death they undergo purification to achieve the holiness to enter Heaven. Where does this purification take place?"

"Purgatory, Brother Raymond."

"And what is the process that releases a soul to Purgatory?"

"Putrefaction, Brother Raymond."

"And if putrefaction doesn't follow death, and the body's not frozen, what must we conclude?"

"That the corpus mortuus is, in fact, a corpus strigus."

"Striga, novice. The default for this noun is feminine."

"Yes brother." Novice Perry knits his brow. "Since the order is called Mors Strigae, are we focused on female vampires?"

I raise my hand. "During these examinations, I ask… " My hand comes down. "We pursue any and all children of Satan."

"Thank you, brother."

Normally, I don't allow thread drift during examinations, but Novice Perry raised a theme that long preoccupied me. Namely: how gender assignment can reveal a word's benign or malignant nature. Still, I worry about imposing advanced interpretation on someone so young. While waiting for Heavenly Father to guide me, I fill my lungs with incense and slowly let it out. A candle on a nearby offertory burns brighter than the others, and I realize the number of flames equals the current number of novitiates. My feet begin a slow journey around Novice Perry while my lips give freedom to long-imprisoned ideas…

"When I was a novice like you, I wondered: Why is the Latin noun striga feminine? Could this ancient language be whispering to us, hinting about the nature of vampires – of evil itself? After much prayer and reading of scripture, plus folklore, I've come to believe that femininity is at the heart of this scourge we are pledged to exterminate."

"I've had a similar thought." Novice Perry's eyes light up. "Vampires hunt under the moon, which is associated with women – including menstrual cycles."

"Excellent observation!" I clap once; the crack echoes off the sanctuary walls. After pausing, I begin another circle. "You might remember the Latin word for blood is sanguis which is masculine. How interesting that strigae nourish themselves exclusively from human blood. I could go on about reports of vampires' sexual arousal while feeding – a double abomination. Ignoring that, it's still easy to see how femininity drains masculinity." I clasp my hands behind me. "You can see this in the Bible where two of the most infamous women, Eve and Delilah, lead their men into sin and downfall. Could these women have been vampires? The Bible doesn't say because the prophets wouldn't have known about these creatures. But from Adam and Samson, the prophets understood that the erosion of manhood creates the conditions for evil to flourish."

"Does this explain the vow of celibacy?"

"Yes it does." I stop. "You're catching on quickly. Let's go outside."

~

I hate not being able to move. Not being able to feed myself. I am completely helpless thanks to silver restraints historically used by our enemies. That this metal is being employed by my own kind is galling enough, but adding a period of isolation is a special kind of cruelty. You see, when you're free to roam, it's easy to keep ahead of unpleasant memories. Now, 250 years' worth of forgotten images play over and over and over. Since my capture, I've mourned Agripina dozens of times, but I'd stay forever in this dark hole of silence rather than listen to Ferdinand. What my prosecutor hopes to achieve with this visit I'm not sure. Perhaps he's enjoying a moment of schadenfreude. I wouldn't mind this ego puff at my expense if he had a message from my grand-sire.

"Where's Miklós?"

"I'm afraid he's busy." Ferdinand's eyes land on the silver surrounding my neck, hands, feet, and pelvis. "Does that hurt?"

"Has he asked about me or mentioned my name?"

"No."

"Could you at least bring me some O negative?"

"This is not a hotel, Fiona. And I'm not your concierge."

"Then why are you here?"

He shrugs. "I suppose I'd like to know why you're representing yourself."

"We both know you're the family's only lawyer. And, forever needing to prove your worth, you chose to prosecute. You're here for another reason."

"I was hoping you'd tell me why."

"Why...?"

"You burned our gathering place."

My lips curl. "Is your case so weak it hinges on a motive?"

"It's open and shut." His chest swells as his hands go to his hips. "Your motive is a mere ornament."

"Then why ask?"

"Look, I know I haven't been a kind uncle. I was brusque, imperious, disinterested..."

"Not when you wanted sex."

"But I don't relish the idea of you – blood of my blood – receiving a death sentence. The hole you'll leave in our hearts will almost eclipse the stain you left on our family history."

"That was charming. Thank you."

"Will you tell me or not?"

"350 years."

His brow wrinkles. "What's my age got to do with it?"

"It was also Agripina's."

"Right." He straightens before laughing. "Miklós was busy in the 17th Century. Sired both of us in the same year."

"She six months before you."

"True." He folds his arms.

"And yet you sat ahead of her on the Council."

"That wasn't my decision."

"You decided to say nothing. And in doing so, you stole what was hers."

"Gender before age – that's how we're seated. The males of our species have always led. You can't demand that we change centuries of tradition!"

"I will keep demanding. Right up to the moment I burn."

"All right, how about this – and this is my final offer." Ferdinand's gaze meets mine. "If you apologize to the elders, and beg for their mercy, I'll ask the Council to consider your petition – "

"What petition?"

"– to allow females equal access to Council seats."

"No."

"Why?"

"I don't need to apologize. I don't need their mercy. And I definitely don't need you to ask for my equality when I am already equal."

"Fine. Have it your way." He turns and walks toward the door. "I'd say bon chance, but we both know your luck has run out."

"Careful yours doesn't run out as well, Ferdinand."

"Who do you think you are?" He approaches again, aiming a nail at my face. "You've shown no remorse after exposing us – threatening your family with extinction!" The nail retreats. "And yet you sit there, smugly suggesting that some Deus ex Machina will fly in and save you." He leans in, close. "250 years. That's all you'll get, Fiona. Make your peace with us. Show some contrition and grace. And tell us how we should dispose of your ashes."

~

"Remember, you must hit her heart." My right hand makes the sign of the cross over the gun. "St. Gabriel, Protector of those who bear arms. Hear our prayer and intercede with Christ our God that he may make our barrels straight, our triggers swift, and our aim accurate."

Novice Perry shields his eyes as he looks downrange. "What's the distance?"

"50 feet." I point at the ground. "Stand firmly at this line. You may bend your knees a little." I check to be sure his finger rests on the trigger guard. "Thumb on the safety?"

"Yes."

I motion with my hands. "Extend your right arm, but leave the elbow relaxed. Now take

your left hand and rest it under the pistol grip, like a saucer beneath a cup."

"I have a question."

"Go ahead."

"Did you see that video of our brothers burning a vampire in Michigan? They dragged her out of a house using a winch."

"Yes. I drove the truck that pulled her."

"Then you saw her burn to ashes in the sunlight."

I cross myself. "Divine vengeance is at once terrible and awesome to witness."

"But if the current tactics work so well, why do we need guns?"

"The abbot..." I sigh. "He wants to engage the enemy at all times, including when they're most powerful."

"I've seen them move. It's like the speed of light."

"Then you know the odds. At 50 feet, you'll get one shot. To prepare, you'll have ten rounds for your first practice, with one less for each consecutive session. At the end of the course, you'll need to hit the heart with your first and only shot."

"Are these the wooden bullets?"

"No, practice rounds." I squint at the life-size torso and head printed on cardboard. The thermal image shows the wavy blue outlines of a freezing body. But one can still see her undulating hair, large eyes, and a neckline that's a huge distraction. I regain focus. "Ready?"

"Yes, Brother."

"Slowly fire ten times."

~

My eyes barely believe the results. I stare at the target between my hands, count eight holes in her heart, and shake my head. Only the most experienced brothers achieve such a score, which plays into another aspect of our order: economics. Our combat-issue bullets, tipped with the hardest hardwood, cost $200 each or $10,000 per box. I continue to push for furniture oak – wood is wood, for Heaven's sake – but the abbot insists on these. Under this regime, even a marksman like Novice Perry could be expected to waste $2,000. Still, the abbot considers this "acceptable given the importance of our mission." Never mind him. After lunch, I invite Novice Perry to my office.

"Is Wolf your birth name?"

"It's the name given by my adoptive mother. Short for Wolford."

"Hmm." I pour two glasses of wine. "Rome was founded by two brothers raised by a wolf: Romulus and Remus."

Novice Perry accepts a glass. 'Thank you."

I swallow and let my imagination flow – something I rarely do because it detracts from His holy mission. But Heavenly Father must be speaking when I remember Romulus murdered Remus after the latter ridiculed the wall his brother built to protect our future spiritual home. Eyes closed, I nod certain that God delivered a righteous warrior to me. My eyes reopen. "After your initiation, I shall name you Brother Romulus."

Wolf's eyes go wide. "You mean I've been accepted?"

I rise and stretch out my hand, allowing him to kiss my ring, a ruby overlaid with a silver crucifix. "The ceremony starts at dawn tomorrow. After breakfast, you'll begin your first mission."

A knock on the door. Father Abbot walks in and abruptly stops when he sees the novice on one knee. "Brother Raymond, what did I tell you about meeting alone with novitiates? We can't afford another compromising incident." He notices the stemware. "Really, Brother, is he old enough to drink?"

My hand quickly withdraws. "I've identified a talented prospect for our team."

Father Abbot glares. "I'm the one who selects our members." He turns to the novice. "I don't believe we've met. I'm the head of this order. Who are you?"

"This is… "

"He'll speak for himself, Brother Raymond." Father Abbot extends his hand. "No kissing required, a simple shake will do. Your name again?"

"Novice Wolford Perry." Their hands clasp. "My friends call me Wolf."

"Are you ready for graduation?"

"Yes Father Abbot."

"Let's be sure." The abbot glances at me and I see his skepticism. "Novice Perry, When King Jehu arrived in Jezreel, he saw Jezebel looking down at him with contempt. So he ordered three eunuchs to throw her out the window. After running her over with his chariot, Jehu issued another order. What was it?"

The young man straightens. "Jehu mistakenly ordered them to bury her."

"Mistakenly?" Father Abbot is incredulous. "I wanted a simple answer – not outlandish interpretation."

I motion to our student. "Answer his question."

"Forgive me, Father Abbot," the novice hesitates, "but Jehu skipped a step that's central to our mission."

The abbot raises an eyebrow. "Go on."

"We would hold a special vigil to watch for decomposition."

"Would we?" Father Abbot glances again at me. "What do you suspect about Jezebel?"

"Based on her infamy, we'd want to be sure she wasn't a striga."

The abbot scoffs. "Jezebel might have been wicked, but the Bible says nothing about her being a vampire."

Novice Perry nods. "The Bible also ignores this possibility about Eve and Delilah, but their harmful actions against men make them suspect."

"Do they?" The abbot locks eyes with the novice. "And what experience do you have with vampires?"

"I…" the novice hesitates.

I step forward. "The time has come for you to answer this question. You'll go no further without doing so."

~

Dusk. A mailbox opens on a suburban street in front of a townhome. Daniel reaches in, turns briefly toward the twilight, and takes a small stack of envelopes inside. He drops the bills on the counter, junk fliers in the trash, and keeps a postcard of a baseball diamond in the desert. He takes it to the living room, pours a glass of scotch, and sits in one of two large wingchairs flanking a cold fireplace. He flips the card over:

Spring training underway. Started with bench coach, then met Skipper who was uncertain at first. After some debate, I'm in the starting lineup.

W.

"Is he in?"

Daniel looks up at Søren stretching his slender arms and feels a phantom urge to do the same. "Yes. The abbot cleared him."

"Any friction between the top two?"

"The note refers to 'some debate.'"

"As I suspected." Søren sits in the opposite chair. "Looks like my plan is working."

"Your plan?"

"Oh, I'll give you some credit, not that the elders will care." He looks around. "I hope you scored some A positive today. Fiona's bags of O neg are about to expire."

"I brought home twenty pints." Daniel nods toward a decanter on the mantle. "You owe the house $6,000."

"Good. My palate's growing weary without my favorite." A pause. "Well?"

"Glasses are on the shelf. I'm not pouring again."

"Excuse me?" Søren's eyes smolder but Daniel returns his stare, daring him to escalate:

"Fiona may be detained, but I still work for her. Not you."

~

"I..." Novice Perry takes a deep breath. "I used to work for a vampire named Fiona." He points to the target on the desk. Brother Raymond picks it up. "This is Fiona?"

Novice Perry nods.

"How old?"

"250 years."

Raymond starts writing on a notepad. "Do you know her sire?"

"Agripina, the one you burned."

"Where is Fiona?"

"She disappeared a month ago. Around the same time, members of this order torched the home where Fiona met with the elders."

"Chicago. Large Greystone."

Novice Perry turns to the abbot. "Yes sir."

Father Abbot folds his arms. "Did you know Fiona contacted us to reveal the location of that building?"

Novice Perry's face drains of color. "No. I didn't." He turns to the target. "Is that how you got this image?"

"And you haven't seen her since the fire?"

"No Father Abbot."

"Who else works for her?"

"No one else."

The abbot's face betrays his doubt. "How old are you?"

"Twenty one."

The abbot shakes his head. "She'd have a more senior guardian managing her supply."

Novice Perry's hands go up. "That's all I'm going to say -- I'm not a traitor."

"Fiona is the traitor." The abbot's voice is sympathetic. He walks to the young man and places both hands on his shoulders. "She abandoned you and caused three of your fellow guardians to die in Chicago. I saw them go down." He lowers his head until their eyes are level. "You already said too much for her to take you back. She'll read your mind, discover what you told us, and kill you. You know this." He straightens. "We are your family now. Let us in. We can help you."

"I don't know." Novice Perry turns and leans on a window sill. "Just because she's gone doesn't mean she betrayed me."

"You say that," Raymond holds up the target again, "but you put eight bullets through her heart. I'd be lucky to group half that many." He taps the cardboard. "Whether it's you, or God working through you, this says everything."

~

Søren picks up one of Fiona's napkins and polishes a large ruby ring. "Our law is clear: A guardian becomes communal property when his employer is absent."

Daniel leans forward. "Your law allowed the elders to arrest Fiona. Your law allows them to kill your sire."

"Watch your tone, mortal." Søren's eyes briefly glow red. "They won't destroy her if we succeed." He aims a long finger. "You love her, admit it, so you have just as much to lose."

"All the more reason to regard me as an equal." Daniel raises his glass. "This evening starts a new contract. I'll keep investing Fiona's money and paying the bills. I'll get your supply. And I'll guard the place when you're asleep. That's all."

"You're not doing a good job on that last part."

Daniel nearly chokes on his scotch. "What?"

Søren indicates his head toward the street. "There are two men watching this house. White van, six doors down. They were here yesterday too." His eyes follow Daniel as he walks to the window. "We may have to adjust our plan."

"What are you suggesting?" Daniel slowly pulls the curtain

aside.

Søren rises, grabs the decanter, and fills his glass. "We need to draw Wolf out so I can read his mind."

Daniel narrows his eyes. "You've already decided what's in there. You think the monks turned him."

"You know it's a possibility. I'll be sure once I see him."

"You're not going anywhere near him." Daniel disappears down a hallway and returns seconds later with an M4 rifle slung across his chest. His hand holds a suitcase. "Go back to the elders. I'm going after Wolf."

"You have one arm – can you even reload that thing? The monks will kill you."

Daniel opens the front door. "They'll kill you, too, if you stay here."

GUNFIGHT AT THE OK TURNPIKE

"Call Fiona." Daniel slows as he approaches an exit on the Roy Turner Turnpike in Oklahoma. As is the case for several weeks, the call goes straight to voicemail:

"Chances are very good you arrived at the wrong place. Check your number carefully before dialing again. Those who know me may leave a message."

Daniel clears his throat. "It's me again, just outside Tulsa where I'm supposed to meet with Wolf. Here are some more details since my last message. A few weeks ago, Søren and I asked Wolf to join the monks and work undercover for us. Unfortunately, he may have been turned – not by choice, but by blackmail or other means. I'm going to try to flip him back. It's risky but he knows too much about our organization, and theirs, not to try. The rendezvous point is just ahead. I will proceed and hopefully call with an update." A pause. "Fiona, I refuse to believe that you are not alive. Please contact me the minute you're able."

~

Abandoned Mors Strigae Training Camp, Illinois – site for Fiona's trial.

"The court will come to order."

I look up from the witness box to see Miklós with the gavel. Next to him sits Konstantin, my granduncle. Based on the scale of my crime, however, I'm expecting a judge more senior than their combined 1,500 years.

"Is the defendant hungry?"

My head shake is the only move I can make. My hands and feet remain anchored by silver bracelets, and a harness of the same metal keeps my pelvis and back still. Eyes and mind are free to roam, though, and I see Miklós and Konstantin lack the customary wigs; part of me feels validated that someone more powerful will decide my fate.

"Due to the seriousness of the charges – conspiracy to commit fratricide on multiple counts – this trial will be presided over by the oldest member of our family tree, Caius Drusus." Miklós scans the courtroom. "Caius may be the grandsire of myself and Konstantin, but during this trial we will call him Magistrate. I understand he will join us presently."

"I am here."

All eyes turn to the back of the room where a curly-headed male stands draped in Roman robes, crowned by a golden laurel. Miklós and Konstantin rise, step back, and bow as the 2000-year-old passes. As he does, I hear him whisper to Miklós:

"You picked a site that belonged to our enemy? It smells of human food and human waste. Decamp immediately after this trial and find a more fitting place to live."

"As you wish, Magistrate." Miklós and Konstantin bow again.

My judge sits and examines the evidence before him. I never met Caius Drusus, but know his history of non-leniency. Still, he has a reputation for fairness, often in unexpected ways. He looks at me. "You are Fiona, sired by Agripina?"

I nod.

"You are aware of the charges against you?"

I nod.

"Have you been nourished with the required ten pints of blood each night? Please speak."

"Yes, Magistrate."

"Are you ready to defend yourself?"

"There will be no defense, Magistrate."

~

Wolf said to meet him on a dirt road, two miles from the exit. It's pitch black, so Daniel drives slowly. After a couple of minutes, his headlights find Wolf standing in the middle of the road, hand raised in a greeting -- or warning. Daniel gets out, arm bent, holding the M4 rifle pointed at the sky. Body armor covers his torso, groin, and thighs, and thermal goggles rest on his forehead.

Wolf notes the second magazine taped to the gun. "Wow, you're not taking any chances." He walks slowly toward him, stopping at thirty feet. "I assume you're alone?"

"That was the brief. As you can see, I've already guessed you're not."

"You always said trust no one."

"Are you armed?"

Wolf gives a slight smile. "You asked that question when we met. Remember my response?"

"Remind me."

"I have two to your one, so better armed than you."

"Right." Daniel smiles just a little. "Then Fiona appeared out of thin air. You should've seen your face."

Wolf laughs. "My heart actually stopped for, like, three seconds." The smile disappears. "It's a shame she won't be coming back."

"If you know something, this would be a good time to tell me."

"Hold that thought." Keeping his eyes on Daniel, Wolf tilts his head left, then right. Next his eyes dart behind Daniel.

Daniel breathes in deeply, then slowly exhales. "Your shoe's untied."

"Yeah?"

"I think you better tie it."

Wolf crouches and Daniel jerks the goggles into place. Yellow blobs appear to the right and left. He fires short bursts at each. When they fall, he gets behind the right front wheel of the car and fires toward the rear. The return fire comes heavy and close, forcing Daniel to lay flat. He shakes the glass from his hair and flips to full auto. Then he kneels, raises the gun above his head, and sprays through the now-windowless car. Two seconds later, he's empty. He sits against the wheel and holds the weapon between his knees, looking for a nearby blob that might be Wolf. There's no sign of him, and the voices are closing in. He releases the empty magazine, flips it, and inserts the fresh one. Then he reaches up and sprays again, fighting for time. After switching to single-fire, Daniel keeps the intruders at bay for a few more minutes until the rifle is useless. He tosses that aside, opens a flask, and enjoys a long swallow of scotch.

Did he expect this to end differently? Hardly. But with Fiona gone, his own life became less important and, well, Wolf was the last thing worth fighting for. Without help from him, Daniel was down to one .45 caliber pistol, two magazines, and a derringer for himself. As he prepares for one last battle, he sees a blue blob coming fast from the left. The attackers grow excited when they spot it too:

"Vampire -- switch rounds!"

Søren smacks Daniel's head as he crouches next to him. "Fool. Couldn't you tell this was an ambush?"

"Got anything useful, like ammo?"

"Not for that." Søren hands him an antique machine gun. Daniel looks down, confused. "What the fuck is this?"

"My old MP 40. Still works." Next, Søren lifts a rusty helmet over Daniel, who pulls away. "It says SS. I'm not dressing like a war criminal."

"Look, you ungrateful piece of shit." Søren's icy fingers grab Daniel's face. "This is a rescue mission and I'm in command -- and you're wearing this fucking helmet!" He slaps it on Daniel's head. Suddenly, Daniel's phone rings and Søren can't believe his ears. "Really? You're going to take that?"

Daniel answers. "Wolf, is that you?"

"Look at my text."

Daniel pushes up his goggles with the phone and reads: *They have wooden bullets. Show this to Søren.* Daniel does and Søren's expression turns grave. He looks toward the rear of the car where their assailants are now within twenty yards. Then he taps the gun. "This fires full-auto. When I count to three, open up. You need to keep their heads down for five seconds. Got it?"

~

My words prompt gasps and rumbles throughout the court. Caius gavels once, his disapproving eyes still locked on mine. "Are you pleading no contest?"

"Yes."

"Just to be perfectly clear, this is a capital case and your life is in my hands. I'm giving you thirty seconds to change your plea."

"Magistrate," I strain my voice above the din. "My crime, though one of passion, posed an existential threat to my family. I throw myself... "

"It continues to pose a threat." Ferdinand steps between them. "Who knows what else she told the monks? Fiona is attempting to derail these proceedings with a surprise plea to elicit mercy. We cannot allow her to escape the ultimate punishment."

"The prosecution will speak only to recite the facts." Caius speaks calmly, but his eyes betray a sudden urge to squash Ferdinand beneath his sandal. "Note carefully that your next improvised utterance will be your last."

Chastened, Ferdinand retreats to his seat. Caius turns again to me. "Have you told the monks anything else that could threaten your family?"

"No, Magistrate."

"You swear upon your honor?"

"I swear, I gave them nothing beyond the location of our meeting place. But..." From the corner of my eye, I see Ferdinand struggle to contain himself. This was supposed to be his moment to wow his elders with soaring rhetoric and dramatic poses. Now he sits, arms folded and petulant, like a student accused of disrupting class. Poor baby. Now excuse me while I push some more of your buttons. I turn back to Caius. "I know someone who divulged much more."

~

From a distance, Wolf shakes his head in wonder as Daniel stands, lit by the car's remaining light, wearing an SS helmet and night-vision goggles – a Nazi/Steampunk mashup worthy of Comic Con. Then Wolf laughs as Daniel raises a World War II machine pistol and fires, forcing the monks to dive for cover. When was the last time anyone saw anything like this? When Daniel stops firing, Søren speeds through the Mors Strigae soldiers, taking wooden bullets while breaking necks and smashing heads. The attack ends in seconds with no prisoners, no survivors. Staring through a thermal imager, Wolf shakes his head at the carnage. He liked most of his dead colleagues. Still, he'd give anything to be by Daniel's side, fighting with someone he often doubted but now admired more than ever. Too bad fate intervened. For the first time, Wolf thinks he's fighting for the wrong side, and it may be too late to cross back over that line. One day, if they reunite, he'll tell Daniel how proud he was to witness him in action.

~

"Time's up." Caius's voice registers his impatience. "Will the defendant change her plea or not?"

"No, Magistrate. But I have information vital for the protection of everyone in this room – including you."

"Magistrate, please!" Ferdinand leaps from his chair. "It's too late for her to introduce evidence."

"Magistrate," I raise my voice, "at the beginning of these proceedings, you ordered my family to abandon this compound after the trial. I urge you to reconsider your advice."

Caius hushes the crowd with a wave before glaring at me. "You have abused my patience, but I will suffer you for a few more seconds. Why do you recommend they remain here?"

"I've learned that one of my guardians abandoned his duties and joined the monks. We must assume he gave them information about each of us."

"Betrayed you, eh? I wonder where he learned that." Ferdinand mugs at the crowd which is growing more hostile to me. I press on:

"This compound is your best defense. Scatter and you'll get picked off one by one, like Agripina."

Ferdinand prances between the bench and witness box. "First, she gives up the location of our meeting place. Now she wants to save us?" He faces Caius. "Fiona has no credibility, yet you allow her to poison this process!"

"The process is the problem," I strain to be heard, "because it stays the same. Nothing in our society evolves. Meanwhile, our enemies continue to improve their weapons and tactics."

"ENOUGH." Caius stands and motions to Miklós and Konstantin. Both rush forward to place a black hood over the magistrate's golden laurel. Then they stand back as he locks eyes with me. "Fiona, sired by Agripina: You will immediately be chained to a pole in the courtyard, facing east. There, you will watch the sun's rays slowly approach until you burst into flames and burn to ashes." He motions to Konstantin. "Take her outside." Then he turns to Miklós. "Arrest Ferdinand. He will burn next to her."

~

"Wolf!" Daniel walks away from the shattered car.

"He's gone and not coming back." Søren steps between the corpses, sniffing. His shirt has several holes where the wooden bullets passed through; none hit his heart. "Why do you keep believing in him? He's just a tool for the monks, Fiona, or anyone who pays attention to him. Like an orphaned puppy. Ooh, this one's A positive." He points. "Stay over there and keep watch." He lowers his face toward a dead man's neck.

Daniel lifts the flask, swallows more scotch, and stares into the dark landscape. For the tenth time since the gunfire ended, he checks his phone. This time there's a message:

Forget about me. Fiona is a prisoner at the old Mors Strigae camp in Illinois. An attack is imminent.

~

Grabbing Ferdinand's arm, Miklós can't decide which is worse: participating in the death of his scion or playing the bailiff for Caius. He wonders how Konstantin feels as he escorts Fiona; maybe it's less painful losing a grandniece. Walking into the courtyard, they pass Caius waiting for his bare-chested guardians to lower a *lectica*, an ornate portable bed. Ferdinand spits in his direction. "Abortu Justitiae! Fiona's crime is far worse, and I get the same sentence?"

Caius, about to settle in, turns. "Do you think I haven't been watching? Your entire existence is characterized by waste, sloth, recklessness, and avarice. Insubordination is just your latest offense, but the one that put you over." He nods toward Fiona. "She's right, you know. Agripina should've sat ahead of you on the Council."

"But can't you show some mercy?" Miklós places his hand on

his heart. "For all his failings, Ferdinand did not put his family in danger."

"Up!" The guardians lift on Caius's command, placing the wooden posts on their shoulders. The 2000-year-old scowls at Miklós, his chiseled visage unsoftened by a frame of purple curtains. "You are to blame for his weakness, encouraging his dissipation with too little discipline. The same holds for you, Konstantin, and your progeny. It will be a miracle if this family survives the monks

-- and they are coming."

"We will defeat them," Konstantin tightens his grip on Fiona. "Like we always have."

"Such confidence," Caius gives a sly smile. "You realize you'll be two less by morning."

"Wait." Ferdinand struggles to free himself. "Are you deliberately undermining us?"

"Watch your tongue." The ancient roman growls. "If I wanted the monks to win, I'd have killed you all myself." An olive-skinned woman wearing an Egyptian dress hands him a golden goblet.

Fiona chimes in: "I have nothing to gain since I'll be dead by dawn. But you, Caius, are the most powerful among us. Why not assist in their defense?"

"It's too late to pretend that you care for your family, Fiona." Caius empties the goblet, hands it back, and dabs his mouth with a cloth napkin. "Besides, my strength only works when added to strength." His eyes briefly land on each of his descendants. "You're in the hands of nature now, and her justice is far more stringent than mine. Forward!" The guardians start moving.

Miklós follows for a few steps. "What's to prevent the monks from coming after you?"

"Friends in high places." Caius leans over the rail. "Whichever one of you survives may join me in Rome. Vale liberos meos."

THE REMAINS OF THE DAYLIGHT

"You think there's a heaven?" Søren looks out of the passenger window, eyes scanning the stars.

Daniel glances over. "You mean for humans or…your kind?"

"I mean for Fiona."

Daniel's eyes leave the road for several seconds. "Don't you dare give up on her."

"Watch your tongue."

"If you are giving up, you need to get out." Daniel slows and signals right. "I'm not going on a rescue mission with someone who's already surrendered."

"Stop the drama and keep driving." Søren keeps his eyes on the heavens. "I just think we need to prepare ourselves."

Daniel kills the signal. "Wolf said an attack was 'imminent' but I don't know how soon."

"That text came six hours ago."

"Why don't you flap your arms and fly there? You flew in to save me from the ambush."

Søren glares. "We don't flap our arms – and you're welcome." He looks away again. "I'm too tired now."

"You get tired?"

"Yes, as a matter of fact, we do." Søren checks his watch. "Daylight arrives in one hour. I'll need a hotel."

"You won't find any out here. A fleabag motel, maybe."

"The cheap ones have bathrooms without windows. I could sleep in the tub."

"Next one's in five miles. Try not to attack the clerk."

"I'll need a snack before bed."

Daniel sighs. "While you're doing that, I'll steal another car and get going."

"You're not staying?"

"Hell no. You can catch up tomorrow night."

Søren finally looks at him. "When do you sleep?"

"I take pills so I don't have to."

~

Father Abbot squints through binoculars at the former Mors Strigae ranch a thousand feet down. "I need a closer look." His voice crackles in the pilot's headset. "Take us down to 500." The pilot tilts the helicopter into a spiral around the central compound, just out of range of small-arms fire.

"Father Abbot, see anything from up there?"

"Hold on." He taps the pilot's shoulder. "The light – I can't see." The pilot puts the rising sun behind them, and the abbot resumes scanning the familiar grounds and buildings: "Negative, Brother Raymond. No guardians, no vehicles. Move in."

~

"Fire in the hole!" Brother Raymond accelerates, leading a dozen pickups toward the chain link fence topped with razor wire. Seconds later, an explosion leaves a 20-foot gap for them. Once inside, the monks pour out of their vehicles and hit the dirt, weapons aimed toward the buildings at the center of the camp.

No response, no movement of any kind. Wolf stands and motions for his squad to advance. Seven men follow him toward the center of the compound while the rest begin to encircle the buildings. Once again, Wolf is ambush bait. But this time he encounters no resistance as he enters the meeting hall Mors Strigae built two years ago. His men begin calling "Clear!" from various corners, but a glint outside prompts Wolf to signal caution before keying his mic: "There's something in the courtyard. We're investigating." He turns to the two closest monks. "Leo, Casey – with me."

The two men flank a door, nod, and throw it open. Weapons aimed, they cover Wolf as he runs to the nearest building, a guardhouse at the edge of the courtyard. Wolf waves the other two forward as he enters this smaller building. A second later, he peers through a window to see the glint again. His shoulders relax when he sees two sets of chains hanging from a pole at the center of the yard. As monks close in from every direction, Wolf sees a pile of ashes at the bottom of the pole; the mound shifts and shrinks with each gust of wind. Wolf's stomach tightens as he scoops a handful of ash with one hand. The other grabs a chain made of soft, light metal. "Jesus..."

"What is it, Wolf?" Brother Leo approaches.

"Silver." Wolf appears astonished at the ash falling through his fingers.

Leo glances back at the meeting hall. "They said one of them was on trial. This must be the execution ground. You okay, Wolf?" Both men press their earpieces as someone calls:

"Uh, Wolf, can you come to the security building? I found a letter for you in a cell block."

~

A Honda Fit with an Augustana College sticker speeds east on Interstate 80. Inside, Courtney Kim is singing along to her playlist when she gets a call. "Yo, Ricky."

"Hey, baby. Your room is empty. Where are you?"

"Going home. I've got baskets of dirty clothes and everyone's taken over the laundry room."

"Yeah, I gotta do that myself. My sheets are gettin' rank."

"Ya think? I almost took them with me, but then I thought 'No, I'm not his mom. He can wash them himself.'"

"Hey, it takes two to mess up a bed, you know?"

"I know." Courtney smiles. "I'll be back on... Wait." She slows as she sees a sedan on the shoulder with its hazards on. "There's a guy with car trouble. He might need help."

"Hell no. He's got a phone."

"Holy shit, he's missing an arm. I've never seen a one-armed man before."

"People do all kinds of stuff with one arm. Like you only need one to strangle someone."

"No, he can't even get the hood open. His engine is steaming."

"He's probably got Triple A, he's fine."

"What if it was your girlfriend? You'd want someone to stop and make sure I'm okay, right?"

"That depends. How many arms does she have?"

"Goodbye Ricky." Courtney ends the call, stops in front of the disabled car, and gets out. "Woah, that doesn't look good."

The man struggles once more with the hood before facing her. "I need to get to the oasis at I-39." He squints as he looks toward the sun. "And soon."

"You don't have a phone?"

"Triple A can't get here for another hour."

"Any family nearby?"

His gaze finally meets hers. "Alas, no."

Courtney eyes him up and down. What kind of murderer says 'alas'? And how threatening can a one-armed man really be? Still, she adopts a firm tone. "You better not have too much stuff. I got a lot of laundry."

~

100 acres from the compound, a woman in desert fatigues lies prone with a pair of high-powered binoculars, watching the invaders. A Twizzler hangs from her mouth as she chews. Nearby, between scrub bushes, sits a pickup truck beneath camouflage netting. A steamer trunk sits on the ground behind the woman, along with a flatbed trailer with a deflated tire, both hastily covered by camo blankets. Ophelia Cortez tilts the lenses toward the sky, searching for the abbot's helicopter.

The chopper recedes in the distance, slowly disappearing into the blue. It won't be long before the monks depart after inspecting the ash pile in the courtyard. Had it not been for Ophelia, there would've been two.

In all her time as a guardian, Ophelia never saw a vampire look afraid. But a few hours ago, as the sun broke over the horizon, Fiona and Ferdinand shivered and moaned, teeth bared and eyes peeled like cornered animals. They looked a lot like Ophelia did fending off snipers in Fallujah. Holding a full-length cloak, Ophelia froze for a second before throwing it over her employer. The silver chains fell easily to bolt cutters. Then Ophelia locked the screaming creature into a steamer trunk – all while the other begged for help. Ophelia's orders were clear, however: Leave the other to burn. As its skin ignited, Ophelia dragged the trunk onto the trailer and secured it with belts. Then she climbed into her truck and sped away from the fiery effigy of an immortal.

Ophelia wanted to get on the Interstate and drive until sunset, but the flat tire limited her speed. Knowing the monks were near, she dragged the listing trailer to the edge of the ranch. After covering everything, she lay flat and waited.

And watched.

~

Courtney grins as Daniel adjusts to the snug interior. "Sorry it's kinda small, unlike that Lincoln you left back there. Did you see *Suicide Kings*? Christopher Walken had one like that."

"Who?"

Courtney rubbernecks -- is he kidding? She forces her eyes back on the road as Daniel realizes how that sounded: "I've been out of touch with popular culture since the mid-80s. My work keeps me…It's almost like I'm frozen in time."

After an awkward silence, she looks through the mirror at the guitar case resting on her laundry. "You play guitar?"

Daniel glances back. "I'm borrowing the case for my prosthetic arm which needs repairing."

"Oh okay." She nods. "Hey, you remind me of Antonio Banderas in Desperado. Except you're not a Spaniard and…" She trails off.

"I'm guessing he had both arms."

"Yeah." Her voice grows excited. "But that guitar case was cool. It had a machine gun and rocket launcher. What would it take to convert yours into that?"

"A little engineering, plus the right weapons." Daniel smiles a little. "Not a bad idea."

She pops in a wad of gum as she merges into the fast lane. "So what's waiting for you at the end of this journey?"

Questions, questions. Daniel takes a deep breath before giving his rescuer the diversion she craves. "A woman I've known for many years. I liked being with her, but the time has come for me to move on. And for her to let me go."

"Do you love her?"

"Really?" Daniel looks at her. "You're starting there?"

"Journalism major," she smacks her gum. "We're taught to go for the jugular."

"Huh." Now he looks ahead. "The answer is yes."

"Then why leave her?"

"It's...complicated."

"Life is complicated."

Daniel scoffs. "What are you, twenty?"

"But going on thirty." She blows a bubble, takes it from her mouth, turns it around and pops it with her teeth. "I'm very mature for my age."

"I see."

In goes the gum again. "And what's her name?"

"Uh...Roxanne."

"And what does Uh Roxanne do?"

"She's my boss – and don't ask me what I do."

"Hmm." She glances sideways at him. "Does she boss you around at home, including in bed?"

"We don't sleep together."

"Really? You said you love her. Does she love you?"

"It's not like that. She needs me."

Courtney looks confused. "So if she's not getting sex from you, what does she get?"

Daniel sighs. "I make her problems go away. Plus...I cook for her."

She shakes her head. "You better be one hell of a cook."

"I am."

"She pays you, right?"

"I don't work for free."

"But you want more."

"And if more is impossible, I'd rather be alone."

Courtney is silent for a few seconds. "What does 'alone' look like to you?"

Daniel shrugs. "A Greek island. Sandy beach. No obligations."

"You want to be the island."

"I suppose."

"Men. You're all the same."

Daniel wrinkles his brow. "That's a bit unfair."

"Maybe." She locks eyes with him. "But it's the truth."

"You have first-hand knowledge, huh?"

"Woah-woah, I'm the interviewer. That's the price for this ride." She slows to let a truck pass another car. As it merges back into the right lane, she continues. "What benefit do you expect from being alone, as compared to being with Roxanne?"

"Freedom."

"Freedom from what, exactly?"

"I'm tired of answering to others, including her. I want only to answer to myself." Daniel pauses. "Does that make me a bad person?"

"I got a C in Philosophy so you don't want my opinion." Courtney wags a finger. "But office romances don't last, so you're probably doing the right thing."

Daniel looks out the window again. "It took me a long time, but I've finally learned my lesson."

~

Dear Søren, Daniel, and Wolf.

I had hoped to write each of you separately, but my captors gave me one sheet of paper and no pen. I hope you'll excuse the blood.

Wolf: I know you betrayed me, but I suspect you were manipulated by enemies stronger and more experienced. I do not forgive you but will grant you the one thing I can't have: a reprieve. Go and live.

Søren: Please note that Wolf is not to be harmed. Of all my accomplishments, you are my proudest. When we met, you were a mass murderer infected by a malicious ideology. Since your transformation, you've learned the value of human life. You also became a cherished companion – even after I stole Daniel from you. My selfish desperation put you in a difficult position, and for that I am truly sorry. Believe me when I say you returned a valuable lesson about forgiveness and friendship…

Søren is bouncing off second-story walls when Daniel arrives at the compound. Thinking there's a fight, he opens the guitar case, grabs his M4, and runs toward the courtyard. Windows shatter and roof tiles fly in all directions, causing him to duck for cover. He turns on the headset and scans the courtyard; no one else is around. The sound of vandalism mixes with words like "Meine Geliebte," "Mein Herz ist gebrochen," and "Müssen alle töten!"

Finally, Søren drops from the sky and kneels in front of the ash pile. His hands reach in, each grabbing a fistful, then he lets it fall between his fingers. "They destroyed her. They didn't even wait for an appeal. WHERE'S THE JUSTICE?" Blood streams from his eyes as he throws the ashes in the air. Then he falls on his rear and weeps, hands covering his face.

Daniel stands silently, keeping his distance, wiping his eyes and nose. A balled-up piece of paper rolls toward him in the breeze. As if in a trance, he picks it up and skips to the part with his name:

Daniel,

Long ago, I told you that Søren would reclaim ownership of you after my death. More recently, I told Søren that you deserved to retire after years of competent service. He agreed, with the stipulation that you find, and train, a suitable guardian for him – a process that could take months, as you know. It pains me to ask you to defer your dream yet again, but I must impose this final wish. I hope you will forgive me. And if I never thanked you properly for all you've done, please know that I owe my last 35 years to your care and concern. I am deeply grateful. Yours in sadness at our final parting,

Fiona.

"So, Daniel."

Søren's voice startles him. Daniel drops Fiona's note and lets it disappear in the wind. "Yeah?"

Søren's ash-streaked face resembles war paint. "I need you to score some A positive."

"The nearest hospital is an hour away. It'll be dawn by the time we get there."

Søren's eyes, normally chilly, harden into a glacier. "Then I'll need a pint from you."

Daniel drops the rifle and draws a pistol. "Allocasuarina luehmannii."

Søren laughs. "What are you, Harry Potter?"

"These bullets are Australian buloke, courtesy of a dead monk."

"You're old and slow, Daniel. You'll never hit me where it counts."

"Try me."

"Your memory is going, too. Fiona said you're mine until you find a replacement."

"I don't care what she said, I'm a free man." Daniel keeps the gun steady. "Anyone or anything that challenges that notion will have to kill me. Or die trying."

"So that's it, huh?" Søren puts his hands on his hips. "You declare you're free, despite what the law says, and I'm supposed to accept it. Is that where we are?"

"You know," a smile crosses Daniel's lips, "Fiona always hinted you weren't the brightest, but I think your bulb is a bit shinier than she let on."

"Know what she said about you?" Søren begins to circle his adversary. "'Oh, I'm so tired of him desiring me, always looking for an excuse to meet with me. Every time I read his mind, I see his hands on my body.' And then she'd shudder." He circles a little closer. "She played you for a fool, holding herself just out of reach so you'd always think you had a chance." He stops. "I have caressed every inch of her, tasted her liquor, and felt her body shake like a moaning volcano at the bottom of the ocean." He pauses, looks at the ground, and wipes away a tear. "The planes of pleasure we reached you could never imagine."

"Well." Daniel begins squeezing the trigger. "Now that she's dead, we can both move on."

"Schnauze!" Søren stamps his foot as if missing an old jack boot. Then he sneers: "Giftzahn. Hurhensohn. FICKFEHLER." Daniel fires, but by the time the bullet leaves the barrel, Søren's flying overhead.

"Come on, you old fraction of a man. Catch up!"

"That'll be easy." Daniel turns, aiming in several directions. "You're slowing down."

"Oh yeah? Where am I now?"

Daniel spins around again. Nothing but laughter greets him. He slides down the thermal imager and sees a blue dot hovering at ten o'clock high. Søren's voice surfs the wind:

"One time I joked with her: 'Do you think a one-armed man could give you pleasure?' Know what she said? 'Only if he brings another amputee with the opposite hand.' Oh, how we laughed as I fondled both her tits. Feeling jealous yet?"

Daniel steals a glance at the eastern horizon. "It'll be dawn soon. Where are you sleeping today?"

"I'll leave extra room when I dig your grave. Just for one night, of course. Too bad you'll stay and rot there."

"Dig?" Daniel steps forward. "I thought you vampires were allergic to work."

"Ooohhh, we're using forbidden words now." The dot grows quickly into a human-like form. "You really have a death wish, don't you?"

"Maybe you'd prefer some others that describe your kind. I myself like the ancient ones. Lamia. Succo. Sanguisuga -- that's a good one." The blue image suddenly doubles in size. "Or my personal favorite..."

"Don't."

"Surely I can use it in a proper noun, as in Mors Str..."

Søren swoops past, knocking him down. "Uh-oh. Leftie has to get up now." More laughter. "Look at you, like a turtle on its back. Poor old man. Perhaps I'll leave you to die that way."

Daniel sits up and aims the pistol again, keeping his elbow close to his body. "Ah, but you're starving, aren't you. There's no one around for miles, Søren, so you're stuck with me." He bares his throat. "Come on, striga. Dinnertime."

The blue image dodges left, then right, then zooms in until it fills his view. Daniel waits until the last half-second to roll on his back -- gun straight up – before firing.

~

Courtney Kim is still thinking of the one-armed stranger with the guitar case when she sees another vehicle on the shoulder. Her headlights illuminate a pickup truck with a listing trailer and a short woman dragging a large trunk into the truck bed. Courtney stops, gets out, and circle-waves. "Hi. I see you've got a flat. I'm good at fixing those – my dad taught me."

The woman, nearly out of breath, grabs a tire iron. "My dad didn't teach me anything."

"Great – I mean, sorry to hear that. So let's get started." Courtney walks up and kneels next to the deflated tire. "You're the second person I helped today. The other was a middle-aged guy with one arm. He was okay, though, which proves not everyone you meet on the side of the road is a bad – "

Ophelia wipes the tire iron with a handkerchief before dragging Courtney's limp body into the truck bed and laying her next to the trunk. Then she inserts a key, opens the lid and lifts the body over the occupant.

Two blackened hands grasp Courtney's bleeding head. Ophelia shuts the lid, locks it, and drives east toward Indiana and beyond – leaving Courtney's car and the trailer behind.

~

"Hello, it's me again – this time with a message for the man who killed several of my buddies yesterday." Wolf looks up at his iPhone. "Gotta say, Daniel, that was some nice shootin.' Still, I can't let it go unanswered so…Take that!" He dangles a crucifix in front of the screen. "Not sure this'll affect you, but it might keep Fiona away. I'm constantly looking over my shoulder expecting to see those long nails aimed at my face." He curls up the rosary and puts it aside. "You probably want to know why I'm hangin' out with the guys you sent me to spy on. This has nothing to do with you, I always respected you, but I kinda cooled on Fiona." His face sours. "Look, she doesn't seem to trust me, or even like me, and I guess I got tired of feeling underappreciated." A pause. "And I gotta admit, I'm not 100 percent comfortable living with a creature that can read my mind, and who might kill me because of what I'm thinking. And I've been having a lot of thoughts lately..." He shakes his head. "I don't know how you survived all those years with her. You must really love your job. I know you're good at it. Maybe you love her, I don't know. I loved her, at first, I think. But right now, I'd rather live with a bunch of sweaty guys who are armed to the teeth with wooden bullets." He laughs. "Yeah, it smells like a locker room around here, and sometimes it smells like a sewer. But we get three squares a day, plus wine or beer at dinnertime. Not like your scotch, though, which I could really use right now." He looks away. "Look, I don't know how this is going to play out, but you should take these guys seriously." Back to the camera. "Each one would give his life, without hesitation, for a chance to kill Fiona, Søren, and the others -- and they won't stop until they're all dead. And that means you, too. I'd say get out while you can, but I know you. You'll stick with her 'til the end. Just know that when we meet next time, I won't be able to help you. But I won't pull the trigger on you, either. You, however," a slight bow, "are free to dispose of me as you wish. I guess I owe you that after abandoning you." A sigh. "Maybe I'll find a way to send you this message on the DL. Otherwise, it'll just sit up there on the cloud, waiting for you. I wonder if that's what heaven is like: one big fluffy place where people watch messages sent up from here during tense times." A smirk. "I guess that would make this hell, wouldn't it? And on that note...Oh, I learned a new word today, which means good luck: *Benediximus,* my friend. I'll understand if you don't wish the same for me."

~

It's mid-morning when Daniel reaches the interstate on foot. With any luck, he'll hitch a ride to O'Hare today. There, a locker waits with a fake U.S. passport, Illinois driver's license, and credit cards. Next, he'll fly to Switzerland where a safe deposit box guards his retirement package: another new ID, new passport, gold coins, and wads of euros.

"Just try and find me," he exhales as his arm extends over the asphalt, thumb pointed at the sky. Hungry, sunburned and thirsty, Daniel realizes this is the first time in 35 years that he is free. If that

Augustana girl stops again, he'll buy her breakfast and tell another, more truthful story about what he hopes from his new life in Greece. He'll even pay the rest of her tuition. He'll do it secretly, so it'll be a huge surprise when she opens her student loan statement. And when she graduates, he'll buy her a guitar case with machine guns and a rocket launcher. That's when she'll remember the one-armed stranger, and hopefully think of him as a good person.

Because if one person believes you're good, you are good. Right?

~ PART THREE ~
"ARCHIVUM ARCANUM"

Epistles

Diary of Cardinal Massimo de Luca
Dec. 21
The Vatican

Such a strange occurrence on this first day of winter, one perhaps more in keeping with the Solstice traditions of our pagan ancestors than the supposedly enlightened proceedings of the Church. Today, Holy Father finally allowed me to join the College of Cardinals, though my appointment isn't the one for which I'd hoped. For years, I've been petitioning His Holiness, or rather his vicar, to elevate me to Prefect of the Sacred Congregation for the Doctrine of the Faith, the body that promotes and defends the Church's core values. I should note that Cardinal Ratzinger held that title before becoming Benedict XVI, so anyone securing this commission is viewed as next in line to the papacy.

It's tempting to use the word "Mephistophelian" when describing the backroom dealing, even backstabbing, employed by those striving for this hallowed prefecture. My elimination as a candidate was so swift and bruising, I considered leaving the Church to help my brother run his winery in Tuscany. This potential future acquired even greater urgency when I pondered the position Holy Father did grant me. I am now Prefect of an obscure and rather arcane institute called The Sacred Congregation for the Inquiry into All Things Preternatural. As the name might suggest, this body is charged with investigating occult phenomena, a responsibility that includes paranormal investigations and demonic possession. His Holiness – that is, his vicar -- said the time had come to re-establish accountability for this jurisdiction which lacked cardinal supervision for more decades than he could count. But not too much accountability, it seems. I was instructed that no one under my authority should ever be quoted, cited anonymously, or even hinted about in official communications or the news media. "Not to put too fine a point on it," he added, handing me a key, "His Holiness must never, ever, be asked to confirm or deny anyone or anything pertaining to your Sacred Congregation. And this especially applies to the order called Mors Strigae."

You read that first half correctly, "Mors" meaning "death." I now supervise the only lethal branch remaining in the Catholic Church. As for the second part...we'll get to that in a moment.

Still thinking wine country would be more hospitable than Rome, I unlocked the archives. I was curious as to why His Holiness – his vicar -- presumed I would be an ideal match for a death-dealing monastic order. So, I grabbed random scrolls and started reading. And here's where a warning is in order: If you're Catholic, worship with another denomination, or do not acknowledge God, be prepared to accept that He allows a host of unholy entities to wander among us. I'm speaking beyond those things which desire to haunt and possess us. It includes creatures that look like us, and behave like us – in fact, they used to be us – but now prey on their former cohorts. Which brings us to the second part of the name Mors Strigae.

Strigae (singular: *striga*) is difficult to translate because early Latin speakers didn't have a noun for the thing to be killed: a heretofore unknown monster that hunted humans at night, feeding on their blood. The closest word they had, *striga*, meant "evil spirit" or "witch" so they used this identifier for the new threat. Later, we in the west adopted the eastern word "nosferatu" – meaning "not dead" – to refer to these creatures, and "striga" was soon forgotten. Meanwhile, Mors Strigae kept its name, allowing its mission to fade from memory and leaders in Rome to deny the existence of "i vampiri" even as our monks hunted them.

Vampire hunters. My head keeps shaking at this discovery which makes the Congregation for the Doctrine of the Faith look like a quilter's group. Suddenly, my ambition is piqued: Who needs doctrinal authority when I have the tools to assemble my own private army? True, the soldiers are long gone, but the papal charter remains. And now, for the first time in decades, there's a budget.

Still, I remain suspicious. Who wants this order revived, and why now? Perhaps this bound stack of letters to and from my predecessor will offer some direction. They date from the last time Mors Strigae engaged in armed conflict, more than a century ago...

March 20, 1900
To Cardinal Gianluca Soriano, Rome
From the Abbot Adolpho Martinez

Your Eminence,

Greetings on this first day of spring in the new century. I hope this letter properly conveys my excitement at receiving news of great importance to our order. Without further ceremony, I'll get right to it. I've just received intelligence that, if true, could lead to the realization of our goal of eliminating that elusive scourge to all that is holy: the bloodsucking strigae.

According to my second in command, Brother Matteo, several of our Lord's enemies have retreated to the village of Campoleone, about a day's journey south of our blessed city founded by St. Peter. During interviews with local peasants, Matteo learned that about ten "i vampiri" (as they call them) have during the past month visited their nightly depredations upon the villagers, before at dawn taking shelter in a catacomb previously unknown to us. Your Eminence might well remember my reports from late last year estimating a similar number of strigae plaguing Rome and the surrounding area. I can't yet prove these are the same foul creatures, and I am without explanation as to why they may have moved, but it appears the Lord has given us an opportunity to destroy all his enemies in one location. To this end, I am preparing to join 100 of our brothers already in the field who are setting up camp near this Den of Devils. However, one important item begs for your consideration before any operation can proceed. And here I must temper my passion by grappling with the comparatively prosaic matter of infrastructure.

A scouting mission has revealed only one entrance to the catacomb, with a tunnel that appears limited to single-file passage.

One entrance presents both a challenge and an opportunity. A single cave-in could be enough to cut off any team we send below ground, possibly long enough for them to perish. On the other hand, the lack of a second opening makes it easier to trap our enemy. It goes without saying that any incursion would be conducted during daylight hours when the strigae are asleep.

After much prayer, I've come to believe the Lord has given us a rare (and possibly brief) opportunity to finish this nearly thousand-year war on His behalf. I humbly request that upon reading this news (and after what will no doubt be a profound moment of prayer) your Eminence will grant approval for my proposed incursion. Such a mission would be made even easier with the arrival of 200 more fully armed brothers to Campoleone, plus engineering tools. You have my most heartfelt gratitude for devoting whatever time and resources you can spare to this rather urgent petition.

Vivat Mors Strigae!

Your faithful servant in Christ's mission,

Abbot Adolpho Martinez

March 22, 1900
To the Abbot Martinez
From Cardinal Soriano, Rome

Abbot Martinez,

Vivat Mors Strigae indeed! After years of struggle and limited victories, it seems Heavenly Father desires our order to finally live up to its name. Your report of this hidden harbor for Satan's children has renewed my faith that we will prevail in this centuries-old struggle. However, after spending the last hour seeking our Lord's guidance (the "profound moment of prayer" you predicted), I've concluded that we should balance our renewed spiritual fervor with a measure of caution. Two concerns now settle heavily on my mind. First, we should confirm the reports from Brother Matteo's peasant sources that possibly ten strigae are indeed hunting in the area around Campoleone. Second, we must be absolutely certain that these alleged blood drinkers are, in fact, residing in this newly discovered catacomb.

I have no doubt about the godliness and good intentions of our local informers. Still, I've had occasion to learn that rural folk benefit greatly when large groups of hungry strangers arrive, bearing coins. I also worry that some of our less experienced brothers may fall victim to the charms of fortune tellers or women of questionable virtue.

With all this in mind, I must ask that you provide confirmed contact with a striga or strigae before I send additional brothers and equipment. It would also be greatly helpful if you would search for other places where our enemies might retire during the day, thereby proving beyond all doubt that the catacomb is to be our battleground.

I'm releasing two horses for your journey, plus an extra steed for your courier. Safe travels, brother, and please address my twin concerns as soon as you are able.

Yours in Christ,
Cardinal Soriano

March 24, 1900
To Cardinal Soriano, Rome
From the Abbot Martinez, the Lord's Blessed Battlefield

Your Eminence,

Thank you for your quick reply and wise counsel. Such qualities are the sign of a right and true leader, and our order is clearly blessed to be placed under your stewardship. Another characteristic of a great leader is forgiveness, or at least forbearance, which brings me to the following confession: Immediately upon my arrival in Campoleone, and alarmed at the gaunt faces and growling stomachs of my brothers who greeted me, I unlocked our order's treasure to purchase milk, bread, and eggs from our local hosts. Seeing now your desire to discourage excess entrepreneurship among these rustics, I shall therewith halt this outflow of coinage by ordering a fast. Such discipline should be made easier during the current period of mourning felt by those under my command, which leads me to my report:

It is my sad duty to inform your Eminence that last night, shortly after midnight, at least ten strigae assaulted our encampment. Our losses amounted to the deaths by exsanguination of Brother Matteo, plus nine more from our order. Their bodies were found scattered across the countryside. After collecting the corpses, we followed the protocol for those felled during this holiest of wars: staking their hearts, separating heads from torsos, and burning the remains while reciting prayers for the souls' quick ascension to Heaven. Having witnessed these measures myself, I am confident that none of our dear brethren will return as cursed creatures of the night.

I should note that my 90 surviving brothers found the ceremony beautiful and filled with meaning, and I assure you that each of us continues to be moved by the Holy Spirit and a desire to finish this mission. I also appointed Brother Francesco as my new second-in-command. Nevertheless, the sun is getting low again, and I fear our numbers may decline from further predations. In order to stem our losses from attrition, I must now reiterate my request that you send 200 more brothers, armed with wooden stakes, holy water, and crucifixes. If granting such a request is not convenient at this time, I beg you to allow us to retreat to Rome so we can regroup for a return expedition to this village.

I remain your faithful servant in Christ's mission,
Abbot Adolpho Martinez.

March 26, 1900
To the Abbot Martinez, the Lord's Blessed Battlefield
From Cardinal Soriano, Rome

Abbot Martinez,

It is with great sadness that I read of the demise of Brother Matteo and the nine other members of our blessed order. Matteo, in particular, will be missed since I have fond memories of his service as an altar boy in our beloved Basilica. Please accept my condolences. I have no doubt that each of the fallen has assumed his rightful place in Heaven. Please also extend my salutations to Brother Francesco as he assumes his new post as your second.

Despite my disconsolation at our losses, the Good Lord has seen fit to provide me with half the proof I requested in my letter of March 22: You have confirmed that approximately ten strigae are hunting in the area around Campoleone. That's one box we can check. Unfortunately, your most recent letter didn't provide me with a list of alternatives as to where these evil creatures might be sleeping. I make no reproach since your letter clearly conveyed the distress which has arrested your attention. I look forward to learning in your next letter whether the catacomb is our main target or one of several possibilities.

Yours in Christ,
Cardinal Soriano

March 30, 1900
To Cardinal Soriano, Rome
From the Abbot Martinez, the Lord's Blessed Battlefield

Your Eminence,

Please excuse my delay in replying. The reason for my tardiness will become clear later in this message. First, allow me to provide the answer you sought in your letter dated March 22, which I neglected to include.

After conducting a wide search of the area, and failing to find any other shelter that could possibly be useful for a striga to take its ill-earned rest, I've concluded that the catacomb must be the only location where these bloodthirsty monsters hide when the sun rises. My suspicions were confirmed the night of March 27-28 during a visit to the crypt's entrance which we've been guarding since our arrival. While chatting with the sentries my own eyes witnessed, for the first time, a striga. It flew out of the tunnel, naked and borne by some wicked force that allowed it to arrange its arms and legs as if it were posing for a prurient artist's paintbrush rather than propelling itself through open air. Such a frightful thing to behold: a female with hair the color of glowing embers, piercing green eyes, milk-white skin, and a most fiendish smile punctuated by those long canines so often mentioned in folklore. Since it was my first time witnessing such a creature, I stood transfixed as she swooped down upon the sentries, undeterred by the crucifixes they employed to keep her at bay. Grabbing my hapless brothers by their collars, she lifted them up and smashed their heads against each other. Then, God as my witness, I heard her utter a lascivious moan of pleasure as their lifeless bodies crumpled to earth and were quickly set upon by her unholy kin. As I ran toward our camp, the unclad female descended light as a feather in front of me. When she approached, my feet were paralyzed by a debate raging in my mind. Should I avoid looking into her eyes, which, according to our instruction, could hypnotize in seconds? Or do I risk my eyes being diverted to her pale breasts, hips, and thighs, which were so sinfully curved and well-proportioned that I now understand it to be a sinister trick to keep me from attacking her with the holy water I carried. I hope you and Heavenly Father will forgive me for being duped by such a simple yet diabolical ruse.

It is with some hesitation that I provide further details of this encounter, because doing so will reveal how profoundly my soul has been corrupted, and how unfit I am to continue service in our sacred order. Nevertheless, share I must because it may provide information about what to expect when future warriors of God confront these terrible yet astonishing creatures.

"My name is Agripina," she said without any solicitation from me. "I want you to convey a message to your cardinal." I agreed, hoping she would spare my life. My reprieve was merely temporary but that is far less important than the information she offered which, if true, could save hundreds of our brothers.

"The catacomb is rigged to collapse," she warned. "Should you monks enter you will all perish."

"Why do you tell me this?" I asked, uncertain as to whether I should speak to this evil creature. She answered, "Nature requires a balance between predators and prey. Nothing upsets that balance more than a massacre." Then, taking my hand, she turned and led me toward the woods, adding, "Still, the laws of nature say nothing about playing with your food."

I don't remember being bitten, but one of my brothers found me early next morning with twin punctures on my neck. I was laying amongst the leaves in a state of nature, barely conscious and shivering from exposure. I can only conclude that this wicked monster fed off me, leaving just enough blood to allow me to relay her message to you, however suspicious it may seem to both of us. I still have doubts while writing this, wondering if the Devil might profit from our hesitation to enter the crypt. Nonetheless, I will probably hand this letter to the courier and leave this matter to be decided by your wisdom. And now I have one more confession for you to hear:

Added to my bodily injury is a spiritual unmooring which results from my shame at having to admit that, with the help of this concupiscent demon, I have broken my vow of celibacy. I am left with little faith that even Heavenly Father, for all his power and goodness, will find my decrepit spirit worth salvaging.

As I write this, the sun is about to set and I fear that venereal vixen will return to finish me off. Even if she spares me such a visit, my weakened state makes me doubt I'll witness another sunrise. With every cough, with each labored breath, I can feel life slipping away from me. I have already written a note to my brothers instructing them to dispose of my remains according to our doctrine, and informing them that Brother Francesco has command until you decide on my replacement. I can only hope that my soul will be allowed to enter Purgatory, so I may have a chance to expiate my sins, as I am too unclean to enter Heaven.

Despite the gravity of my circumstances, I continue to find comfort in prayer, plus the thought that our holy war will continue under your steadfast leadership. Thank you, your Eminence, for allowing me to serve you in His mission. And may the good Lord bless you and keep you from harm.

Vivat Mors Strigae!

Abbot Martinez

April 1, 1900
To the Abbot Martinez, the Lord's Blessed Battlefield
From Cardinal Soriano, Rome

Dear Abbot Martinez,

My shock over your injuries and concern for your spiritual well-being continue to haunt my thoughts after a most difficult night. Following much prayer and reflection, I've become certain that your unblemished record of service, plus the kindness and generosity you exhibited to each member of our order, will bless you with enough indulgences that Heavenly Father will speed your redemption and grant you the everlasting salvation you so richly deserve.

I hope this letter finds you at peace and surrounded by angels ready to sing their praises for your exculpation. For my part, I will pray every night, asking that the Good Lord embrace you in the hereafter.

God speed, faithful friend. And Vivat Mors Strigae.

Cardinal Soriano

April 1, 1900
To interim commander Reynaldo Francesco, the Lord's Blessed Battlefield
From Cardinal Soriano, Rome

Brother Francesco,

It is possible that your esteemed abbot, Adolpho Martinez, will have expired by the time you read this. It is with great sadness that I read his letter of March 30th, in which he described the assault upon his honorable person by a striga, and his subsequent failing health. If he passes, I charge you with the disposal of his remains according to our rules.

Responding to one of the abbot's final requests, that for reinforcements, I am dispatching 200 brothers who should arrive at your encampment no more than two days from now. They will be led by your new abbot, René Jean-Baptiste, who will assume command. Please be ready to receive him and provide updates regarding the strength, both numerical and spiritual, of your team, and report your latest intelligence about the dreaded strigae.

There is another item in Martinez's most recent letter which requires your awareness but not immediate action. Martinez said he received a warning from the striga who attacked him the night of March 27-28. This succubus, named Agripina, informed Martinez that the catacomb had been rigged to collapse after we enter. To verify this claim, I ordered your new abbot to bring a team of engineers who will inspect the tunnels. I'd like you and eleven volunteers to provide security for this team while they do their examinations underground.

On a more disturbing note, Martinez also informed me that our holiest symbol, the crucifix, did not deter Agripina during her attack on two of our sentries on March 27-28. If Martinez was not mistaken, we'd need to rethink how we engage these creatures in future combat. I hardly need to tell you that it is essential for you confirm the potency of our sacred symbol during your next encounter with these foul demons. Additionally, I'd like to confirm the efficacy of our other weapons including silver and holy water. There's no need to confirm wooden stakes; this long ago proved a most devasting implement.

I realize this is a most detailed communiqué for a temporary command, and I thank you for your attention to my concerns. Thanks also for your continued service and loyalty to the cause.

Vivat Mors Strigae!

Cardinal Soriano

April 3, 1900
To Cardinal Soriano, Rome
From the Abbot René Jean-Baptiste, the Lord's Blessed Battlefield

Your Eminence,

It thrills me to deliver this, my first report as leader of the divinely inspired band of brothers you assembled to exterminate our Lord's enemies. And while the latter may have gotten the better of us last night, I have every confidence that, God willing, we shall prevail. No doubt, you'd prefer to read more details about our latest action (this being a report, after all), so here are the main points:

We lost 15 brothers last night during an attack just before midnight by about ten strigae. All our brothers' corpses have been recovered and disposed of in the prescribed manner.

Silver works! Brother Himmelman, a Master Metalworker, created a 6' x 6' blanket made of silver rings, all tightly linked, and for a brief time we captured a striga. During the attack, Brother Himmelman courageously positioned himself as bait next to the blanket which lay on the ground under a bed of leaves. When the striga, a raven-haired female of exceptional beauty, landed on it she immediately collapsed like a rag doll. Himmelman wrapped her in the blanket and was in the process of dragging this captured devil when a loud shriek assaulted our ears. An anguished call for FIONA echoed off the trees, quickly identified as coming from a red-haired female my brothers call Agripina. This banshee grabbed another of our German brothers, Bauman, and held him with nails like eagle's talons poised to pierce his neck. Despite Bauman's offer to sacrifice himself, Himmelman unwrapped our prisoner. A third demon – male, name unknown -- flew down and picked up Fiona and all three flew off, to our dismay, with the doomed Bauman. He was discovered the following morning, bloodless, with multiple bite marks the length of his body. All of us are furious at the treachery the strigae displayed during their feigned hostage negotiation. Nevertheless, our feelings at Bauman's loss must be tempered by our newly gained knowledge about the power of *argentum*.

Crucifixes don't work. I'll admit, this causes me to question other objects central to our faith -- even the wine and wafer we use for communion. I truly hope this is not a sign that God has seen fit to abandon us. I am still awaiting a report on the efficaciousness of holy water.

Tomorrow morning, my engineers will return to the catacomb

to continue searching for evidence of the alleged trap set for us. I should mention the majority of brothers killed during this latest attack – nine -- were engineers. With this development, I can only conclude that the strigae are targeting them.

I hope my second report from the field brings better news. In the meantime, I remain your loyal partner in service to Heavenly Father.

Vivat Mors Strigae!

Abbot Jean-Baptiste

April 5, 1900
To the Abbot Jean-Baptiste, the Lord's Blessed Battlefield
From Cardinal Soriano, Rome

Abbot,

If your faith has wavered, hand command back to Brother Francesco and return immediately to Rome. If, on the other hand, the flame of devotion to our Lord and Savior continues to burn within your breast, remain on post and read on:

Assign additional protection for your remaining engineers in the form of extra guards and, if possible, clothing or ornaments made of silver. This was the most useful revelation of your April 3rd letter, which otherwise I found objectionable for the breeziness of its tone and content. For example, your first item describes in the briefest possible manner the slaughter of 15 of our brethren – but no context. Were they ambushed as previous reports suggest? Could they have survived if they were better prepared? I am becoming increasingly concerned that the deaths on our side result from poor leadership which allows our brothers to be caught unawares. You are hereby also ordered to establish new protocols for night watches and assemble a fully armed team in reserve that can quickly respond to sudden attacks.

Let me remind you that the loss of any member of our sacred order carries great significance because they died while serving Heavenly Father. There is also the more worldly consideration of recruiting and training new brothers, which takes time, effort, and treasure. So remember: You are your brothers' keeper – take better care of them!

In the meantime, I'll order a team here in Rome to add silver rings or threads to our standard battle garments. I'll advise you when these are ready to be distributed among your men.

Cardinal Soriano

April 7, 1900
To Cardinal Soriano, Rome
From the Abbot Jean-Baptiste, the Lord's Blessed Battlefield

Your Eminence,

Please accept my humble and heartfelt apologies for the perfunctory manner with which I related the deaths of our 15 brothers the night of April 2nd. I will make sure that future *notitia mori* properly convey my own feelings of loss, plus awareness of the Church's investments (material and spiritual) to prepare each soldier for the Lord's service. I am also reserving extra time for prayer in hopes that I may receive further strength from Heavenly Father. Now to my report:

Your Eminence surmised correctly that ambush is the leading cause of expiry for our brothers serving near the catacomb. I have adopted your advice about increasing the number of sentries, and establishing a team armed and ready for rapid counterattack between dusk and dawn.

I have ordered our hallowed silversmith, Brother Himmelman, to add rings of *argentum* to our cloaks, and already he issued one to the head of our engineering team. I am pleased to report this cloak repelled the much-feared Agripina during a raid last night. Unfortunately, two more rank-and-file engineers were slain, one each by Agripina and the raven-haired Fiona. Hopefully, the garments and weapons you promised will arrive soon. Brother Himmelman has enough material for two additional cloaks, and I plan to issue the next one to myself.

Holy water is not a deterrent. I myself attempted to douse the blessed drops onto a male striga who promptly ignored me and flew away with another of our precious engineers. I am ordering our brothers to reserve their vials for worship, along with our crucifixes.

The claim of a rigged tunnel or tunnels has yet to be proved during inspections. The engineering team spent two full days in the catacomb, advancing 50 meters each day. The eight surviving members hope to advance another 50 today. All they've discovered so far are the skeletons of Capuchin monks from long ago, supine and

intact. I can assure you the remains have not been disturbed during our work.

I hope to have more tangible progress to report during my next dispatch.

Vivat Mors Strigae,

Abbot René Jean-Baptiste

April 9, 1900
To the Abbot Jean-Baptiste, the Lord's Blessed Battlefield
From Cardinal Soriano, Rome

Abbot,

The next cloak of silver produced by Brother Himmelman should go to an engineer. If Himmelman produces a third, and my promised shipment has not yet arrived, you may have that.

Cardinal Soriano

April 9, 1900
To Cardinal Stefano Mancini, Vicar to His Holiness
From Cardinal Gianluca Soriano

Your Eminence,

Happy belated birthday. I do hope Heavenly Father continues to grace your worthy person with good health, good spirits, and the steadfast determination for which you've become legendary in service to His Holiness.

It is with sincere hope that a humble request from yours truly will in no way spoil your celebrations, but an emergent state of affairs compels me to prevail upon you, my brother, for the distribution of certain assets. I'll avow it is not currency I seek, rather a quantity of silver that could be melted down quickly for a purpose which, I am obligated to remind, cannot be disclosed under the terms of my Congregation's rather esoteric charter. Nevertheless, you have my utmost assurances that the material I seek would forthwith be employed in direct service to our Lord.

No doubt, Heavenly Father has blessed you with an exceptional memory, which I truly envy at my age, but I seem to recall hearing about a vault somewhere in the Holy See containing hundreds of bars of precious metals, including many of pure silver. I assume that such a collection, were it to exist, would fall under the supervision of His Holiness. Would your Eminence be so charitable as to inquire on my behalf to Holy Father? I will admit the unorthodox nature of this request causes me to blush more than a little.

I remain your faithful colleague in Christ's service,
Cardinal Soriano

April 10, 1900
To Cardinal Gianluca Soriano
From Cardinal Vicar Stefano Mancini

Your Eminence,

Unorthodox, indeed! Of course, most requests from the Prefect for The Sacred Congregation for the Inquiry into All Things Preternatural are bound to raise an eyebrow. Still, I must admit the earnestness of your query nearly convinced me to melt down all the silver goblets and flatware I keep in my household! Fortunately for my discriminating dinner companions, I am happy to report that, verily, the Holy See maintains a collection of .999 silver in the form of 100-ounce bars. And while it remains under the authority of Holy Father, I see no need to interrupt his sojourn in Capri with this matter. How much *argentum* do you require?

I remain your fellow servant in Christ's holy mission,
Cardinal Vicar Stefano Mancini

April 11, 1900
To Cardinal Vicar Stefano Mancini,
From Cardinal Gianluca Soriano

Your Eminence,

Blessed news! Many thanks for your assistance which, I assure you, will greatly further our combined mission in service to our Lord in Heaven. I think 100 bars should be enough to meet our current need. I shall immediately alert the metal workers under my authority to prepare for this shipment.

I am at once humbled and inspired by your generous and expeditious offer of help.

Your dear friend in Christ's service,
Cardinal Soriano

April 15, 1900
To Abbot René Jean-Baptiste
From Cardinal Soriano

Abbot Jean-Baptiste,

A shipment of 100 cloaks fitted with silver rings left this morning for your encampment. I hope to send another 100 in a few days. What news from you?

Cardinal Soriano

April 17, 1900
To Cardinal Gianluca Soriano, Rome
From Abbot Jean-Baptiste, the Lord's Blessed Battlefield

Your Eminence,

Many thanks for the silvered cloaks which arrived today. Since there is approximately one such garment for every two monks, I asked during our morning muster which brothers would forgo a cloak so another could benefit from its protection. My heart became full and my eyes watered when, to a man, each raised his hand. Still, proper leadership demanded that I distribute these garments, so I asked my brothers to count off, and then asked Brother Francesco to choose odd or even. The odds won the cloaks which were promptly issued. Among the evens, I noticed more than a few faces trying to conceal their relief when I announced that more of these cloaks were on the way. I include this anecdote merely to underscore how brave these men are despite the terror they feel. And now for the difficult news:

Nearly all of our blessed engineers, who worked tirelessly to inspect the catacomb's main tunnel, have succumbed to the predations of the evil strigae. I am deeply saddened at the loss of such dedicated and pious men. Only one survives, Brother Paolo, who lately has been displaying symptoms of the dreaded dysentery and joined a growing number of men in our makeshift infirmary. I've lately been reading a scientific journal which warns about how diarrheal diseases spread and I've concluded that our training could benefit from a course on personal hygiene, with particular attention to the burying of excrement. Much fouling of the landscape has occurred since our first group of men arrived more than a fortnight ago, and I fear the flies that swarm during our mid-day meal are polluting the food. I humbly suggest that we could prevent future outbreaks by adding a small shovel to each brother's standard kit. In the meantime, I must prevail upon your Eminence to send whatever shovels you can spare during the next supply shipment.

With the emergence of a second opponent, disease, I must also ask that we quickly agree on a course of action. Each day we remain encamped costs dearly in lives, plus valuable resources needed to sustain us. And for what? So the strigae may continue to gorge themselves? So the flies can carry our own feces back to our meals? I believe the time may be right for us to return to Rome, regroup with proper equipment, and then return here for a decisive battle. Your thoughts, Eminence?

Yours in Christ's service,

Abbot Jean-Baptiste

April 19, 1900
To the Abbot Jean-Baptiste, the Lord's Blessed Battlefield
From Cardinal Soriano, Rome

Abbot,

I do hope for the sake of your eternal salvation that your hours spent perusing the latest science don't outnumber those praying or reading scripture. It seems your study of the worldly literature has enervated your attacking spirit and engendered a wandering state of mind, as evinced by your sudden interest in human waste and shovels. Really, brother – is this what preoccupies you?

For too long, I have refrained from running this operation from afar, but now I see your lack of initiative has further enfeebled a once proud fighting force. As you've no doubt ascertained, my patience has run its course over your inaction which has imposed a drain on capital, both financial and political, for our sacred order. With this in mind, my next directive is a metaphor in keeping with your sudden fascination with all things scatological: Evacuate your bowels or else remove your posterior from the latrine. And expect no shovels from Rome.

Cardinal Soriano

April 22, 1900
To the Abbot Jean-Baptiste, the Lord's Blessed Battlefield
From Cardinal Soriano, Rome

Abbot,
What news?
Cardinal

April 24, 1900
To Cardinal Gianluca Soriano, Rome
From Brother Reynaldo Francesco, the Lord's Blessed Battlefield.

Your Eminence,

It has fallen upon me to inform you that the Abbot Jean-Baptiste has, like so many of our brave brothers, fallen in battle. During an attack the night of April 17-18, I personally witnessed the abbot succumb to bewitchment by the malevolent enchantress Fiona. Myself engaged in combat, I was unable to prevent him from removing his silvered cloak and following her alone into the catacomb. The next morning, I entered the crypt to begin a search which required me to venture twice more until, on the third day, I finally recovered the abbot's exsanguinated corpse about 1000 meters into the main tunnel. And here, if your Eminence permits, I'd like to add to our growing body of knowledge about strigae and those unfortunates who become their prey.

Upon my discovery of our late abbot, I'd noticed the normal process of putrefaction had begun to take hold. After his removal to our camp, and an overnight vigil with brothers holding sharpened stakes at the ready, I have concluded that merely being drained by a striga does not lead to one's reanimation as a similar foul creature of the night. Once again, it seems our order has been fooled by the gross simplification of the common folklore. After burying the abbot, and saying prayers for his speedy ascension to Heaven, I now feel I can safely recommend the cessation of our current method of disposing victims, as this consumes not only time but valuable resources like firewood.

And now, I must humbly seek your Eminence's forgiveness for resuming, without your order, the interim command I briefly held from April 1st to 3rd. I have today deferred to a special appointment by my brothers who unanimously affirmed their wish for me to finally lead them in an attack, which shall begin as soon as I hand this letter to our courier. Before I sign off, you will no doubt require assurance that during my three days underground, I encountered no evidence of our enemies' alleged plan to welcome us with a cave-in. I found none. Furthermore, I'm certain that the infamous warning issued by that harpy Agripina was a ruse designed to keep us in the open, exposed to repeated nocturnal hunts. As I write this, my blood boils at the realization that we've become handmaidens to our recurrent slaughter. Now at last, with Heavenly Father's grace and assistance, we will catch these evil creatures while they slumber, at last employing our disposal methods on their cursed bodies instead of ours.

Upon returning victorious to Rome, I will gladly accept any punishment you deem fit for exceeding my authority. However, I must humbly ask that you spare my brothers from blame as their unanimous support for my command was inspired, not by mutinous feelings against your person or our order, but a sincere desire to complete our sacred mission.

I look forward to personally sharing with you the details of our blessed victory after so much struggle and loss. The thought that we may deliver such a devastating blow against evil fills my entire being with the light of the Holy Spirit. May God be pleased to witness such a triumph achieved by those fighting on His behalf. Vivat Mors Strigae!

Interim Abbot Reynaldo Francesco

~

Diary of Cardinal Massimo de Luca
Dec. 22

I can't stop shivering after reading these "Catacomb Letters." Only after a second cognac was I able to calm my nerves and feverish brain. Then I got on my knees and prayed, thankful for the unwavering faith and bravery exhibited by these brothers while facing terrible odds. Their story is at once heartbreaking and inspiring, and I am privileged to be their witness. How awful not to be able to share this! The Abbot Martinez, in particular, arrested me with the sheer desolation of his prose. The interim abbot, Francesco, made me so terribly worried about his inexperience, but

I had every confidence in his faith and the spiritual readiness of those who placed themselves under his command. Even the Abbot Jean-Baptiste, for all his brusqueness, astonished me with his certainty.

As for the strigae Agripina and Fiona, I can only say they represent the most profane confluence of savagery and cunning. I doubt I could survive for two seconds after encountering either of them, which makes the absence of a victory message from Francesco weigh heavily on my mind. I've searched everywhere in this archive for a hint of the outcome, but to no avail. Other than a notebook about strigae and the weapons employed against them, the only item I found is Cardinal Soriano's diary which I dutifully read. It's a long and often boring chronicle of his career, a story I nearly abandoned several times, but the ending wrenched me awake and caused me to jump out of my chair. Soriano's final entry comes two years after the Campoleone letters end, and contains a startling revelation – no, confession – about a most unholy wager.

Diary of Cardinal Gianluca Soriano, Rome
March 20, 1902

When a cardinal seeks confession, where can he go? Normally, I could obtain absolution from a brother cardinal or even Holy Father if the sin is not too bad. But when a transgression is so great it threatens the authority of the Church, then it – like a disease – must be contained. I must not infect my colleagues' spirits with the colossal military failure that weighs solely on my shoulders. Nor should I burden any person other than the one who reads this entry that I am also a traitor to God, having consorted with, and been duped by, an emissary of Satan.

One night, a little more than two years ago, I received an unexpected visit from an ancient striga dressed like a Caesar in white robes and crown of gold leaves. He did not attack me. Instead, Caius Drusus introduced himself and offered something:

"Have you noticed a sudden decline in the population? No doubt, you've heard from certain armed monks that ten of my…associates…have been hunting around Rome."

Before I could finish uttering the word "strigae," five of the coldest fingers I've ever known clamped shut my mouth. "Imagine the scandal when your worshippers learn that their Sunday offerings are paying for a secret army that fails to protect them." Then his tone brightened a bit. "Are you a sporting man, Cardinal?"

I nodded once.

"Let's test the strength of your order. I'll send my army of ten south to Campoleone, where they and your monks will meet in battle."

I backed away from his fingers. "And if my men win?"

"Then you, sir, shall become pope."

Here I sought to correct my visitor. "The College of Cardinals elects the Holy Father."

"Yes, and His Holiness appoints the cardinals – it's all very incestuous, like my own system of governance." Then he leaned closer, his voice like whispers from a crypt: "All that's needed is for the papal vicar to instruct the College to approve his successor."

"You left out an important step. His Holiness would have to die."

"Look who's connecting the dots." Caius's lips curled into a smile, revealing two long canines. "I would handle that bit, of course."

Only the most Machiavellian ambition could tamp down my horror at the thought of such an assassination, and I am here admitting my most baneful weakness. "And if my men lose the battle?"

"Surely the Cardinal doesn't admit that possibility."

"The Cardinal must be prepared for every possibility."

Caius chuckled at my resoluteness, but then turned serious. "If your men lose, you will be my agent for as long as you live."

"Agent for what? Your agenda is unknown to me."

"And so it shall remain."

I never thought that an all-powerful and merciful God would allow His army to fail. But fail we did, and now I'm reminded of our Savior's last words while dying on the cross: "My God, why hast thou forsaken me?" I hope you, Dear Reader, will not consider my quoting these words a blasphemy.

My orders from Caius were few and far between, at the start. Befriend Cardinal Vicar Mancini, buy him gifts, gain his confidence. Listen to his concerns, offer suggestions, stroke his ego. Then one day my tormentor announced "an escalation in intimacy" was required so that I may gain access to the most sensitive information about papal offices and appointments.

I am too ashamed to write more. After violating nearly every proscription in the Bible, I shall debase myself no longer. My soul beyond salvation, I have decided that only my absence can stem this pernicious corruption. I have procured poison which I will ingest immediately after composing this warning for whoever succeeds me.

Beware: The visitor who won my eternal damnation is certain to know of your appointment and will soon approach you. I pray that you'll resign immediately and halt the evil that I helped promulgate. To continue your appointment would only prove this city is not a place for men of God, only men of power – the very kind our Savior warned us about. I hope your moral compass is truer, and your faith in God greater, than mine ever was.

Yours in disgrace,
Gianluca Soriano.

~ PART 4 ~
UNA STRIGA VITAE

ELEVENS (2001)

"You count the money, I'll count the blood." Daniel pushes the open case of cash toward Jesús who in turn opens a large cooler releasing a cloud of mist. The cooler is tied to a dolly. Daniel's gloves lift blocks of dry ice, revealing pint bags labeled O negative, A negative, A positive, B positive, etc. All will be consumed during the next Council meeting.

"Looks good." Daniel replaces the ice and shuts the lid. "Let's do this again."

"You got it." Jesús shakes hands and nods toward the twin-engine plane fronting a skyline of red rock formations. "Baron, huh? What's it cruise, 200 knots?"

"I'm not a pilot." Daniel grins. "I just hire them." He tilts the dolly back while Jesús opens the door. "I need a steady source for O negative. What can you get me every other week?"

Jesús shrugs. "80 or 90 pints. Maybe 100."

"Get me a hundred and I'll pay $200 a bag." Daniel pushes his cargo into the morning sun. "See you in two weeks?"

"You got it. I'll have a hundred for you."

Outside, today's pilot – Bud -- opens the baggage door. When Daniel unstraps the cooler, each grabs a handle and lifts. Bud groans. "This feels heavier than what we agreed."

"132 pounds, like I told you." Daniel grunts through his teeth.

Bud shoves it into the cabin. "Same as my daughter who flew with me yesterday. Of course, she's at the age where she'd kill me for telling. You got kids?"

"None that I weighed recently." Daniel looks at his watch. "It's after six. Let's go."

Bud starts the engines. "Sedona traffic, this is Baron One-One Two-Two Alpha taking off runway two-one, left turnout."

"That you, Elevens? It's Boxcar on your six. Where you headed?"

"Chicago with all that money I won last night." He turns onto the taxiway.

"*Me too.*"

"Uh, I recall you leavin' more than you came with."

"*I meant Chicago. And I was doin' all right until you dropped triple Jacks. I'm staying at the downtown Hilton. Sure would love a chance to get my five hundred dollars back.*"

"Game on!" A smile creeps across Bud's face. "Of course, we could bet that five hundred on a race to Chi-Town."

"*Hmm. Where you stopping for fuel?*"

"Garden City, Kansas." Bud enters the runway. "Wanna make it double or nothin'?"

"*That's a Texas-sized 10-4.*"

Bud opens the throttle and the engines roar in stereo. Seconds later they're airborne, white wings disappearing into a cerulean panorama. He looks in the mirror at Boxcar's single-engine Mooney lifting off. "So, Mr. Strange, what're we haulin' today?"

Daniel is so entranced by the Mars-red surface he almost forgets his "business" name, Robert Strange. "Uh, lab samples. Tissue. Can't say much beyond that."

"Long as it ain't stem cells – or clonin'." Bud shakes his head. "So sick of people playin' God when they should be worshipping Him. You a church-goer?"

"It's been a while. I might come back."

"Don't wait too long. Never know when Judgement Day will arrive."

"So why do they call you Elevens?"

"My lucky number. Born November 11. On my eleventh birthday I went to church and got moved by the Holy Spirit. At twenty-two, I became a father for the first time. And at the age of thirty-three, after wanderin' the desert so to speak, I came back to Jesus. Yessir, born again." He pauses. "Of course, you heard about my last winning hand."

"Three Jacks."

"Which was the eleventh hand of the game." His right hand goes up. "God as my witness, I kid you not."

Daniel wrinkles his forehead. "I'm trying to remember the

significance of eleven in the Bible. All I remember are twelves."

"Right, the number of apostles, and the age Jesus was when he questioned scholars in the temple. Plus, twelve sons of Jacob who formed the twelve tribes of Israel. Yep, the good book likes an even dozen. But eleven is connected to the main event for people in my church – hold on." Bud listens to frequency traffic for several seconds. "Chatter on the east coast. Reports of a plane crashing into a skyscraper." He shakes his head. "Where were we?"

"Eleven in the Bible."

"Right. Eleven appears less often in scripture but when it does, it usually signifies judgement. Take the Book of Genesis. In Chapter 11, mind you, mankind rebels against God and builds the tower of Babel. God responds by confusing their language – literally, they start babbling -- and the result is chaos." He pauses to listen again. "The apostle John had eleven visions in connection with the final judgement. And the Gospel of John tells of eleven promises God makes to mankind, beginning with everlasting life if you believe in Christ and ending with a call to obey Jesus. My takeaway: Eleven is a sign to get right with the Lord before Judgement Day." Listening again. "For the sake of completeness, I'll note that our savior was thirty-three when he was crucified." He presses a headphone tight against his left ear. "Another plane hit the World Trade Center – South Tower this time – and now they're saying both were airliners. Looks like an attack of some sort."

"Let me hear."

Bud switches to an AM channel and they listen silently for several minutes. The news gets worse as reports come in about another airliner crashing into the Pentagon. Even the distance of two time zones can't deaden the reality that the nation is under attack. There's confusion about a fourth plane which, at first, was headed for the White House but now lies burning on the ground in Pennsylvania. Aboard each plane, the hijackers shouted *"Allāhu akbar"* – 11 letters spelling "God is greatest" -- as they used boxcutters to slit crewmembers' throats. Now the media is sharing voice messages from those trapped in the burning towers. Daniel keeps swallowing to quell his emotions. Bud just lets his moans, groans, and tears flow unchecked. He improvises a prayer:

"Dear Lord, it's Elevens here, your perennial sinner. I know we haven't spoken directly about my little gamblin' problem, but I'd like to make sure we're square. If this is your Final Judgement, please have some mercy and take this flawed but well-meaning servant to sit by your side. If, however, this is a trial you've set for us, I'm ready to show my devotion by givin' up cards. Just, please, give me a sign. Show me the way." He turns to Daniel. "If you need help prayin' – maybe you forgot some of the words – I can help."

"I'm sure my fate has already been decided."

Bud looks forward. "And Lord, let's not forget our quiet friend here, Mr. Strange. He may be a mystery, but I'm guessin' his intentions are just as noble as mine. That, I believe, makes him worthy of your protection. Amen."

Albuquerque Center to all aircraft: All flights are to immediately land at the nearest facility. This is a nationwide order from the FAA. Repeat: Land immediately.

"Ask for a sign, receive one." Bud clears his throat. "Albuquerque Center, this is Baron One-One Two-Two Alpha. Message received. Over." He spreads a chart across the control wheel. "No long runways in front of us, so we'll have to turn around."

"No." Daniel holds a pistol in his right hand. "Keep going."

"You out of your mind? I'll lose my license – and my livelihood." Bud's eyes land briefly on the gun. "Careful with that trigger. We'll both die if you pull it."

"I'm not pulling anything so long as you keep flying."

Bud sighs. "Mr. Strange, you're makin' a big mistake. And it's a hell of a thing to do, dragging me into whatever scheme you got going on." He glances back. "I'm guessin' that's not lab samples, is it? What are you into, drugs?"

"The less you know, the safer we both are."

"Sounds like you're in deep." Bud softens his voice. "Look, man, it's not too late. I'll testify in your favor if you just give me the gun and let me follow orders."

"We're all obeying someone, Bud. Just get us to Garden City."

"And then what? They won't let you take off. All flights are grounded!"

"Let me worry about that."

Barron One-One Two-Two Alpha, Albuquerque Center. Turn around now and land at Sedona. That is an order.

Daniel pushes the gun closer. "Don't acknowledge."

Bud exhales and puts both hands on the wheel. After several seconds, he shakes his head. "The Lord is testing me today. With signs I do not like."

"When we land," Daniel adjusts his tone, "I'll pay your second installment early, and we'll part ways. The world has no time right now for this little problem between us."

"Problem? You hijack my plane and call it a 'little problem'? That is a breach of trust, my friend, and comes at a time when my very identity is shaken to its core."

"Identity?"

"Eleven has always been *my* number, whether it's cards, horses, or life events. Then this morning happened. I woke up and said, 'It's the 11ᵗʰ of September, gonna be a good day.' But clearly, it's not. It's a shitty day for everyone – possibly the worst in our nation's history. That's one sign." He points at the gun. "Next, I'm held up by a Colt M1911. And now," he punches his door, "111 miles from Sedona, we get intercepted."

"What?"

"LOOK OUT YOUR GODDAMN WINDOW."

Daniel's jaw drops when he sees an F-16 with its flaps open and gear down, slowing into formation. Its pilot raises a hand, finger pointed down.

Barron One-One Two-Two Alpha, this is Captain "Spike" Ripley of the United States Air Force. I'm in visual contact and will shoot you down if you fail to comply with the following order: Land immediately. Repeat: Land immediately.

"There's nowhere." Bud is sweating. "NOWHERE TO FUCKING LAND!"

Daniel snatches the chart. "There's a private strip on a mesa up ahead."

"What's the heading?"

"25 miles straight ahead."

"Length?"

"What, the mesa?"

"RUNWAY!"

"29-hundred feet."

Bud snatches it back. "Shit, that mesa looks half the size of Sedona. It'll be like landing on an aircraft carrier – which I've never done before."

Baron One-One Two-Two Alpha, this is your final warning. Land immediately.

Bud's voice cracks. "Don't shoot, Captain! Gimme two seconds." He switches on the landing lights, decelerates, and snaps his fingers at Daniel. "Airport elevation."

"What?"

"FEET ABOVE SEA LEVEL."

"47-hundred."

Bud clears his throat. "This is Baron One-One Two-Two Alpha, descending. God bless you, sir, and God bless the United States of America." He glances over. "I'm assuming there's no tower at this little outpost we're shootin' for."

"Correct."

"Well, brace yourself, 'cause crosswinds are gonna be a bitch." He scowls when he notices the gun again. "Put that away."

"Are you calm now?"

"Fuck you."

Daniel complies and settles into his seat as the runway comes into view, sitting atop a block of crimson stone. The approach is fairly calm until a half mile out, when a gust knocks them off target. Bud's knuckles are white as he raises the nose and straightens out against the crosswind. Back on track, he finally lowers the wheels, adjusting for the extra resistance which now appears to come from everywhere. At 500 yards, the plane shakes violently while Bud struggles to stay on target. At 300 yards, he pulls back on the wheel, keeping the nose up, while gunning the engine to stay above the rim. At 200 yards, a giant gust pushes the plane below the runway.

Bud yanks back again and accelerates sharply as the rocky face grows bigger. Suddenly, Daniel sees Boxcar's Mooney directly above them.

"Shit, that you Elevens? I'm on top of you."

"THE FUCK, BOXCAR. ABORT LANDING."

"Pulling up."

Too late. The Baron's wheels catch the rim and collapse, causing the plane to skid diagonally across the runway. They knock aside a parked helicopter, then hit another plane before smacking into a hangar.

As he slowly regains consciousness, Daniel hears a gurgling sound. Turning his head, he sees Bud's eyes staring at a long piece of metal in his throat. The gurgling slows to intermittent choking before Bud finally goes silent. Next, Daniel turns to the right and sees his arm hanging out the window, bent the wrong way. A piece of bone sticks out through his bicep.

~

"Daniel." A familiar voice, but not the one he hoped for. His eyes open to see Søren leaning over him, eyes piercing the narcotic haze. He snaps his fingers and waves his hand in front of Daniel's face.

"Stop it."

"There he is." The hand withdraws. "That must be powerful stuff they gave you."

Daniel looks at the tubes hooked up to his left arm. "Where's Fiona?"

"Really? I come to your rescue, and she's all you think about?" He shakes his head. "She's not coming."

"Rescue? Bullshit, you're here for the cargo."

"I did salvage some A positive. The rest will go to waste because the elders canceled the meeting. I suppose you'll blame the pilot for our having to reschedule."

"Waste? Take the O negative to Fiona."

Søren looks indignant. "I'm not your mule – or hers."

"You piece of shit, I nearly killed myself delivering that."

"Well well, the truth comes out." Søren's face comes closer. "I've got some truth of my own to share." Two icy hands grab Daniel's face and turn it to the right. "Look at what's left of you and tell me you're still useful."

Daniel's breathing accelerates when he sees the stump wrapped in bandages. "That's up to Fiona."

"She and I have already spoken." Canines appear as Søren's voice changes to a snarl. "I'm to estimate your value and decide whether you stay employed or remain here. Permanently."

"I have a new source." Daniel struggles to speak. "One hundred bags of O negative every two weeks. That, plus Atlanta and Cleveland, and Fiona is set."

"Where is this new source?"

"Sedona. All we have to do is hire a new pilot."

"All the planes are grounded."

"For just a few days. The economy would collapse."

"A hundred bags of O neg, huh?" Søren regards him carefully. "Add an equal amount of A positive to each flight and I'll let you live."

Daniel's vision fades as the drugs take hold again. A warm, fuzzy feeling spreads throughout his body, and the pain that was rallying begins to recede. At this point, he could care less if Søren brought him home or drained him dry. He wonders if heaven feels this good, and kind of wishes he could slip away forever. Would Elevens be there? His prayer for protection should carry weight, right? With St. Peter or whoever guards the gates? If, however, he must stay here it better be with a steady supply of this shit. The label on the drip bag was hazy but it might've said Dilaudid. Maybe Jesús could add a few bags of this, too. Get rid of the bad dreams. Allow him to forget everything.

The shadows gather again. Søren's voice sounds like it's coming from an old phonograph. Soon, all Daniel can hear is his own shallow breathing. Sure isn't hell, that's for certain…

DILAUDID DREAMS

Søren lies crumpled on the ground about twenty feet away. Slowly, he gets up and brushes off his clothes, and that's when he sees the smoking hole over his heart. His eyes try to lock with mine but they're on fire now. I keep the gun level, ready to shoot again, but each second confirms the ghost of immortality is abandoning this feral Nazi-turned-vampire. Despite everything he said about Fiona and how she mocked me, which is probably true, I still feel relieved she's not here to see this.

"She'd rip out your organs," Søren's voice is harsher now, "and scatter them across the plain, one after the other." Søren goes from standing on two legs to a torso propped on a pile of ashes. "MY GOD HOW COULD YOU LET HIM DO THIS TO ME?"

If Fiona were here, she might leave me just enough pieces to continue functioning – a lung, a kidney, perhaps a leg -- because I saved her life, long ago, and I'd still be useful. Of course, I could forget about retiring. Smoke, bitter and metallic, invades my nostrils as Søren watches his fingers disappear.

"Fiona," he coughs, "ich komme."

I step back and holster the gun. A pithy "Goodbye Søren" seems appropriate but I doubt he can hear now that his ears disintegrated. Eyes merely holes now, his face aims toward heaven as his mouth screams in silent protest.

Like a sandcastle reduced by waves, Søren dissolves into a nurse checking my vitals; a slender, long-haired female from what my blurred eyes can see. Sounds of the hospital return. I whisper, "More drugs" because my right hand is killing me, but she's focused on my chart. My eyes clear just enough to read her nametag and my mouth struggles to speak:

"Camilla. I'm in pain."

Her face moves closer and I see strawberry locks and emerald eyes. "You're Daniel. You belong to Fiona, don't you?" Her voice has a lovely, soft English accent. "You're not supposed to be here."

"What?"

"I'm supposed to meet you after Fiona." She opens a vial, pops on a needle, and sticks it in my IV. "She's supposed to bring me right to the edge of death, then give me her blood. She will be my mother and my lover, and you will end up working for me. Not sure if we'll be lovers, though."

"When do you meet Fiona?"

"Not 'til winter, I think. *L'Inverno*. At least that's the music I heard when I dreamed of her."

"What?"

"The Four Seasons."

My eyes drift right, and I see the source of my discomfort: twine cutting the circulation to my fingers. Somehow, I forgot to unwrap it as I drove back to Fiona's home and didn't notice until now. My breath is stale from thirst and adrenaline as I park in front of her building. Getting out, I glance in the back to be sure the blanket covers evidence of my first murder. In the upstairs unit, Fiona shivers beneath a robe that looks ten sizes too big. Without a word, I slide one arm under her legs and the other beneath her neck. She feels about eighty pounds when I lift. A handful of hair sticks to the pillow, gray strands fanning out like a dusty spider web. As I walk down the stairs, her ribs and pelvis poke my torso. Now her breath is moistening my neck. Twice I feel her lips graze my skin. Then her tongue.

Outside, I crouch as I open the rear door and lay Fiona on the back seat, her face close to the homeless woman's neck. I pull back the blanket, find the corpsman patch, and rip it off her jacket. When I shut the door, it's not for Fiona. I need a break. The way I killed this woman – so sloppy and amateurish -- prolonged her suffering. The last thing I want to see is her corpse violated. I just stand outside, looking at the patch, drinking from a flask of whiskey.

"Well," Fiona wipes her mouth as she emerges from the car. "She tasted like heroin and Mountain Dew. But she was O negative."

Stunned, I watch her silk robe retreat before expanding curves.

With every second, her skin regains color and suppleness. Her breasts, which had shrunk to barely a handful, swell back to DD. I blink once and when my eyes reopen her waist and hips again resemble a Greek amphora. She's within reach now, eyes wide and shining, chin stained with blood: "May I give you a hug?"

"I was hoping for more."

Her expression darkens.

"After what I went through today, I earned it."

A hand goes up. "Enough."

"I can't get that woman out of my head."

She turns and walks toward the condo. "Ditch the car and bring back another. We leave in one hour."

Fiona is here, with me now, wearing her peasant dress. But not *here.* The small hospital window has been replaced by French doors which welcome the moonlight skipping across the lake and resting on her bare shoulders. We're in another home Fiona keeps in Wisconsin. Between us sits a decanter filled with brick-red liquid sitting next to an empty bottle with a faded label.

"I found a rare wine." Fiona stares at the bay. "Open and enjoy."

The label reads Graham's 1948 vintage port. "As old as my mother," I whisper while pouring. I sniff and empty it with one swallow; the alcohol burns while the sugar soothes my parched throat. "I had hoped we could finish our conversation."

"I know what you want. You are forbidden to request it."

"So you read minds, too." I rub my hand across the stubble on my chin. "If you knew what I wanted, but didn't answer, was that because you needed me to bring you here?"

Silence.

"I murdered for you," stepping forward. "I worked one day and already I'm eligible for the death penalty."

"The police won't find you as long as you keep working for me."

"That's blackmail." My hand reaches for her arm.

"Don't." Her eyes remain fixed on the water. "You saved my life, and for that I am grateful. But I will snap your neck like a twig if you touch me."

My hand retreats. Fiona wraps herself in her arms. "I'm

surprised you asked so soon. The others waited a year, sometimes two."

"Tanya asked after she got cancer, didn't she? You denied her eternal life. That's why she sabotaged your network."

"It was Tanya's time to go."

"Are you God *and* the Grim Reaper?"

"In your case, I'm the Angel of Mercy." She moves toward the table, refills the glass, and extends it toward me. "Søren would've made a meal out of you, just like he did with Ramon."

"What?"

"You're both his type." She looks plainly at me. "Are you going to drink this or not?"

Surrendering, I reach for the glass but stop when I notice the tattooed crucifix between her thumb and forefinger. I look at her face but it's not Fiona anymore.

"Ten dollars will feed me and my baby. Can you spare it?" The corpsman's pale blue eyes stare back, framed by dirty blonde hair.

"Where's your baby?"

"Sleeping. All it takes is twenty to feed a family." Her hands grasp mine and begin removing the twine.

I feel an odd sense of relief seeing her again. "I know you'll never forgive me, but I must ask: Was the baby real?"

"She was, for a while."

"And Lebanon...the bombing...you were there?"

"Yes, Daniel. I was there."

"The Marine with rebar in his throat – wait. I never told you my name."

"And I never told you mine. Would you like to know who I am now?"

"Are *you* God?"

"I don't think so." She moves to my side, and I see the hospital window is back again. Slowly, she wraps the twine around my neck.

"The Devil?"

"There is no Devil. Only sin, passed from one to another. Strange how yours came full circle." She wraps another length around my throat. "At least you gave me time to pray before killing me. Would you like to do that?"

"I'm not ready to die."

"I wasn't either. And don't ask me to suck your dick again. One last breath?"

"Please…" She pulls tight, choking my airway. My eyes look up again, but this time it's Fiona holding both ends. Her eyes smolder and her mouth twists with rage. As my face turns purple, her features tremble. Her eyes fill with blood which spills over as she softly wails.

"Why did you betray me?"

Betray you? Søren tried to kill me.

"Blood is the strongest bond. If you had a child you'd understand!"

Here's what I understand: You have the power to choose my fate – decide! A scream wells up, borne on a cloud of repressed rage: *KILL OR SET ME FREE.*

I'm on my feet when my voice echoes off the walls. The sun blinds me, sweat soaks my pajamas, and I nearly trip on tangled bedsheets. My left hand grabs the nightstand while my eyes confirm the right's still missing. Lungs filled with sea air, I know I've finally caught up to the present, but her voice lingers:

Kill. But not now. I need you.

"Stay AWAY." In the bathroom, I splash water in my eyes and watch the drops stream down my tanned face. "She doesn't exist. She's in your head and nowhere else." I stare harder at the mirror. "What do you know now, Daniel, what can you be certain of *now*?" I breathe deeply and slowly exhale. "I am here, Fiona is not. You can't even prove she existed. Was she there when you lost your arm? Are any of your memories of the last three decades true?" My head rests against the mirror. "All you know is you are alone and free. Enjoy what remains of your life."

Back in the bedroom, I decide to record my life in the present. I pick up my phone, press the voice recorder, and start speaking. Like the living do.

DANIEL THE JOURNALIST

Day One, Morning: Visited Apollo's temple, all ruins now except for a tall rectangular stone entrance which still stands. In Greek mythology, Apollo is associated with the Sun and healing. After decades in the shadows, losing a limb and nearly my mind, I need to bask in Apollo's glory before it's too late. I remain standing beneath the temple's entrance long after the other visitors depart.

Afternoon: Didn't bring enough water; my mouth is as dry as the ancient dust that surrounds me. I head for the more fertile ground of Naxos village where I'm craving octopus salad and chilled wine. Then to a bar owned by my fixer, Ian, who has leads on properties. I told him I want something move-in ready, no outside maintenance.

Day Two, Morning: Ian wasn't available yesterday. Bartender said he and his wife were visiting friends in Hora on another island. I texted Ian and told him I was coming and would not be put off. He replied, inviting me to a restaurant. Looked up Hora and noticed a 12th Century castle once belonging to a Venetian lord. Booked passage and tour. While at Ian's bar last night, saw a bottle of Graham's port on the top shelf. Asked the bartender to turn the label toward the wall and drank scotch for the rest of the evening. Hours later, bed spinning, I couldn't wipe the slate clean. Maybe Ian can help.

Afternoon: Loved the Venetian castle with crumbling walls, stone archways, winding paths. Asked Miss Tour Guide how much it would cost to buy. She looked like I was from Mars and said it wasn't for sale. First time I remember someone saying "No, you can't have this for any price."

Evening: Met Ian and his wife at dinner – lovely Greek woman half his age. Good for him. Now the bad news: No islands for sale. Suddenly, Greece is less interesting. Ian asked if I'd settle for a home in a village, at the edge, or away from everybody. If away, contractors might not want to make the trip. I downed my wine and muttered "edge." After my third glass, I nearly asked his wife if she had a sister. Had to pee instead. Saved by the bladder.

Day Three. No tours this morning. I ordered room service and searched for homes myself. Ian was right: no islands for sale. Does the government own everything around here?

Afternoon: Ian drove me to a home just outside the village. Two bed, two bath – perfect size but needs repairs. On the way back, we passed a clinic with a line streaming out the door. "Blood drive," Ian said. I asked if there was an emergency. He shook his head and said a local charity pays 10 euros for a pint. Times are hard; even he has five or six jobs. He offered to find me a car and driver's license. Also, did I want a call girl? I considered that last item but declined.

Evening: After dinner, I looked for another bar, some place dark and lonely. For 35 years, I dreamt of white Mediterranean beaches, but I'm still happiest when the sun disappears. The street was full of people, some sort of festival, but I wasn't celebrating. I kept thinking of those blood donors and wondered how many of them were O negative. Most appeared impatient, waiting for their money, but a few seemed genuinely pleased to give something back to the community. I have no idea how that feels. My only sensation is guilt for all those years stealing from people with good intentions. And for what – to feed a creature who never stopped being hungry? Fuck. I told myself I wouldn't think of her.

Day Four, Morning: Aching head. Must remember: two doubles of scotch is my limit. I don't remember much from last night except nearly getting hit by an Aston Martin. Just like the '69 I drove once before burning. The driver was drunk and didn't see me crossing. Tires screeching, he got out and started yelling. As he waved his arms, I calculated the distance from the edge of my hand to his throat, my palm to his nose, and fingers to his eye sockets. His date saved him. A brunette with pale skin wearing a low-cut dress that left me defenseless. I don't know why but I apologized to her, walked to the nearest bar, took my drink to the darkest corner, and wept.

Afternoon: Ian brought me a BMW, fully loaded, plus a driver's license. I paid cash, then asked for a blonde. He scratched his head and asked if she had to be "a real blonde." I said yes and paid his finder's fee. Finally, after midnight, a blonde knocked on my door. Long hair, mermaid dress, push-up bra. She asked for the bathroom and said to wait in bed.

Day Five, Morning: Drove to a home in another village where Ian was waiting. He showed me the rooms and asked how I liked Daphne. I paused because she didn't tell me her name. Had she, I would've remembered the story of Apollo and his pursuit of Daphne, thanks to help from Cupid. I could've used one of those magic arrows; my Daphne did a lot of work to make up for my...I don't know, distraction. When it was over, she gathered her clothes, but stopped to chat when I added a hefty tip. She said she could be available tonight, which she must've told Ian, so now I think he gets a cut of her fee. Add pimp to his resume. I told him a brunette might be better after all. He stared open-mouthed, like he wanted to slap me, which I probably deserved.

~

"Buon giorno, Father Abbot," Brother Raymond checks the time, then adjusts for Rome. "I mean buona sera."

"Yeah, they're serving dinner in a few minutes, so let's get to your report. What's the body count?"

"I'm happy to announce," Brother Raymond leans toward the conference phone, "that we exterminated every striga in North America." He nods toward his colleagues around the table.

"When you say 'every' that means Miklós, Konstantin...?"

"All eleven of them, after Agripina." Raymond folds his hands and waits for an ovation.

"Who witnessed their deaths?"

"I saw Miklós get shot. Brother Leo here was present when Konstantin burned."

"What about the one that massacred our brothers in Oklahoma?"

"Søren Fillenius? Brother Wolf said he killed him during that battle."

"Ferdinand and Fiona?"

"Fiona's death sentence was carried out at the Illinois camp. We saw an ash pile beneath silver restraints in the courtyard."

"And how did Ferdinand die?"

"We found another ash pile a little further away, plus a spent wooden bullet."

"Who killed him?"

"We're still trying to determine that."

"When you say 'trying to determine' what does that mean?"

"Well, Father Abbot, a lot of brothers were involved, and many fell in battle. It'll take time to sort out who did what."

"Clearly, you haven't heard the news from England or you'd be sorting faster."

"What news?"

"Police are reporting multiple disappearances on a container ship that landed in Portsmouth. When they did an air search, they found three crew members floating along the ship's path. All were drained of blood and had bite marks on their necks. As you can imagine, the cardinal was not pleased to hear this. I'm not either."

Raymond flushes. "I don't understand."

"Tell me about the remains you think belong to Ferdinand."

Raymond leans toward Brother Leo, who murmurs in his ear. Then: "We recovered some clothing and jewelry, but nothing we recognize from our image library."

"So you're not even close to being sure that was Ferdinand."

Raymond pauses. "We're still investigating."

"Last time I checked, Brother Raymond, 'exterminated' means wiped out completely. The strigae are not 'exterminated' if one escaped."

"Father Abbot, are you certain that ship came from the U.S.?"

"It left New York eight days ago."

Raymond is silent for several seconds before clearing his throat. "What do you recommend?"

"My orders are to send everyone to Europe to finish the job. I need to reassure the cardinal that we'll complete our mission in days, not weeks. Don't make me a liar, Raymond."

"Yes, Father Abbot."

"Going forward, assume that any corrective action from His Eminence will reverberate down the chain. Is that clear?"

OPHELIA IN LONDON

"Do you have an account with us?" A sales clerk named Susan scans a crystal wine glass and decanter.

"No." Ophelia Cortez tilts her head, letting her ears bathe in pure British English. Her eyes open. "I'll pay cash." Before arriving in London, Ophelia regarded English as a tool to navigate the U.S. mainland. In her home, whether eating or making love, Ophelia always expressed herself in her mother's Puerto Rican dialect. Now for the first time she imagines sex *en Inglés*. Using her silk scarf to blindfold Susan. Using black stockings to gently tie her hands to each bedpost. Removing her underwear...

"Would you like these gift-wrapped?"

"Yes." Light-headed, Ophelia watches her wrap her items. As Susan reaches for a box, Ophelia leans forward. "Actually, I'd like to ship these."

"Of course." Susan moves to a collection of heavier boxes. "Where would you like to send them?"

"I don't know." Ophelia feels uncomfortable hearing her accent. "I mean, I don't have the address yet. Could you just pack them, and I'll ship later?"

"Certainly." Susan places the new box and paper on the counter. "We do have discounts on additional stemware. One extra glass is 10 percent off, and you deduct 25 percent if you buy a set of four."

"One will suffice." Ophelia is startled by her word choice. Suffice? And that accent she used, stripped of any hint of her background. Her face flushes as she looks for an escape.

"Very well." Susan acts like nothing happened.

Ophelia opens her mouth again, hoping her normal voice returns. "Where's your bathroom?"

~

Father Abbot is anxious when he enters St. Peter's Basilica but relaxes when he hears the choir and sees his favorite sculpture:

Michelangelo's Pietà. He loves how the artist used the white marble to highlight the purity of Mary while preserving the suppleness of her son's body just removed from the cross, foreshadowing his rising soon after.

As his heels echo across tiles rescued from Palace of the Caesars, the abbot is reminded of his place in a thousand-year-old war. Reports of vampires surfaced periodically in the Middle Ages, but church leaders never recorded them. Nothing in approved texts or artwork refers to these creatures. By the 15th Century, Pope Innocent VIII felt it necessary to address these reports. He appointed one person with the rank of cardinal, Sextus, to discretely investigate. In a clever move, Sextus gave these creatures the noun *striga*, which also meant "witch." It was the perfect cover since no one batted an eye when the church announced a witch investigation.

Soon after, Sextus went beyond his mandate to form the secret Mors Strigae order which, unfortunately, came into the open when a bystander filmed Brother Raymond burning Agripina. Still, nothing in that video identified Raymond or linked members of his team to the Church. As a result, the mission to faithfully serve God continues in the Holy See. Not long ago, the new pope continued the ancient tradition of appointing one cardinal to investigate occult phenomena, including *strigae*. This official remains the only Vatican leader who knows the actual role of the abbot moving toward a cordoned off worship area.

A robed secretary approaches. "His Eminence will see you." Father Abbot bows his head as the secretary briefly unhooks a rope separating them from the rest of the faithful. Cardinal Massimo de Luca kneels with a rosary in his hands. He doesn't acknowledge the visitor but speaks after he joins him: "When I was young, I went on a mission to Rhodesia – still a British colony – where an outbreak of hemorrhagic fever was reported in a distant village. Do you know of such fevers?"

"I've heard of Ebola."

"That's the one. But we didn't know much about it." His fingers work the shiny black beads. "It was horrible to witness. Endless vomiting followed by ghastly moans. The stench of diarrhea. I even saw bleeding from the eyes."

"It sounds horrible, your Emin…"

"What I learned," the cardinal raises his voice, "is that one patient can infect an entire village in days. Ergo, you must quarantine everyone who had contact with the patient. If just one slips through, all progress made to contain the disease is lost." He fills his lungs with the incense-laden air and slowly exhales. "So it goes with an infection we thought we eradicated a few days ago, and is now returning to Europe after more than a century. What's your new plan?"

"My team arrives tomorrow morning."

"How many are left?"

"Three dozen."

The cardinal shakes his head. "I'll send word about where to pick up your weapons."

"Thank you."

"You will provide daily reports on your progress. If on a given day, you have nothing to report, I'll need to know that too. I'll need to know everything."

"Yes, your Eminence."

Cardinal de Luca gives a sidelong glance before returning to his beads. "It's been a while since we talked about your career. Perhaps we should do that now."

~

I place the box on the counter and stare into the mirror, my mind replaying that conversation. One will suffice? Who the fuck did I think I was, the Queen? It was like I never even visited Puerto Rico. Susan played along, like nothing happened, but she must've thought I was putting on airs. Or is it heirs? God, the fuck? Everything changed after that visit last night. I glance at the stalls before untying the scarf around my neck, revealing a band-aid with some blood showing.

Peeling it off, I see the bite marks that continue to weep. I don't actually remember being bitten, but I can see everything up to that point: the shadow at my bedroom door, the icy finger on my lips, the hand sliding down my pajamas. I wasn't expecting it, maybe hoped it might happen, but I could've used some information. Was I being granted eternal life? Was I just a snack, or a meal to be discarded like leftover bones? Then a shock of cold, like someone placed an ice cube between my legs. Gradually, though, I grew warmer again and I started to relax. As my head fell back, I heard strange whispers blending with my own. Wave after wave of pleasure flowed through me, taking me higher, each climax making my voice hit notes I never heard before. But then the sucking started, and that's when I got scared. My vision tunneled, and I felt myself slipping toward death. Knowing I was losing the fight for my body, I fought to control my mind. That last orgasm was proof we were locked in combat; it had to be wrung out of me. I don't remember anything after that.

It frightens me to have to go back there. If I had any brains, I'd return to the counter and ask Susan if I could stay with her for a while. Maybe I should start by asking her to show me the jewelry case -- I've seen how they hate silver. I'll buy a necklace with a crucifix or something. And would I like that gift-wrapped? Yes, Susan, that would suffice quite nicely. Whatever it takes to keep us talking. And do you have an extra band-aid? I could really use one.

RETIREMENT: DAY 11

Morning: Woke up for the first time in my new home: a two-level that's completely furnished. I hesitated about three bedrooms and two baths since I'll never have guests, but Ian was prepared. He said I'll need a housekeeper, so why not a live-in one? Then he offered to find me someone suitable. I also balked at the garden, which is small but ornate. Ian brushed that aside, too, saying a skilled gardener has it on his schedule and leaves a bill every month. "Long as you pay, he keeps coming," Ian said. "And it is beautiful." Clearly, he wanted this sale. But the thing that clinched the deal was the balcony. Just off the master, it has stunning views of the islands of Paros. Right now, I'm enjoying coffee and baklava while the sun rises behind me; its rays reflect off sailboats which follow the wind back and forth over the Aegean. This afternoon, I'll read about the history of these islands – the Cyclades – and nap beneath the shelter of the awning. Of course, I'll need to eat. There's a place nearby that serves fresh Octopus salad and chilled wine. Ian says their souvlaki is good, too, which means lunch and dinner are decided.

Late in the evening I'll drink wine, watch the cruise ships pass by the setting sun, and wait for nightfall when their lights go on. And when the moon rises, I'll have a nightcap and dream of another day in paradise.

And what does that look like? Pursuing my dreams, and mine only. I may take up painting. Or write a novel. Whatever I do, it'll be right here. And no one will disturb me. Better tell Ian the housekeeper should live elsewhere.

~

"There are two monasteries that need leaders with your experience." The ancient pew groans as the cardinal and abbot get off their knees and sit. "One is in Assisi, where the Church's oldest abbot died recently, in his sleep. He led a team that translates

149

ancient poems into modern languages." Cardinal de Luca's eyes roll. "Boring, I know, but here's *la cosa importante*." He raises an index finger. "They maintain twenty acres of vines which produce excellent wine. The restaurants buy most of it, but our brothers keep the best for themselves. Would this be a suitable appointment?"

Father Abbot perks up. "Absolutely your..."

"The other is in El Salvador, where the abbot was murdered last year." The cardinal frowns. "It seems our blessed workshop straddles territory claimed by rival gangs." He glances over. "If the Lord saw fit for you to serve there, you would do your best?"

"I would. But I can't do His work from a grave."

"Only He knows for certain." The cardinal gazes at a stained-glass window featuring a white dove in flight. Viewing this symbol of the Holy Spirit somehow makes it easy to tighten the screws on his subordinate. "You're the leading candidate for both positions. Where you go depends on how you handle this crisis. You have two weeks."

~

Daniel pushes away his plate, not quite able to finish his dinner. Next time, he won't stuff himself on olives beforehand. He pays the bill, thanks the manager, and walks into the night, legs wobbly from wine. His flushed face welcomes the sea breeze, and the laughter of young couples prompts him to think of Daphne. Would she give him another chance? Armed with Viagra this time, he resolves to throw her in bed and pound the hell out of any doubts she might have about him. Oh, that's right, Ian has her number; Daniel would have to talk to him first. Why is everything so complicated here? He stops when he sees a tiny red glow. Smoke from a Macanudo fills the air. Daniel places his hand on his hip and shouts toward the balcony:

"Who's smoking one of my cigars?"

"You know who. Don't say you weren't expecting me."

~

Alone in his pew, Cardinal Massimo de Luca pockets his rosary and pulls out a century-old letter he discovered on his desk one morning: the missing "Catacomb letter" to Cardinal Gianluca Soriano from interim abbot Stefano Francesco. De Luca has been carrying it ever since it mysteriously appeared. The words look like those scribbled by a child, with sentences that curve up and down, even crossing over previous sentences. Occasionally, a string of words will start level, dive to the bottom, and then curve up again through the middle. It looks as if a blind man wrote it, which is basically true. Raising it to his nose, de Luca can almost smell the damp and dusty air of a cramped and craggy hole deep underground:

April 24, 1900 to Cardinal Gianluca Soriano

Dear Eminence,

I hope you can read this, if you ever find it, for I am writing in complete darkness – in both the worldly and spiritual sense. I am forced to admit that malevolent striga Agripina was right. Two cave-ins blocked us forward and back. We are trapped with many injured. Some were killed instantly but we'll all die soon as we're running out of air. I am praying that Heavenly Father will quickly receive my brothers. I do not, however, expect or deserve the Lord's mercy due to my foolhardiness. I alone am responsible for this fatal error. God bless you, your Eminence, as you continue our sacred fight against these evil, yet cunning, creatures. I am so sorry I failed you and all these brave men who had such confidence in me. I will pray for them until my dying breath. Vivat Mors Strigae!

Your faithful servant in Christ's mission, interim Abbot Stefano Francesco.

Cardinal de Luca shakes his head. More than three hundred died if you count those who perished from strigae raids before the cave-in. "The Battle of the Catacomb" would be the worst defeat in the history of the order if it were permitted to have a history.

Even Soriano's diary is off limits, except to the person in de Luca's position. Of course, all this secrecy went out the window with that video of the "revenge burning" of Agripina. Now de Luca's fellow cardinals are demanding to know how long he's been running a private army. When pressed, they'll admit they're more concerned about negative publicity than an actual paramilitary force in the Holy See. Several noted with relief that another story is keeping the "Vatican's Secret Warriors" off the front page: *Coppers Keeping 'Vampire File' in Bloodless Bodies Investigation.* One cardinal joked that the supposed vampires being hunted by Mors Strigae are providing real camouflage for the Church, and wasn't that ironic? De Luca replied it certainly was interesting. What he didn't say was his "vampire file" is much older than Scotland Yard's. And with this final "Catacomb letter," De Luca's file is slightly thicker than that of his current abbot, who'd no doubt want to know how he obtained Francesco's last words. But some secrets are too sensitive even for those second in command. De Luca returns the letter to his pocket, makes the sign of the cross, and passes silently behind the abbot praying in front of The Pietà.

~

Daniel steps through the open door of his bedroom. "So, you're smoking now?"

Wolf exhales long and slow. "You gave me one of these the night we met. Didn't appreciate it at the time, but now I get it. Nice place, by the way."

Of all the people from Daniel's former life, Wolf is the least unwelcome, but Daniel remains suspicious. He takes a cigar from the box and accepts a light. "I see you kept my Zippo."

"The abbot's been eyeing it, so I'd better give it back." Wolf leaves the lighter on the table and watches Daniel ease into the other chair. "If you're trying to stay hidden, you're doing a terrible job. I asked about a one-armed American buying property and it took me six hours to find you. They have prosthetics, you know."

"I'm comfortable with what remains of me." Daniel breathes the smoke deep and exhales. "Besides, I'm no interest to your people now that Fiona's gone."

"Yeah, about that." Wolf inspects the glowing tip. "My people are having second thoughts, which means you're in danger."

"What the hell are you talking about?"

Wolf passes a flask and watches Daniel tilt it up and swallow.

"A vampire arrived in Europe from North America. We don't know who it is, but I'm thinking there's a slight possibility it could be Fiona."

Daniel caps the flask and tosses it back. "Get the fuck out of here."

"Crazy, I know."

"No." Daniel stands. "Get the fuck out of my house."

"I thought you'd be glad there's a chance she's alive. You loved her."

"You have ten seconds."

"I'm here to warn you." Wolf raises a hand. "If you don't believe me, or don't want to, I'll go and you'll never see me again. Just hear me out."

"That a promise?"

Wolf takes another pull at the flask and winces. "Got something better? I miss your scotch."

Ian rings and Daniel decides to take it. "There's a bottle on the bookshelf. Glasses, too." When Wolf goes inside, Daniel answers. "What's up?"

"You have visitors."

"Yeah, he's in my house. It's all right."

"Two men came to the bar tonight. Bald and serious. Asked about a one-armed American looking for property."

"And you said?"

"I told them you didn't find anything and left for Cyprus."

"Did they believe you?"

"They were inscrutable, which is a red flag. I could get you a gun if you want." Wolf returns with two glasses, and Daniel eyes him closely. "Let's talk tomorrow."

Wolf hands him one. "I'm guessing that was Ian."

"You know about him too, huh?"

"He'll be dead before morning." Wolf sits again. "I'm guessing you have three hours before we hit you."

"By 'hit' you mean…"

"Kidnap. Torture." Wolf pauses to let the whiskey drain down his throat. "God damn, that's good."

"I'll assume your friends don't know you're here."

"I'm supposed to watch the docks, make sure you don't leave."

"What do they want to know?"

"If you heard from Fiona." Wolf swirls the whiskey beneath his nose. "Based on your reaction, I'll assume no. But my colleagues already made up their minds about you."

"So a vampire arrives in Europe and everyone thinks it's Fiona – and that I'm involved somehow." Daniel points at his chest. "I saw the ashes. They executed her."

"You saw ashes." Wolf sets down his glass. "Let me give you some background. We destroyed eleven vampires – that's confirmed. But as you know, there were twelve."

"You killed Miklós and Konstantin -- Ferdinand?"

Wolf nods. "They're all dead except one." He leans back. "The trouble is, my people don't know which one and..." He pauses. "I messed up their check list when I said I killed Søren in Oklahoma."

"Why did you tell them that?"

"I came back alone, had to tell them something." Wolf shrugs. "And he did come to your rescue. I felt I owed him an escape."

"Ah." Daniel's eyes light up. "If Søren isn't dead, he might be the one in Europe now."

"That's one theory." Wolf knits his brow. "I've always thought of him as a fight-to-the-death guy, not a retreater. But you know him better than I do."

"Perhaps. But you said Fiona might be here."

"Yeah."

"Why?"

"Just wishful thinking, for your sake, but it's probably Søren." Wolf takes another sip. "How do you feel about the possibility of him being here?"

"He's not here."

"How do you know?"

Daniel takes a pull from his cigar. "Did you search the area outside the courtyard?"

"We found an ash pile that we're still confirming."

"That's Søren."

Wolf coughs. "Are you shitting me? How do you know?"

"I took one of those guns from Oklahoma, loaded with hardwood. He made some moves I didn't like. Basically, he turned on me and I killed him. One through the heart."

"Holy fuck." Wolf gets up and starts pacing. "This makes my theory even more plausible."

"About Fiona? How?"

"Did you search the execution ground?"

"I…" Daniel sorts through his memory of the place but Søren's face keeps getting in the way. "No."

"There were two sets of silver chains. And one ash pile beneath them."

Daniel looks up. "You sure about that?"

"I saw it myself."

"OK." Daniel pauses for a sip. "If two were sentenced, and there was only one ash pile, and you're missing a vampire…"

"Then it is possible that Ferdinand died and Fiona survived."

"Wait -- you said Ferdinand *is* dead, along with Miklós and Konstantin."

Wolf takes another sip. "My boss thinks Søren's remains belong to Ferdinand."

"Why?"

"Bits of fabric in the ashes. They don't match what Fiona reportedly wore."

Daniel laughs, gets up, and looks out toward the lighted cruise ships. "I was just starting to enjoy life." He empties his glass and smacks it down on the stone railing. "You know what? I don't care if Fiona's alive. She handed me off to Søren so any obligation I had toward her is over."

"That may be, but my friends are coming for you. They'll turn you inside out until they get what they want."

"And the first thing I'll tell them is that I killed Søren." Daniel points at Wolf. "Then you'll have to explain why you lied, and how you were the only one who survived in Oklahoma."

"Say what you want. They'll kill you anyway before coming after me."

"I guess we're both dead then."

"Not if we split up and leave now." Wolf empties his glass and crushes out his cigar. "With any luck, one of us might survive. Unfortunately, if I'm caught, I'll talk – I can't take even a little pain. I suggest you get as far away as you can." He gets up and extends his left hand. "So long, Daniel. See you on the other side, whatever that looks like."

OPHELIA: PRE-EXPLOSION

The bell rings again as I leave the shop, and before the door shuts I'm overwhelmed by a scent wafting by: Jasmine. I look left and my eyes land on a woman even more beautiful than Sexy Clerk Susan. "Wow." I can't help exclaiming. This town is full of gorgeous women. This one's a red head with very pale skin wearing hospital scrubs. She's standing next to a window poster announcing, "The Four Seasons," a concert happening this weekend. She turns to a man next to her – older guy, big gold watch – and the two talk excitedly. I'm not looking my best, so I try to sneak past, but she almost bumps into me.

"Oh, sorry." Her eyes are bright green. Holy shit, they're like that city in The Wizard of Oz. Her man nods politely toward me, but he's clearly eye fucking her which means it's time to go.

"No, it's my fault. Sorry, uh..." I look at her hospital ID. "Camilla. Nice name." There I go again, saying stupid stuff.

"Thanks. And you are?"

"I'm nobody, really. Nice to meet you – bye!"

~

Daniel stands at the front door watching Wolf cross the street with a baseball cap pulled low over his eyes. Before going back in, he notices a package nearby with "Daniel" drawn in a black marker. The box came from London but has no other information about the sender. It's also cross-tied with twine which makes it easy for him to lift but triggers a bad memory. Was this intentional?

Inside, Daniel ignores the package while he grabs his Go Bag under the bed. Back in the kitchen, he dumps the contents on the table. He pockets a phone and sim card, then selects a Canadian passport with his photo and the name Robert Strange. Next, he fills an empty wallet with an Ontario driver's license, a credit card, and wad of Euros. Every other document goes into the shredder.

Before he exits the house, leaving his keys behind, he remembers the package. He hesitates before cutting it with scissors, wincing as if expecting it explode. Instead, the box reveals a single crystal wine glass and matching decanter. His breathing slows as he recognizes the Lismore pattern, a coded invitation that could only come from *her*. Whoever mailed these, however, left the green Waterford stickers attached – a dead giveaway that a more experienced guardian would avoid. Daniel's body shakes as he realizes Fiona hid way more from him than he realized. Who else was working for her, and for how long? And how did this person rescue her from a fiery death?

As the veil lifts, Daniel feels no joy or relief – only anger and jealousy. Why would Fiona mislead him? Why would she place her life in the hands of someone clearly less experienced? And why is she reaching out now when he's trying to forget her?

Outside, he shuts the door to the "forever home" he kept for less than 24 hours. Without a final look he walks away, ignoring his brand-new BMW waiting by the curb. Without a care, he dangles the wine glass and decanter from his fingers, letting them clink to the point of chipping. After a few blocks, he tosses these over a fence into a bed of bougainvillea.

~

Big Ben bongs slowly nine times. In a candle-lit room near the Thames, red-painted hawks' beaks peck at a laptop, pausing for a page to load. Four violinists appear, along with a violist, cellist, and bassist above the words "Antonio Vivaldi," "The Four Seasons" and "Tonight Only." The box office link appears as *La Primavera* leaps from tiny speakers barely able to contain the joy, abundance -- the hope -- of springtime. Long black strands tickle the sound holes as she leans closer, humming along. Seconds later, another voice crashes in to deliver the latest bulletin. Off goes the speaker. The intruder is a tabloid newsreader accompanied by a crimson-eyed Christopher Lee, fangs bared, above the headline *Coppers Blame Vamp Imitator for Bloodless Bodies*.

"I prefer Langella." Fiona rises, a black silk robe hanging open as she walks into the kitchen. The refrigerator has just five bags of O negative and Ophelia is away, which means the hunt must resume tonight. But first, a snack. She punctures a bag with a nail, fills a glass, and walks back into the living room toward a table covered with charcoal sketches. Each one is a portrait with a name and range of dates underneath:

Ophelia (hair tied back) 2018 - ?
Wolf (hair mussed) 2018 – ?
Daniel (with fedora) 1986 - ?
Tanya (head sideways, decapitated) 1976 – 1986
Dominic (handlebar mustache) 1945 – 1975.

Fiona picks up a pencil and adds shadow under the eyes of another man with the dates 1910 – 1914. His round face sits on a mountain of neck and shoulder, eyes sad and loyal like a neglected dog. Beneath him is the word "Venice."

What was his name again?

THE DEAD OF VENICE (1914)

She promised to do it quickly. I promised to stay out of sight. All bodies float, which is why I brought two anchors – one for me, one for her victim. All she need do is throw us in, then the chains, followed by the weights. This far out, the lagoon is 40 feet deep, maybe 50. From down there our lifeless ears might still enjoy the sounds of Vivaldi performed in St. Stephen's Cathedral. Just as likely, we'll hear the rattle of Europe's emperors as they prepare, once again, to exterminate a generation of working-class blokes like me.

As I row, I point to Italy's newest battleship which dares to keep its lights on; perfect target for a night raid. I ignore that bit as I play the tour guide for Fiona and tonight's meal. "The *Regina Elena*. Faster than the *HMS Dreadnought* wot I helped build. Yup, this next war looks to be a doozy."

In the lamplight, Fiona toys with the gold dragonfly I pinned to her ball gown. I can see her eyes well up and her mouth tremble. Lorenzo, heir to the Duke of Parma, raises his fist at the glowing gunboat. "Viva l'Italia!"

Toff. What does he know of war? I served in the Tibetan campaign, so I know it's a nasty business for those who actually fight. I want to hit him now but we're still within sight of ship and shore. Looking back, I see a city of free spirits being hemmed in by sandbags and barbed wire. Bloody hell, when did the Four Horses of the Quadriga flee the Basilica? Someone said the statue might go to Rome for safe keeping. From what -- so the Turks can't take it back?

I suppose I owe you an explanation as to why three people are in a boat, after dark, and two of them will soon head to the bottom. Hang on: The young swell is giving Fiona his kerchief. Blimey, he even recites a Shakespeare sonnet – in English. She tries to smile but struggles to contain her thirsty teeth and, guessing here, a broken heart? Concern for her future? Both hands cover her mouth as she leans forward, shoulders quaking. This exposes her breasts which prove such a distraction that Lorenzo misses the oars resting and the blackjack falling toward his scalp. I wanted to wait 'til a hundred yards off the Main Island, our usual point, but the fog rolled in so ... Boom. Done. *Colazione* is ready.

I uncork my wine and try not to stare as she sinks her canines into his neck. It always amazes me how efficient she is. No wasted drops. Her lips move gently as she slowly sucks him dry. I've never timed her, but bottle and body usually empty together. Then I chain him to the anchor and over he goes. The rest – hundreds of them – are a little further out in what I call "the cheap seats." This will be my final resting place. I can barely stop my tears now, but they're not for me. Creatures like her are vulnerable these days. She'll need someone to look after her, but my pain is almost debilitating now; I couldn't arrange a replacement.

I take another sip and remember how our partnership began with an ad in the *Daily Mail*:

"Seeking Personal Assistant. Must be physically strong, and willing to work all hours. Compensation: copious. Benefits: worthy of a parliamentarian. *Nota bene* -- People with the following characteristics should not apply: squeamish, weak-willed, illiterate, semi-literate, religious, superstitious, melancholic, alcoholic, xenophobic, agoraphobic, unimaginative, uninventive, uninspired, and with rigid moral standards."

I had to look up *Nota Bene* and, if pressed, would cop to some grumpiness without a few pints each night. But I posted a reply. Benefits worthy of a parliamentarian. What did that mean?

We met soon after sundown in Hampstead Heath, at the gazebo. I wore a suit that no longer fit and she wore a dress that barely contained her bosom. Her coal black hair waved gently across the palest shoulders I've ever seen. I thought she was a courtesan looking for some muscle, and she did nothing to dispel that notion. She gave me money to hire a carriage which took us to Charing Cross. We stopped outside a row of fancy homes and that's when she turned and handed me the dragonfly. All that gold with emerald eyes; I couldn't guess the value of this "down payment" as she called it. Then she lowered her voice and -- without blinking -- said, "A gentleman lives there. I am going to drink his blood and he will die. Your job is to wait in this carriage until I return. If you tell anyone what I just said I will know, and I'll come after you to reclaim my dragonfly. And you. If, on the other hand, you wait as instructed, I will pay a handsome sum. But first you'll need to get rid of the body. Think of a place to bury him. And start thinking of places for tomorrow night, and every night. Welcome to your new career."

She didn't tell me for a week that I was her first. Guardian, I mean. Or caretaker or whatever you call someone that works for a ... Whoops, not supposed to say that word. Anyways, from backbreaking work in a shipyard I started breaking my back for Fiona, digging graves and such. That first week I made more than all the previous year and a half. I quit that job -- Hello new job -- and soon graduated to being the murderer. Things were getting hot for Fiona, what with Scotland Yard improving their detection and all. She needed someone to do the dirty work, which I didn't mind. I killed before, but it always bothered me that the people you shoot, stab, or blow up often go to waste. You seal them in a coffin or burn them and that's it; they serve no further purpose. These days, when a body goes limp in my hands, I know it's about to give life.

She looks ravishing afterwards. Her hair gets full and wavy. Her skin glows like the moon. And her eyes – you could drown in them. They're like a clear lake with a bottom so deep, so full of secrets that you'd need to swim forever to discover them. It's the opposite, though, when she doesn't get her ten pints. That's the nightly quota. The first night without a victim is bad, but her hair starts to fall out on the second. Then her skin wrinkles and begins to smell, and her eyes harden to the point where I think she'd eat an entire schoolyard of children. I work very hard to make sure I never see that look again.

"We have to move," she announced one night. "Detectives, newspapers – I feel like we're surrounded. Did you know Venice has lots of people and very few policemen? It's also easier to get rid of bodies there."

"Where will I dig? It's a city built on water," I said before realizing her point. "Fairly deep water actually, between the islands."

"Yes." She frowned. "The only problem is getting there."

Before the night is over, I'm nailing her into a trunk with an unconscious bloke beside her. The journey would take two weeks by ship so she warned me: Some passengers would have to die. When I asked how many, she wouldn't answer. I think she didn't know the minimum needed to sustain her. In the end, I tossed three bodies over the rail; we couldn't risk any more. To this day, I pity that poor bastard that crossed our path after we landed. I did a rum job of subduing him, and Fiona ripped him so terrible that half his blood painted the alley. Absolute horror show.

We didn't have a boat yet, no weights. Just my blackjack smashing his nose, a knock-down drag-out into the alley, and Fiona attacking his throat like a rabid dog. The musical accompaniment, though, was amazing. A lively melody emanated from a church across the street. I'd never heard a string ensemble perform, so I was unprepared for the effect it had. The bowing and plucking lifted my spirits, opened my heart, and stimulated an awareness I'd never felt before.

A spark of inspiration: Let's make this disaster look like a Mafia hit. I took my knife, severed his head, and tossed it into the nearest canal. Wouldn't you know, that did the trick. The next morning, I scoured the papers and saw nothing. No mention of a blood-sprayed alley, headless body, or bobbing face screaming in silent agony – *niente*. There was, however, an article about another event on that same street: a review of a concert featuring music by the baroque master Antonio Vivaldi. It said they did five shows a week at St. Stephen's Cathedral, and they always sold out when performing *The Four Seasons*.

St. Stephen's became our main hunting ground. Fiona and I surveyed the crowd and she picked the swain who'd leave with her as the musicians stood to rapturous applause. That's how we claimed the cream of European society. Too bad I won't see the job through to its finish. Here, off the Piazza San Marco, this dying East-Ender is preparing for his curtain call. I am not even good enough for an emergency snack because the cancer makes my blood smell bad. When she said that, when I realized I could serve no further purpose, I replied "Enough. Let's end it."

"Well," I stand chained to my anchor, "you found me. You'll find someone else." I wipe my nose and eyes and lower my head toward her. "I'm ready."

Her hands caress my face as her lips melt against mine; I taste a little of bit of Lorenzo. Now our foreheads rest against each other. "You'll feel a brief shock but no pain. I promise you."

"Will I hear the music from St. Stephen's?"

"Vivaldi? Yes. And Bach ..."

I nod, tears mingling with hers in a puddle at our feet. She drapes her right hand around the back of my head, stroking my hair, while her left tightens around my chin. "And Corelli ... Scarlatti..."

I close my eyes.

"... Handel ... Monteverdi..."

I feel the shock but the flash behind my eyelids is a surprise. From inside the boat I hear a series of sobs. Then a splash, followed by a slight wailing sound, which gets wobbly as I sink beneath the waves. Her voice grows fainter and fainter as I take my place among our Venetians.

Her timing was perfect. The concertmaster is tuning up the ensemble. I hear a pause. Then, glory of glories, they launch into the first movement, *La Primavera*. Four violins, one viola, a cello and bass fill my ears. Even the bells of the *Regina Elena* keep time with the bowing. I've seen this show dozens of times and never got tired of it. But the water bends the music in ways I couldn't imagine. Antonio, if you're in the ground somewhere, find a way to get yourself down here. Your *Four Seasons* never sounded better.

Best seats in the house, eh boys? You can thank Fiona for that. Better yet, keep her in your prayers. It's the least we can do for her. God, what an amazing place to spend eternity.

~

"Archie." Fiona smiles as she remembers her first. She lowers the charcoal pencil and adds his name at the bottom. Then she drains her glass and dabs her lips with a napkin. A moment later, she's in her closet staring at a row of evening gowns, whispering: "Seductive or sophisticated? Submissive or assertive? Come hither or conquer?" She holds a strapless Renee Ruiz jacquard mermaid in front of her, then a Marchesa off-the-shoulder feather gown. Finally, she selects a Zac Posen cap sleeve mermaid in gunmetal lamé; the material shimmers like mercury in her hands. She slips into this, spritzes a cloud of lavender perfume, and glides through the tiny droplets like a ghost.

Exit the Conqueror.

WATERFORD

Rested from his five-hour flight, Daniel drives immediately from Dublin Airport to the old Norman city, which takes another two hours without stopping for a meal. By the time he arrives, shortly after 10 a.m., he's craving food and alcohol.

The Gingerman is already filling up. Daniel orders a full Irish breakfast and coffee with a shot of whiskey. The newspaper leads with typical disasters such as *Terrorist Bombs Polling Place* and *Mudslide Consumes Village*. The next page has a smaller article about a "vampire murderer" stalking London -- police perplexed, doctors dumbfounded, politicians panic-stricken – and Daniel understands where he's headed next. He's about to read *Windows Explode Along Lower Thames* when his plate arrives -- bacon rashers, pork sausages, fried eggs, white pudding, black pudding, toast, and a fried tomato -- plus another whiskey for good luck. Then the waitress hands him a small envelope. Inside is a card:

Cathedral of the Most Holy Trinity. Back pew on the left.

Whoever was sent to deliver him will have to wait. Daniel doesn't leave until his plate, and glass, are empty.

~

"Greetings, Father Abbot."

"Brother Raymond, what news from London?"

"I'll begin with the latest." Raymond leans in toward the conference room phone. "We're zeroing in on an explosion that has confused the authorities. Every window within a quarter-mile was blown out, but there was no bomb or gas leak. Rumors are circulating that a supernatural force is to blame. I sent a team to investigate."

"Interesting. What about our exsanguinated bodies?"

"The Coroner is divulging little, but an insider told us the office just doubled their staff, including medical examiners."

"Okay, you know what that tells me?"

"They're dealing with more bodies."

"A doubling of bodies. The cardinal said our rogue striga might reproduce. More investigators indicates that process has begun."

"Shall I redirect all teams to London?"

"First tell me about Daniel, the guardian who fled to Greece."

Raymond squirms. "Brother Leo just flew in. I'll have him explain."

"Okay."

Leo leans in. "Father Abbot, I regret to say Daniel left just before we found his house."

"Left? He's a one-armed American shopping for property. You should've found him in one day. Where did he go?"

"Here's what we know: His fixer, named Ian, warned him of our presence. I personally
interviewed Ian for several hours, and I'm
convinced he did not know where Daniel went."

"Why you? I thought that was Wolf's job."

Leo looks to Raymond for help. Raymond clears his throat. "Wolf also has disappeared."

"By 'disappeared' do you mean 'missing in action' or what?"

"We don't know. There's no trace of him."

A long sigh seeps through the speaker. Then a sharp intake. *"Mother of God."*

Raymond and Leo exchange glances.

"Am I the only one who's having an epiphany right now?"

Raymond leans in. "It occurred to us that Wolf could've warned Daniel before abandoning us."

"Of course he did — they used to work together. I've always suspected Wolf was more loyal to his former colleague. But there's a big clue that just jumped up and said 'Helloooo!' You know what that is, don't you?"

"We're all ears, Father Abbot."

"For Heaven's sake, brothers. The Lord gave better-than-average brains to both of you, didn't He? Connect the dots!"

"Perhaps, Father Abbot, you could...give us a clue?"

"No time. Put your heads together, and I'll inform His Eminence that

we now know which striga escaped from America. And bring all teams to London."

FIONA'S FOUR SEASONS

Why *Le Quattro Stagioni*? My answer is simple: Vivaldi's masterpiece is the most beautiful expression of a cycle of time. Each season, portrayed with vivid color, flows into the next, and again the next, until it renews. This is something immortals experience rarely, if at all; centuries are a blur. Even after narrowly escaping death, I'll soon forget why Ferdinand burned and I didn't. Just like I forgot the name of my first guardian. But Vivaldi transforms time into something gorgeous, and I always remember beauty.

They've just begun: seven bows gliding in unison, strings singing, walls echoing the news that *La Primavera* has arrived. And so has my next meal. She's still outside but I can smell she's my type -- even through her perfume which carries notes of iris, sandalwood, ambergris, vanilla, and…something else. I see her now: red hair, porcelain skin, full red lips. My heart aches as I gaze at her mermaid hips, freckled shoulders, and long, delicate neck. When I see a flash of inner thigh, my lips smack and my tongue figure-8s my canines. Look at me, Dear. Not at your sugar daddy. Look. At. Me.

Her eyes are green. Like Agripina's.

She makes me wait until the final season, *L'Inverno*, before leaving her seat. Her four-inch heels keep time with the musicians' short, insistent bowing. My hands long for the center of her hourglass and the slope of her bottom. When she pees, I smell another perfume and my mind rejoices with the memory of asparagus. She emerges from the stall and I stand behind, nose in her hair, breathing deeply. Looking into the mirror, she uncorks a bottle of Hermès 24 Faubourg, dabs her wrists, touches the anointed skin to her neck, and I nearly faint…

Jasmine.

"Where are you going?"

She quickly turns, notices me, then the closed stalls. She eyes me suspiciously. "You're a quiet one."

"You should hear the storm inside me."

She opens her purse. "I have tummy soother."

"That's not what I mean." I continue to stare, unblinking, which rattles her.

"Sorry, do I know you?"

"No. But it's time you did."

"Excuse me." She shuts her purse. "My boyfriend's waiting." She turns and nearly falls over when I'm in her way. "How did you...?" She looks behind her and then at me. "Please step aside."

I smile as I shake my head.

She reaches for her phone; it flies from her purse and smashes against the back wall. Horrified, her mouth opens but only silence emerges. Both hands go to her throat as she tries to scream again. Turning to the mirror she sees only herself and her head starts reeling. She sways once and falls. I catch that exquisite face before it hits the counter.

~

Back in my flat, I slowly release the hold on her voice, but only for the most selfish of reasons. Longing for more music, I place the right leg of this Stradivarius over my left shoulder. My bowing hand mimics the cellist's long strokes as the blood vessels swell in her left thigh. My concerto begins not with the usual *Allegro*, but a *Menuetto*: My nose grazes the little tuft she left after shaving; she stirs. *Adagio con dolcezza*: The tip of my tongue explores her, guided by her faster pulse and deeper breathing. *Adagietto sostenuto*: Mumbling now, *sotto voce*, her hands crumple the bedsheet. For the first time, I remember custard and how greedily I consumed it as a child. *Andante a piacere*: Her disordered moans and whispers yield to groans. *Andantino con brio*: She cries out, *falsetto*, but I can no longer wait to satisfy me. Retreating lips leave moist kisses on her thigh as I near her femoral artery. My ear presses against her skin to bathe in the rush of blood, *doppio movimento*, waiting to escape.

Then I bite, *deciso*.

Eyes wide, she bolts up screaming, *fortissimo*. Sucking furiously, I place a hand between her breasts and push her back toward the pillow. Her body surrenders as I drain pint after pint after pint...

~

Molto grave. She barely breathes now. Eyes half closed, her head tilts slowly to the left as I decide whether to let her die. If she goes, I'll soon forget her. But isn't this face, this body – this encounter -- worth preserving? Still, I worry about the constant distraction she'd provide.

"What's your name?"

Her eyes roll up beneath her lids. My fingers tap the sides of her face. "Your name, what is it?" Her lips barely move so I listen closely:

"Camilla."

"Camilla the Huntress? What a perfect name for an immortal."

As her breathing stops, I stare at the scar on my right wrist which is my only memento of Søren. If I deface it, I risk losing the moment I transformed him. Still, a new scar will keep me focused on how Daniel cut me deeply and owes dearly. But first, Camilla. I straddle her, knees just below her dead-white nipples, and slit my radial artery. Leaning forward, cradling her head, I hold my wound above her lips and give back a little of what I stole. After a few minutes, her tongue emerges, lapping at the drops. She breathes deeply in and out, and her eyes open. They look at my face, my bleeding wrist, then my body. Her fingers trace the blood vessels from my neck, my right breast, down to the artery in my thigh. Then her head slides beneath me and my eyes close, waiting for the revenge bite, her *morso di vendetta.* My left hand grabs the headboard during her first attempt, which misses. Her second is on target. My right hand grabs her hair as she fiercely reclaims pint after pint. With each pull, Camilla improvises a *concerto stringendo* and my body shakes ever more violently – *Andante, Andantino, Allegretto, Allegro, Vivace, Vivacissimo, Allegrissimo, Presto, Prestissimo.* Head back, mouth agape, a scream wells up but chokes in my throat.

When it finally comes, every window in the neighborhood explodes.

Larghissimo: After I collapse, Camilla lay prone on my back. We listen to the car alarms which are the only sound for a long time.

Suddenly, I think I hear Vivaldi in the distance. But it's just emergency vehicles.

OPHELIA POSSESSED

Since hearing of the explosion, I've been texting Fiona every half hour. No reply. I'm about to return to her, abandoning my mission, when Daniel enters the cathedral – fedora, missing arm and everything. He sizes me up, then sits a short distance away.

"You're late." I speak through grinding teeth. His attention turns toward the large crystal chandelier hanging nearby. "Hey." I jab his shoulder. "I don't have much time."

"Stop acting like an amateur."

I want to stab him with my knife when he says this. "You're the amateur, eating like a pig and smelling of alcohol. You should've been here an hour ago."

He glares at me. "The Waterford stickers were a dead giveaway. You should've removed them."

I start to speak but he cuts me off.

"And that card you had the waitress deliver. It might as well have been a billboard for anyone following me. I had to scan these grounds for fifteen minutes to be sure it was safe. How long have you been here?"

"None of your business."

"You sure no one's tailing you?"

"Nobody's looking for me, *pendejo*. I don't exist."

"What's the message?"

"There is no message. You're coming with me."

"She wants to see me? Why?"

"Why would I know? You worked for her. You know how she keeps things hidden."

"It doesn't matter." Daniel rises. "My presence would put her in danger so it's best I leave. Good luck to both of -- "

"You're the one in danger." I hear a shushing sound. In a pew across the aisle, a nun wags her finger. I lower my voice. "They captured Wolf this morning."

"Where?"

"Madrid. The airport."

"Who's your source?"

"The only thing that matters is you need Fiona's protection."

"The monks are coming for her, too." Daniel shuffles sideways toward the aisle. "The last thing she needs is one-armed fifty-something dragging her down."

"You don't get to decide." My knife comes out and my hand holds the blade pointed at the floor.

He scoffs. "What are you going to do? Stab me in a church?"

"She won't. But I will if you continue disobeying me."

What the fuck? Have I been hijacked? Daniel looks around for her while my mouth starts moving again:

"Now that I have your attention, come closer."

Daniel's eyes are on me again. I try to speak independently but can't. I want to cover my mouth, but my arms are frozen. My feet are stuck too.

"How do you like Ophelia's new scarf? I gave it to her after I got a little...impatient...the other night."

Daniel reaches for my neck, and I'm powerless to stop him from untying the knot. The scarf falls, revealing the holes above my jugular. I feel naked. My mouth opens again but it's like I'm not here. Only *her* voice comes out:

"You've put on weight. I liked you better when you were in constant motion on my behalf."

Daniel tries to glimpse her inside me. My lips move again:

"I hope you can recover from the news of Wolf's untimely demise. I know you liked him."

"How did it happen?"

"Our hero was waiting for a connecting flight to Mexico. Our villains were watching. When he went into the men's room, they followed. He was drugged, put in a wheelchair, rolled out of the terminal and into a waiting van. You should take heart, though. He made up story after story about you as they removed bits and pieces of him."

"What did he say about you?"

"A few truths, which he didn't know as he screamed them. That's the thing about Wolf. He told so many lies that he stopped believing his words meant anything. I guess it made sense that they cut out his tongue."

Daniel winces. "Is there a moral to this story?"

"Each of us gets the end we deserve."

"And what end awaits you, Fiona?"

My blade swipes across his face. A red line appears. Shocked, his hand goes up. When he removes it, his fingers are soaked in blood. He takes a kerchief and presses it against the split cheek. "My suspicions were correct." He examines the cloth. "It's more dangerous with you than without."

My arm extends the knife as my feet follow his retreating steps. "Your freedom is hereby revoked. Our agreement became null and void when you murdered Søren. Did you think you could declare war on my family and not answer for it?"

The nun, horrified, moves swiftly toward the exit. My legs propel me over the back pew and suddenly I'm in front of her. Her last move is the sign of the cross, which she doesn't finish because she's on the floor now, choking as a river of blood flows toward my shoes. My feet turn and march toward the door, locking us in.

Daniel's kneeling, lifting the woman's face, but he can't save her. He looks through me. "I don't know Ophelia, but I'm sure she'll never forgive you for this. Good luck finding another guardian."

"I already have one. I know him thoroughly, though I can't say intimately. Perhaps we should correct that."

"What are you talking about?" Daniel rises to his feet.

My hand turns the blade toward my chest. Horrified, I watch it slice the buttons off my jacket. Next, the blade tears open my shirt and cuts through my bra.

"Your crime is serious, but I find it amusing that you killed Søren as a way to defend my honor." My bare breasts face him, nipples hardening from the chill. "Go ahead, feel me. You always wanted to." My hand grabs his and presses it against my left. "Mmm, your hand is smooth. I like that. Go ahead, squeeze."

His hand retreats.

"Something wrong, my dear? These aren't to your liking?" I lift my breast and hold the knife underneath, sharp edge up. "Maybe you'd prefer them smaller." The blade moves like a saw, back and forth. Hot blood streams down my abdomen. I saw again and again...

"STOP IT." Daniel tugs at my fingers. Thankfully, they open. He tosses the knife across the sanctuary.

"Ohhhhh, you really are a knight in shining armor."

"WHAT DO YOU WANT?"

"Don't be silly. You know how much I've missed you." My face moves forward, attempting to kiss him. "I long for your experience and dedication. Your clever solutions. Only this time, I choose the end date."

"When I'm no longer useful."

My lips stretch into a smile. The blood is running to my ankles now. Daniel keeps his eyes on mine.

"I'm guessing you'll kill her in front of me if I refuse."

"And I'll send my newest creation to amuse herself with what's left of *your* body."

"Newest...?" Daniel's eyes narrow. "What have you been up to?"

"Wouldn't you like to know. Her name's Camilla, by the way. Camilla the Huntress."

"How poetic."

"Beware, Daniel: She's in striking distance."

"Will I have to work for her, too?"

"Stop boring me and listen. If you're alone when she rises, you'll be her next meal. I'd advise you to stay close to Ophelia as she makes her way home. And see to her wound."

A second later, I'm on the stone floor howling in pain.

SATURDAY AND SUNDAY
ROLLED INTO ONE

"All right, brothers, listen up." Raymond addresses the remaining three dozen monks, now gathered in a warehouse along the Thames. He clicks a remote and a blueish headshot appears on the wall next to him. "This is the one that got away, according to our latest intelligence. Her name is Fiona, sired by Agripina who we destroyed last year in Michigan. You might be thinking, 'Wait, didn't Fiona's elders sentence her to die?' You'd be correct. She was slated for execution but escaped under circumstances that remain unclear to us." The slide changes, showing two sets of chains and one ash pile. "We're still trying to determine whose ashes those are." Back to the headshot. "Fiona is 250 years old which means full maturity. She's as strong as a hundred men and fast enough to dodge all of us shooting at the same time. What's more, based on the doubling of local exsanguinees, she likely sired one striga. When we engage Fiona, we must assume this new creature is nearby. Now for some encouraging news: Fiona fled here without her senior guardian, so there's a good chance she has minimal daytime protection. That, of course, would make a dawn-to-dusk raid much easier. Brother Leo prepared plans for just such a mission and has more. Leo…"

"Thank you, Brother." Leo steps to the podium and clicks open a map showing a mass of Xs within a large circle superimposed on the city. "Brothers, the Xs are the exsanguinated bodies discovered within the last two weeks. The circle shows their furthest range. If you connect all the Xs to the center, you arrive at an area on Lower Thames Street here. This is also the area where our mysterious explosion occurred." Another click switches to windowless buildings. "These luxury flats are especially interesting because of the blast wave." Now a close shot of blown windows. "We've obtained police reports which show this blast resembles a conventional explosion in that damage at the origin is caused by an initial wave of positive pressure. Damage further out is caused by negative pressure passing by. Experts determined the origin of the initial shock wave is between the 10th and fifteenth floor of this building, ranging from flats 6 to 12."

A hand goes up. Leo points. "Yes, Brother Xavier."

Xavier stands. "What repairs, if any, are being done on the apartment building?"

"Excellent question." Leo changes the slide. "It certainly pays to be rich. All the windows were quickly repaired except in the three flats I've circled. "Two of the owners are out of the country and still arranging to let in contractors. The owner of the third, Number 1111, has not been reached as of this morning."

Xavier points to the display. "So we have an apartment protected only by a dark curtain?"

Leo turns to the image. "Which should make ingress very easy."

~

"She ever do that to you?" Ophelia shivers, looking out at the metal wing which bisects the setting sun. "It's like I was possessed."

"Never." Daniel stares down the dimly-lit aisle at the flight attendants near the galley. They chat easily, sipping coffee and juice. He knows they have his favorite scotch, but are keeping it for First Class. "Guess she has to bite you first." He turns. "When did she hire you?"

"Around the time you hired Wolf. She always had doubts about him."

Daniel grimaces as he sips inferior whiskey. "She ever say anything about me?"

"Dedicated and competent. Said I should learn investing from you." She shifts in her seat and stifles a cry. "God, it hurts like a motherfucker."

"I wonder why she kept me in the dark about you."

"She hid things from me, too. It's like the Army. Each direct report gets enough information to do their job, and only the commander has the big picture."

"I noticed your 'My Life, Your Freedom' tattoo."

"Yeah." She sighs. "I wore it proudly in Iraq. But even there I didn't fully appreciate its meaning. Now that I've worked for Fiona, I can't stand the sight of it." She looks around them. "I gotta change this bandage."

~

Brother Raymond returns to the podium and clicks to a birds-eye view of the roof. "Tomorrow is supposed be a beautiful Sunday, at least weather wise. At 07:00 hours, Team One will access the roof from inside the building. When they're in position, Team Two will secure the eleventh floor by disabling the elevators. Team Three will wait on the ground with the escape vans. When I say 'Go,' Team One will rappel down to the 1111 balcony and Team Two will force their way into the room. Any armed human will be shot on sight. Sleeping strigae will be dispatched with wooden rounds. Then Teams One and Two will rappel to the ground. If all goes well, the vans will depart no later than 07:10." Raymond pauses. "Any questions?"

Brother Shaolin stands. "The police are edgy right now. What do we do if they interfere?"

"They won't." Raymond signals for the lights. "That's all I can say."

~

After flushing the toilet, Ophelia stands in the cramped lavatory, ears popping as the plane descends. She washes her hands and disinfects them with a mini bottle of vodka. Then, facing the mirror, she removes her top and gently pulls back the tape holding the bandage, exposing her wound. She opens another vodka, takes a sip, moistens a paper towel, and lifts her wounded breast carefully to clean the wound. A sharp intake: her nostrils contract, then flare as she struggles to contain the scream. Teeth grinding hard, she discards the old bandage and secures a fresh one. She pauses a moment to rinse cold water on her face. As she pulls her shirt over her head, a familiar voice speaks low in her ear:

"When you land at Heathrow, wait. I'll have further instructions."

~

179

"Team One in position."

Brother Raymond, wearing a headset, stares through binoculars at the target site. The Thames rolls by in the foreground, empty of floating traffic on this fair Sunday the Lord was pleased to provide. What a shame to shatter such blessed silence.

"Team Two in position."

"Team Three is ready and waiting."

Raymond waits a few seconds before speaking. "What about Team Four?"

"Give us a second."

Raymond scans downriver. "What's the problem?"

"We're stuck on a sandbar. Working on it..."

"Team Four, this is Leo. I can see that sandbar extends another twelve feet. Just keep pushing straight and you'll have it."

"Okay. Give us a minute."

Raymond's voice is tense: "I have men waiting and exposed. They don't have a minute." Needing distraction, he scrolls through his mental checklist. "Brother Leo, how's your remote control working?"

"Swivel and axis are fine. We're locked and loaded."

"You sure you ordered blanks and not the real thing?"

"100 percent."

"So no chance of a mistake?"

"They look completely different. If anything goes right today, it'll be this."

"OK, we're ready. Team Four is in position."

"Halleluja." Raymond raises his binoculars. "All right everyone, heads up: Team One, go. Team Two, go. Brother Leo, open up."

The sound of gunfire erupts. A barge appears in the distance with a machine gun firing short bursts; its barrel traverses every direction. While Team One rappels, Raymond switches to the emergency scanner. It takes almost a minute for the first 999 call, but then dispatchers are quickly overloaded. When Team One lands, Raymond returns to the secure channel.

"Team One reached the balcony. We're going in."

"Team Two breached the door. Going in."

"Team Three is starting engines."

Raymond keeps his eyes on the 1111 window, still blocked by a heavy curtain. "Team Four, well done. Begin your escape." Then he switches to the monitor worn by Brother Xavier, the Team Two leader. Xavier is shouting as he approaches someone.

"Hands up -- get 'em in the air now! Oh shit, look at that. DO NOT MOVE, you hear me? Brothers, check her for weapons."

A second later: *"Brother Raymond, we got a human in need of medical attention. We're bringing her down through the elevator."*

~

Daniel is exhausted when he and Ophelia walk through the Aer Lingus gate at Heathrow. On autopilot, he starts toward ground transport but Ophelia grabs him. "Wait."

He looks impatient. "What?"

"We wait."

"For...?"

"She spoke while we were flying, when I was in the bathroom."

"And?"

Ophelia glances at the surrounding passers-by. "She said she'll have further instructions."

Daniel sighs. "Well, there's a bar there. Food court over there. Restrooms over there."

"Everything we need for a Saturday night." Ophelia smirks. Then she nods toward his face. "You need a fresh bandage."

"All right." Daniel points. "Let's meet at that coffee shop."

~

Daniel stands at the sink, slowly peeling the adhesive off his face. A moment later, he feels a presence. The mirror shows nothing but he turns anyway.

"Poor one-armed man, let me help you." Her tongue licks her lips, and he sees a flash of canines. Long, icy fingers rip off the bandage and wave it under her nose. "What type are you – A, B, O? Doesn't matter." She sidles up to him. "You're scrummy."

Daniel backs against the counter. "You must be Camilla."

She grins. "My reputation precedes me." Her hands turn him toward the mirror. In the glass, he sees a fresh bandage lift off the counter and float toward his face. His neck tingles as she breathes on him. "There." She smooths it with her fingers. When she turns him again her eyes are glowing red. "It's time to go."

"I'm not going anywhere with you."

"Frightened? You looked so brave and battle worn." Both hands lift her hair as she leans against him, pelvis pressing against his thigh. Their noses touch and he catches a whiff of fresh blood.

"That better not be Ophelia I smell on you."

"Oh her? She's off to another party." Her hand massages his crotch. "But the real soirée, the one I'm not invited to, is a short walk away. She's waiting for you."

"Fiona? She's here?"

Camilla squeezes his balls. "I'm not that interesting?"

"You're fascinating," he winces. "But we both have our orders."

"Hmm, she said you were clever." Camilla releases him and fusses with his shirt and jacket. "Go to the private jet terminals. Everyone is waiting for Robert Strange -- that's your assumed name, correct?" She licks her fingers and smooths his rumpled hair. "We want you looking your best, don't we?"

Daniel tries to leave but she grabs his wrist. "Don't I deserve something," she presses his hand inside her thigh, "for being so informative?"

"Best not to keep her waiting." Slowly, Daniel pulls his hand away, but she keeps hold of him. Her eyes remain fixed on his as she gradually lets him go.

"See you later, lover."

~

"So who's the prisoner?" Raymond walks with Xavier down a dim corridor. Together, they arrive at large rusty door.

"U.S. soldier, based on her tattoo." Xavier knocks three times. "Looks like she's been in a knife fight. Got a bad gash on her torso that seems infected."

"At least we know she's human."

"Yeah, but she's acting rather un-human."

"What do you mean?"

"You'll see."

Raymond looks worried. "Any word from Brother Leo?"

Xavier shakes his head. "He should've been back by now." The door opens. "Maybe she knows."

They walk past two guards toward a dark-haired woman with olive skin sitting in a chair, wrists handcuffed to each wooden arm. Her stare grows more intense as they approach. When they stop, her lips form a sinister smile:

"Well, look who finally arrived. Brother Raymond, murderer of Agripina."

Raymond stands over her. "What's your name?"

"Don't you know? I'm the one that got away."

Raymond sets down a chair and straddles it. "You don't look like Fiona."

"Sorry to confuse you. I'm borrowing Ophelia for a while."

"Who's Ophelia? May I speak to her?"

"You may not."

Raymond glances at Xavier: "Prepare the Rituale Romanum."

"We're to have an exorcism? How exciting! But wait..." Her tone mocks them. "Isn't Brother Leo your expert in this area? That's too bad."

"What's too bad?"

Her lips form a pout. "Leo's been missing ever since he left to ditch his van."

Raymond stands, kicking over the chair. "Where is he?"

"With that nymphomaniac I created. Did you know he gave up the names of your abbot and cardinal? Jared Neeley and Massimo de Luca." She chuckles. "Funny how the most celibate men forget their vows when they feel the inside of a woman's thighs."

Raymond's hand sails across her face. "WHERE'S LEO?"

"My, what a temper. Need a proper release?" Her legs part. "Give her a try, if you're up for it." She winks. "Or do you monks still prefer little boys?"

Xavier starts for her, but Raymond puts an arm out. "Where can we find Leo?"

"Floating. Near the London Eye about now."

Raymond looks at Xavier. "Take a team. And weapons."

When he leaves the prisoner's eyes harden as Raymond picks up the chair and places it again in front of her.

~

"Welcome, Mr. Strange." A man in a pinstriped suit extends his arm toward an exit. "Your Bombardier Global Express awaits. Follow me." The noise and smell of idling engines rushes through the open door. The man smiles as he holds it open for him. "Have a good flight, sir."

Daniel approaches the narrow white jet with blinking lights. An attendant stands at the bottom of the stairs, motioning for him to climb. Inside, a white carpet leads toward a wood-veneered bulkhead. Tables on one side bear serving dishes with a whole fillet of smoked salmon, beluga caviar, toast points, Belgian endive, pasta salad, and champagne.

"I thought you might be hungry."

Daniel turns and nearly blacks out when he sees her wearing the same low-cut gown she wore when they met.

"Those who cook say revenge is a dish best served cold." Fiona extends a hand toward him. "I don't, so this is how I serve a truce."

Trembling, unable to hold back tears, Daniel bows and kisses her fingers.

"Please," she waves toward the cabin. "Make yourself at home."

He sits in an armchair next to a decanter filled with amber liquid. She reclines on a coach, elbow in a silk pillow, hand in her hair, looking at him. "Try it."

The words "The Macallan 72 Years Old" are etched in the glass. He pours two measures of whiskey and sips, letting the sherry and oak flavors roll around his tongue before swallowing. "Why do I deserve this?"

She smiles. "Sometimes, all you need to do is show up." A look of concern. "I do hope you'll forgive that scratch."

"It's healing. Where's Ophelia?"

"Tidying things up for me."

~

Father Abbot is about to go to sleep when he gets an urgent

message to FaceTime with Brother Xavier. He picks up his tablet to see the monk standing in what appears to be an abandoned warehouse. His expression is grave:

"Father Abbot, I have terrible news. I found Brother Leo's body in the Thames about an hour ago. He was completely drained of blood."

The abbot exhales and drags a hand across his stubbled chin. "Which striga is responsible?"

"We were told by our prisoner that the new one did it."

"How would the prisoner know this?"

"Well, she claimed to be Fiona, the one that escaped from America."

"Claimed to be Fiona?"

"She didn't look like her but sounded like her. I think she was possessed by Fiona. Whatever the case, the prisoner knew Brother Raymond killed Agripina."

"I see. Please don't take this the wrong way, Brother. But why did you call with this news and not Brother Raymond?"

"Unfortunately, I must also report the news of Brother Raymond's demise."

"WHAT?"

"Shall I show you what happened?"

"Yes -- immediately."

Xavier 180s the screen to show the shattered remains of a wooden chair. *"Our prisoner broke free after I left to find Leo. While still handcuffed, she grabbed Brother Raymond and put him in a choke hold with a piece of wood. Then she used him as a shield between her and the guards. When it became clear that Brother Raymond was suffocating, they advanced."*

"This, according to whom?"

"One of the guards, Novice Mbutu." Xavier's face fills the screen again. *"May I show you Brother Raymond's body?"*

"Show me the prisoner first." The abbot's voice grows harsh. "Is she dead?"

The screen zooms in on a woman lying in a pool of blood. *"Novice Mbutu says it took a full magazine, plus five more rounds, to stop her. Sadly, Novice Kumar also perished."*

The abbot shakes his head. "I want an ID on her as soon as

possible." He exhales long and slow. "All right. Show me Raymond."

~

Daniel pours himself another. "So where are we going?"

"Zurich, for starters." Fiona uncaps another decanter filled with O neg and fills a glass. "We're going to the money."

"I wondered if you had any left."

"All that you were managing is gone. But there's more gathered by one of your predecessors. I met Dominic after the war, the last big one. He worked thirty years for me, building up a reserve of gold, mostly coins. Also Nazi bullion that..." She lowers her eyes.

"That Søren helped you acquire."

She looks away. "I don't know, Daniel." She takes a sip. "I understand he threatened you, but I've always known you were waiting for the right moment to destroy him." She wipes away a tear. "I warned him about you. Of course, he laughed it off."

Daniel nods slowly. "I hope you can move on."

"And you? You were supposed to retire to Greece."

He shrugs. "Doing nothing wasn't as satisfying as I imagined."

"You'll be very busy with me."

"I remember." Daniel pauses for a sip. "There is the question of what happens when I'm no longer useful to you."

"You mean, out to pasture again or – wait, you're bringing *that* up again."

"I see no harm in discussing it. As an option."

"There are no options with my path." She leans forward. "You wake up thirsty, acquire blood somehow or go to bed starving. That's my life -- night in, night out."

"There are no options for me, either. In twenty years, maybe thirty, I'll be gone forever."

"At least you'll find peace."

He starts to speak but her hand slices the air. Their eyes remain locked for several seconds before she yawns. "Since we're speaking of mortality, you might find this amusing. I'm sleeping in a coffin today." She nods toward an envelope on a nearby table. "That's the permit for transporting my corpse. Give it to Carlo when we land."

"Carlo?"

She rises and sets down her glass. "Dominic's son." She turns. "Unzip?" Daniel stands, suddenly aware that he had two hands the last time he did this. He slowly, carefully lets down the zipper while she continues. "A tall, white-haired gentleman who prefers tailored suits. He'll take possession of my coffin and put you in a separate car. You're to rest at a hotel and meet us at the vault tomorrow night." Bare back exposed, she bends to remove her heels. Then she straightens and drags her fingers gently across his shoulder as she passes by. "I've missed you. See you in the evening."

~

"Brother Xavier," Father Abbot rubs his forehead, "did this possessed woman give any indication of Fiona's whereabouts?"

"No." Xavier redirects the screen from Raymond to himself. "But she did indicate where she's headed."

"What do you mean?"

"She specifically mentioned your name and that of His Eminence."

Adrenaline floods the abbot's system as he digests this. "You have command. Bring everyone to Rome." He ends the call, reaches across his desk, and presses a buzzer.

A groggy voice answers. "Yes, Father Abbot?"

"I need a courier right away. Let me know when he arrives."

"Yes, Father Abbot."

The abbot fills a snifter with cognac, downs it, and pours another. Then he places a sheet of stationery on the blotter, dips a fountain pen, and starts composing:

Your Eminence,

I must warn that your safety is in jeopardy. I just received intelligence that our escapee from America knows your identity and mine. Furthermore, I learned that my second and third in command perished this evening in London. With ten brothers remaining, plus 21 novices, I am without enough experienced fighters to protect your person from one striga, much less the two we know exist.

Let there be no doubt: Fiona intends to decapitate our organization.

My heart is heavy as I realize how deeply I failed the trust you put in me. Nevertheless, I remain undaunted. I will assume direct command of what remains of this order, gather them here in Rome, and fight by their side until I can fight no more.

Vivat Mors Strigae!

Father Jared Neeley, Abbot of Mors Strigae

GOLD MINE

"Ever see a Krugerrand, Mr. Daniel?"

"No. They were banned in the U.S., weren't they?"

"For the last decade of apartheid, yes." Carlo holds a gold coin under a light. "Here's one of the first minted in 1967." Daniel sees a bearded man in profile between the words *Sud-Afrika* and *South Africa*. Carlo flips it to show a running antelope. "That's one troy ounce of fine gold."

"What's it worth?"

"Last I checked, about $1,800. We have at least twenty of these coins from every year issued."

"So that's..."

"Two million, just in Krugerrands."

"What else do you have?"

Carlo waves a hand over another display. "American and other coins of slightly less value."

"He wants to know about the Nazi treasure." Fiona steps toward a heavy wooden table and removes a white cloth. Two dozen gold kilos lay fanned out like a deck of tarot cards. In the middle sits a 400-ounce gold bar. Fiona's fingers glide over the swastika stamp. "These are the only physical reminders I have left of Søren."

"Sentiment aside," Carlo leans toward Daniel, "these items present philosophical challenges."

"I'm guessing they contain stolen gold." Daniel picks up a kilo; it features an eagle above the words *Deutsche Reichsbank*.

"Probably half their weight." Carlo gently takes the kilo and returns it to the table; it thuds like a brick. "Nearly every bank in Europe can claim them because the Germans looted their vaults."

"All you had to do was melt them down to sell them. Why didn't you?"

"My point will become clearer," Carlo points to the 400-ouncer, "when we consider the provenance of that."

"I'm listening."

"It was cast after Hitler announced his Final Solution in 1942." Carlo locks eyes with Daniel. "It very likely contains gold used in dental work."

Daniel nods as he recalls a concentration camp photo of a pile of human teeth. "And here we arrive at the moral question."

"Exactly." Carlo wipes the dust off his hands. "I prayed I wouldn't have to decide the fate of anything on this table. Thankfully, I'm off the hook."

Fiona steps toward Daniel and hands him a set of keys. "You're in charge of this vault now." Daniel looks again at Carlo who inclines his head.

"I'm retiring."

"I hope you have more fun than I did," Daniel looks around the room. "We'll sell the Krugerrands and those over here."

"What about Søren's gold?" Fiona eyes him carefully.

"Don't you want a memento?"

"We need the money."

"The rest should be enough."

"The Krugerrands are apartheid gold," Fiona stops in front of him.

"That's correct," Carlo interjects, "for those minted before 1995."

Fiona's eyes search Daniel's. "But you want to sell the older ones, going back to 1967, don't you?"

"I do."

"The people who mined that material were second-class citizens." She points to the separate piles. "What's the difference between gold taken from dead Jews and that harvested by black miners who perished by the thousands?"

"The Nazis killed millions."

"And the miners were paid," Carlo interrupts again. "Not much but they received wages."

Fiona's face twists with scorn. "Both of you reek of white privilege."

Daniel is stunned. "Are you aware of the irony of that statement?"

Her eyes burn as they return to him. "What do you mean by that?"

"For thirty-five years, I've been *your* second-class citizen. The only reason I have any value now is you're desperate to save your kind from extinction."

"Tread carefully, Mr. Daniel."

Ignoring Carlo: "I will not prevent one genocide by profiting from another."

"All right then." Fiona cools. "Sell the kilos." She scores one with a fingernail. "They're just stolen gold."

"They fueled genocide."

Fiona tosses it – crash -- across the room and folds her arms. "You've crossed lines for me before. What's different now?"

"I'm leaving a landmark for those who succeed me." Daniel softens his tone. "I'll invest carefully. We don't need anything from Søren."

She turns and walks briskly toward the exit. Carlo gazes at her retreating figure. "Now those are some lines I'll really miss." He lifts a bottle of champagne from a cooler. "You argued well. Let's savor the victory."

~

"Welcome, everyone, to the Holy See." Father Abbot addresses the monks standing around a dining room table. Most had never visited the Vatican before. A portrait of Cardinal Massimo de Luca looks down on them. "Here are the ground rules. First: We are not supposed to be here because our order does not exist. Not even Holy Father knows of us. If questioned, say you are a guest of His Eminence." He points to envelopes in front of each man. "Those are permits which you will present to any gendarme or Swiss Guard who demands them. Second," he indicates his head toward the window, "cameras are everywhere. When you step outside the cardinal's home, assume you're being watched." He spreads out a yellowed floor plan of the administrators' apartments. The others lean in as he points. "We are here. Starting at dusk, Team One will patrol the path leading to the front entrance. Keep your weapons hidden. We don't want to create suspicion among residents or employees."

Brother Xavier raises his hand. "We'll need to wear thermal goggles. We'd be sitting ducks without them."

The abbot frowns. "And with them you'll be subject to unwelcome curiosity." He looks around. "Suggestions?"

Brother Shaolin snaps his fingers. "They're virtual reality. We're testing an education tool."

Father Abbot snaps back. "What's it about? Quickly."

"Uh…The Emperor Constantine's path to Christianity."

"Excellent, Brother." The abbot scans the assembled. "Everyone got that?" Satisfied, he taps the paper again. "Here's the corridor leading to this apartment. Starting at dusk, I want Team Two patrolling up and down, with Novices Mbutu and Cahan guarding the door. Brother Xavier and I will stay inside with His Eminence accompanied by two novices. Any volunteers?"

A dozen hands go up, prompting the abbot to grin. "Looks like you've all heard about our host's wine cellar." His voice resumes a tone of command. "There will be no drinking while on duty."

Brother Xavier chimes in. "His Eminence is famous for his generosity and might be insulted if we refuse. Perhaps we could accept a glass before turning in at dawn."

"Fine." The abbot points to two novices. "Okay, you and you. Now for the roof." He places another sheet on the table and smooths it before continuing. "Team Three is up here, led by Brother Shaolin. Here's the access door. I want two guards on the stairway – one top, one bottom." He pauses. "Regarding combat: We cannot have collateral damage so use extreme caution when firing your weapon. I've procured suppressors which the team leaders will distribute. Please keep in mind that Holy Father sleeps less than two hundred yards from here."

"I don't mean to question the cardinal's priorities," Brother Shaolin again, "but shouldn't we be protecting the pope instead?"

The abbot straightens. "His Eminence assured me there's no danger to him."

"Forgive me, Father Abbot, but I'm astonished that you just accept this."

"We must assume the cardinal knows something we don't." The abbot rolls up the maps. "That will be all for now."

~

Needing a break from my guests, I walk down to the cellar to pick a bottle of Brunello. As I'm entertaining, I'll also grab an Altemasi Brut, a Falanghina for the fish course, and Meletti anisette to accompany espresso and dessert. I have no idea if Abbott Neeley and his soldiers will appreciate these, but I have a reputation to maintain. Sometimes, when alone and impatient about my career, I like to fondle the dusty French bottles I'm saving for when I become pope: 1986 Chateaux Margaux, 1989 La Mission Haut Brion, and Chateau Latour from the same year. A dozen 1990 Latour lay untouched in their case with a note on papal letterhead:

To Massimo on the occasion of his elevation to cardinal. Congratulations and remember: God also made wine so we could be happy.
  Francis

Tonight, however, before entertaining my guests, I'll visit a neighbor who lives down a hidden stairway behind my cellar. He cares not for alcohol but enjoys the company of prostitutes, so I hired one. "Mind your head," I point to the rather short entranceway as I lift an ancient candelabra.

The male escort bows and waves toward the stairs. "After you, your Eminence. That is the proper salutation, right?"

"It is." I lead the way down. "And what may I call you?"

"Maurizio. That's my real name actually," he laughs. "But people get uncomfortable when I give my last name because, you know, it's the Vatican and I'm not supposed to be here."

"Oh, God welcomes everyone. But I think within these walls your first name will do."

"Right. And you can trust my discretion. I have some regulars here who are paying my tuition."

"Good." I make sure to use the railing. "And what are you studying?"

"Weather. I'm going to be a meteorologist."

"Really? Around here we say, 'God makes the weather just to fool the weatherman.' What do you think of that?"

"I don't mind being fooled. Long as I get paid for it."

"Well played, my son. You'll go far in this world."

"I hope so. It is unusual though."

"What's that?"

"Most of my clients are cardinals, but I've never been led around by one. Am I seeing the pope?"

"Around here we call him Holy Father, and the answer is no."

We stop before a heavy wooden door with a padlock. "Hold this, please." I hand off the candelabra and take out a ring of long keys. Maurizio laughs again. "Ooh a sex dungeon, huh? My client a master or slave?"

The lock opens. "Let's just say he's the tail that wags the dog. You can blow out the flames and leave the candelabra here." I push the door and it swings inside, revealing another stairway brightly lit by torches.

"Call me intrigued." He pokes his head through the door. "How far down are we going?"

"Funny, I've never counted the stairs." I put away the keys and lead the way again. "Shouldn't be much further though."

~

"Did you sell the gold yet?" Fiona drinks from a large glass while sitting on her coffin. Daniel turns from the blinking wing lights to his laptop.

"I got the best price available for the Kruggerands. Now I'm working on the U.S. and Canadian. Still figuring out how much to invest versus how much cash we'll need."

"Let's wait to find a bank in Rome."

"Are we staying?"

"Possibly. I should know in a day or two." Fiona reaches for a decanter and does little to conceal Søren's favorite playthings. "Gives me chills to think about it, though. The belly of the beast."

"We'll blend in. It's a city of three million."

"And three million crosses I'll bet." Her lips wrinkle with distaste as she pours.

"I thought they had no effect on you."

"Not outwardly. But each one is an insult."

"How so?"

She takes a sip and thinks. "There must be a symbol that reminds you of your...otherness. Can you think of one?"

"Plenty, actually." Daniel sets the laptop aside and reaches for his scotch. "Anything that suggests happiness is a pair of arms, a pair of kids, a hot young girlfriend, exotic vacations, ecstatic sex.

Humans are bombarded by messages saying we're not living to our full potential."

She grins. "We really need to get you laid, don't we?"

Daniel grins back. "And here's where I'd hold up a crucifix if I had one."

"Watch it."

"Seriously, though." Daniel leans forward. "What makes the Christian symbol so offensive? Why not the symbol of Islam, the Crescent Moon and Star?"

"Actually, I like that because the feminine moon envelops the star."

"Which is masculine, deriving from the Latin *aster*." Daniel pauses. "But a cross is just two sticks stuck together."

"It's not the shape. It's the righteousness behind it – a male righteousness that never ceases striving for power." Her expression darkens. "Convert or die. Obey or face exile. Believe or be damned for all eternity."

"I think they've eased up since the Middle Ages."

"Did you hear what you just said? Have you forgotten the near extinction of my kind?"

"But Mors-" Daniel checks himself. "The monks are a fringe group that's..."

"...allowed to exist. Official or not, they embody an ingrained belief that those who can't fit in shouldn't be here."

"Well, we can't eliminate the Catholic church so the fringe element will always be there. What's our goal?"

"To have a voice." Fiona sets down her glass and climbs into the coffin. "Maybe even get a seat at the table. See you in Rome." She's about to close the lid when she sits up again. "Did you just say you want to borrow Camilla?"

"I was thinking it. I might need her tomorrow."

"For what?"

"Nothing." Daniel whistles a random tune to keep her out of his head.

"Okay," she smirks, "I'll respect your privacy. But what makes you think you can trust her?"

"I can't. But as long as I have your protection..."

She regards him carefully. "Even I have limits, Daniel. The further you stray from me, the stronger her power becomes."

THE ETERNAL ROMAN

"Really? One more door?" Maurizio laughs but I can hear his growing impatience.

"This is the final one." I slide in the key and hear a click. "You go first."

From behind, I can't see Maurizio's face but I'm certain his eyes are wide as he takes in the white marble tiles and columns reflecting light from hundreds of clay oil lamps. No doubt, his eyes grow even wider as we approach the white robed figure sitting on a gold-painted throne between statues of Jupiter and Pluto.

"Wow," Maurizio walks forward, mouth agape. He pauses to run a hand over the edge of a marble bath. "I've never seen a room like this – and I've been all over the Vatican. It's like a Roman palace in original form, untouched by time."

I bow. "Caius Drusus, this is tonight's guest."

"Thank you, Cardinal." Caius's laurel-crowned head turns to Maurizio. "You're right, young man. This palace remains in its original form. The Gauls and Visigoths never found it when they sacked the city. The armies of Napoleon and Hitler – they missed it too." He points to the marble tub. "Have a bath. My assistant will take your clothes."

Maurizio jumps a bit when he sees a man in a short toga next to him. After catching his breath, he starts undressing. Then he pauses to address Caius. "I see no crosses, no images of Jesus or Mary – no connection with the Church. Does the pope know about this place?"

"No." Caius smiles.

I chime in: "Holy Father is a busy man. He doesn't have time to explore every nook and cranny of this city."

Maurizio is naked now. "Anyone filling that?" He shivers as he points to the tub. "It's a bit chilly in here."

Caius aims a long fingernail. "Get in first." He watches Maurizio lower himself into the basin. A second later, a knife glides across his throat. A wet gasp follows, then a rush of blood which an assistant collects in a gold chalice.

"NO." I rush toward the tub. "The last rites."

Caius chuckles. "You'd better hurry."

I stand over Maurizio's upturned eyes as a fresh chalice appears beneath his wound. More assistants line up in a sort of sinister bucket brigade. I quickly make the sign of the cross:

"Per istam Sanctam Unctionem et suam piisimam misericordiam adiuvet te Dominus gratia Spiritus Sancti, ut A peccatis liberatum te salvet atque propitius alleviet."

He's already dead. I walk back toward the center of the room, quietly beseeching God to welcome this poor sinner in case the sacrament came too late. Caius, of course, could care less; he empties ten chalices in two minutes. When finished, he wipes his mouth with a red napkin. "I keep meaning to save you some, Cardinal, but I'm always too thirsty. I want to see you reverse what priests do at the altar, turn blood back into wine."

"The wine is symbolic of the covenant with Christ. Real blood is never involved."

"Too bad." Caius frowns. "I thought surviving might be easier if I could just take communion."

"You'd have to go to confession first. Would you like me to hear your sins?"

"Only humans know sin." Caius glares at me. "That's why God created immortals -- to keep evil in check."

I glance back to see Maurizio's corpse being carried from the room. "I'm curious to know your definition of evil."

"Ambition is a good place to start." Caius fusses with a blood stain. "I was surprised at how quickly you bet against your pope. He seems a pleasant enough fellow."

"Holy Father is the chief defender of the faith. And the current one is badly miscast."

"Well, we're about to find out if I'm speeding his ascension to Heaven." Caius casts his eyes toward the ceiling. "But wait: My last and best soldier is near."

I cross my arms. "And my last, and best, are ready for her."

Caius strolls past Jupiter. "Have you chosen your papal name?"

"Julius the Fourth."

Caius nods appreciatively. "I remember when Cardinal della Rovere took the name Julius the Second. He said it wasn't to honor Julius the First, but Caesar."

"They called him the Warrior Pope."

"Indeed." Caius stops in front of me. "Think you'll revive the Roman Empire?"

"We'll have to free Italy first, from liberals and materialists."

"We? Our agreement was that I'd clear the way for you, Julius. Now I'm to serve in your administration?"

"You could be my chancellor or vicar." Suddenly inspired, I snap my fingers and point. "Nuncio to Brussels. You could take us out of the European Union!"

Caius ignores my finger. "I was hoping to retire."

"Why? We'd make a good tea...Wait a second." My eyes narrow. "Would you retire if I lost the bet?"

"Surely, the Cardinal doesn't admit that possibility."

"The Cardinal must be prepared for any possibility."

"Shh." His hand goes up for several seconds. "The battle has ended." His hand comes down. "How prepared did you say you were?"

"What news?"

Caius turns and walks toward his throne. "Go see for yourself."

~

Hello gorgeous, this is Camilla. The Huntress. Did you miss reading about me? I sure missed seeing all your throbbing vessels, and I might visit you for a snack before dawn. Right now, though, I'm sucking and fucking a cardinal named Silvio Ferraro. Fiona's pet human, Daniel, is sitting nearby telling me to slow down and get more information. This is especially challenging because *Signore* Ferraro is dee-lish. Daniel checks his medical card and says "AB positive" which I must remember. Anyway, we're here because the cardinal manages the *Istituto per le Opere di Religione*, known more boringly as the Vatican Bank. Daniel says it's one of the richest in the world, and he's hoping my victim will divulge more user names and passcodes to drain more accounts.

Look at him, face bathed in the glow of his laptop while he cracks the bank's security. I'm naked, hair and boobs flying -- giving a porn-star performance -- and he's focused on numbers. What. A. Square. Still, there's something sexy about all that determination. One day, I'll steal him from Fiona, maybe even transform him if it suits my purposes. I wonder, though: Would his arm grow back if I sired him? I've gotten used to his damage and I kind of like the way he is.

Daniel's asking for deposit codes now. He says he's going to surprise Fiona by laundering the Nazi gold he refused to accept earlier. He wants the cardinal to approve the deposit, melt it down, and convert it to Euros. Oh, how sweet: It's her transformation day gift – a belated one which will be even more of a surprise.

My wet lips smack above the cardinal's broken skin. "When was it?"

"March 21." He taps away. "First full night of spring."

My heart melts. "La Primavera." I wonder if he'll remember my transformation day. Come to think of it, I wonder if I'll remember it; Fiona warned me about the forgetting. Anyway, back to the cardinal whose *erezione* was quite large and satisfying but is wilting now. He'll be gone in a few seconds. As for Daniel, he's thrilled with what he got. I just wish I had something more to do with that look on his face. I suspect he doesn't smile often.

Ooohhh, I'm full; looks like you're safe for tonight. Better watch out, though: The longer you live the more likely our paths will cross. Have your passcodes ready because I might have a thief at my side and your savings could be the start of my financial empire. Might have to change my name then. How does this sound: Camilla the Empress.

~

There was no way I could've prepared myself for what I'm seeing now in my apartment. Fiona clearly wanted to make a statement with blood covering the walls, bodies strewn across the floor, and Abbot Neeley slouched at my dining room table, his cracked head poking through my portrait which rests on his shoulders.

I take out my phone but there's no one left to call. The

gendarmeria would put the Vatican on lockdown, and I would sit for hours, possibly days, in an interview room explaining how I came to have such a powerful enemy. Of course, when nobody's looking, Fiona would slip into my cell and make it look like I hanged myself. A breeze rushes past me toward the open cellar door, and I realize I've been given a reprieve.

I take a deep breath and follow her. Better to learn my fate now than be surprised. If today is when I meet the Lord, I'm confident I have enough good deeds on my ledger to outweigh all the other, more questionable things.

~

The 23rd Psalm is my companion as I walk back down to Caius's lair, but my lips stop moving when Fiona's bare legs come into view. They dangle over the throne as she reclines sideways. Their voices bounce off the walls toward me:

"You're my great-great grand sire, right?"

"Let's see. Agripina is your sire?"

"Was, yes."

"I could give you the begats, like in Genesis, but I prefer to work backwards. Agripina was sired by Miklós. He and Konstantin were sired by Isis in the 13th and 14th Centuries. I sired Isis – right on that rug over there. She insisted I drink from her thigh, as high as I could go."

"Ach, I don't need to hear that."

Caius smiles. "She was delicious. A real beauty, too. Like you." He claps his hands and rubs them together. "All right, business."

Fiona raises a hand. "Before we get to that, I need you to explain something."

Caius becomes stone-faced. "Why did I let all but one of my descendants perish?"

"Yes."

"They grew weak from routine and lack of imagination -- just like you said during the trial." He stares at the floor, head shaking. "I was convinced they'd rise to the occasion when they realized how far our enemies had evolved, but obviously that didn't happen." He looks up and points. "You prevailed, though." A smile creeps across his face. "You preserved my bloodline. Now I can retire and watch you extend it."

"Extend?" Fiona pretends to check her nails. "Let's see how my latest creation fares." She sits straight now in the throne.

"How is The Huntress?"

"Oh, let's get to business, shall we?"

Caius assumes an official tone. "I'll give you a full pardon for your crime in exchange for ten million Euros."

"Is this for your home in Alexandria?"

"It belongs to Isis, but she'll let me live there if I pay for improvements."

Fiona looks around the room. "And I get this?"

"If you can keep it."

"I'll need half your attendants."

"You can have six. The rest go with me."

I decide to come back later but – "Cardinal" – his voice stops me before I reach the steps.

Turning, I see him standing next to the throne, one hand on her shoulder. "Meet your new boss. Fiona has an updated career path for you which should provide an excellent springboard when Holy Father finally passes."

My eyes follow him as he steps aside. "And what position would that be?"

"You'll address her from now on."

I look in her direction, avoiding eye contact, mind scrolling through appropriate titles. "I confess I don't know the proper salutation."

"Bow first, and I shall tell you." She crosses one leg over the other, proffering a foot more beautiful, more shapely, than that seen on Canova's *Three Graces*. It amazes me that a mass murderer could be so delicately endowed. Enchanted, I take her foot in my right hand. My left strokes her instep while I kiss her toes. When I straighten, she stares down confidently from her new perch:

"Mother Superior."

I hesitate to speak. "May I recommend another title? Mother Superior is rather lowly being the head of a convent."

"Not anymore."

"And, Mother Superior, what is your first assignment for me?"

"I hear Cardinal Ferraro is no longer in charge of the Vatican Bank."

"Silvio? I had lunch with him yesterday, he never mentioned..." My words trail off as I realize this latest casualty. "I assume you'd like me to replace him?"

"Your lack of sentimentality will serve you well." Fiona rises. "Press the pope's vicar on this matter, starting tomorrow." She grins. "Use your charm."

~

"This is me." Camilla stops in front of an apartment block on the Via Marco Aurelio.

Daniel nods toward the building. "You're in there?"

"Temporarily." She doesn't bother to cover a yawn. "I still have to get rid of the tenant who's starting to smell. Unless you want to move him for me."

"I don't work for you."

"No need to get cross." Camilla pouts and twirls her hair. "Doesn't matter, I'll move on tomorrow. Of course, I could always use a companion."

Daniel looks askance at her. "I assumed you'd want a guardian."

"Same thing."

"They are not even remotely related."

"Why not? You're friends with Fiona."

"You don't pay someone ten million a year to be your friend."

"Wow." Her eyes go wide. "That's more than I realized."

"You could probably get one for a million, to start."

"I don't know." She cups her breasts and bumps her hip. "What if I offered side benefits?"

Daniel shakes his head. "You don't want emotions messing up a business partnership."

"What would you know about emotions?"

"Just hire someone you're not attracted to. Want to share your bed? Get a boyfriend."

Twirling her hair again. "Can you help me find one?"

"Guardian or boyfriend?"

Miffed, she looks away.

Daniel looks around helplessly. Finally: "Sure."

"What if I want you?" Camilla leans in, smiling wickedly. "You're the best. Fiona told me."

"You can't afford me. Besides, she'd kill us both if she knew we were having this conversation."

"She'd be daft not to expect it. She knows my situation – and yours."

"And how would you describe my situation?"

"Free agent."

"Hardly."

"She's in a good place now. Hidden palace, bodyguards. She doesn't need you anymore."

"She needs someone to invest her money."

"And so do I. Name your price."

"If you're sitting on a gold mine, show me. Otherwise, stop wasting my time."

She points toward the Vatican. "We just stole 50 million. Fiona can't use all of it."

He points to himself. "I stole that money as her employee."

"And who gave you the passcodes?"

Daniel's hand goes up. "You want to claw some of that back, talk to Fiona. But there's no guarantee she'd let me go."

Hands on her hips: "If I convince her, will you accept my offer?"

"I won't take a pay cut."

"I'm not asking you to."

"And I get to leave any time after one year."

"No, ten."

"Two."

"Five."

"Three."

"Five is my final offer."

Daniel refuses to blink. "Four."

Slowly, she extends her left hand and Daniel reluctantly grasps it. "I still think you're wasting your time."

"Don't leave town until you hear from me." Camilla's eyes glow as she tightens her grip. "You should've asked for more money." Long canines accent her grin. "I have big plans for us."

A NOTE FROM MOTHER SUPERIOR

What a nice couple they make – don't you agree? Daniel's right, of course: I will have the final say regarding his future, and I won't allow any change that doesn't benefit me. Still, there may be an upside if he agrees to protect my offspring. The problem is, Camilla will never be a good employer because she's too impulsive. For a moment, I liked that about her. Setting that aside, I can't imagine Daniel working for someone who doesn't behave professionally. Did you see how she flirted with him? A guardian with less experience might think there's more than money in the offing. It shows just how reckless she is. One lovers' quarrel is all it takes for her to wake up burning beneath the sun. That's why I stick to my own kind, even though I was attracted to Daniel at the beginning. I know he felt the same for a long time. Funny, I can't remember when that feeling changed for him. Or why.

Clearly I, for all my powers of observation, missed something. Could it be that Daniel enjoys playing with a fiery redhead? I've never known him to before. I've never known him to feel anything because, while I can hear his thoughts, I can't interpret whatever emotions he buried inside. In this one area, Daniel has always been a cipher. But enough of this guessing game. Let's see who he prefers: Camilla or me.

Show us who you are, Daniel. Give us your Big Reveal even if you don't know what beast you'll free. I like to think there's a wicked, funny demon in there that will make the most of your remaining years. At the very least, I hope this new creature avoids calling Nazi gold "tainted" in one moment, only to consider it gift-worthy when my new bank washes it clean. Yes, I heard that bit of hypocrisy. I wasn't amused.

Regardless of what Daniel does, I'll never worry about money as soon as my cardinal controls the pope's purse. Massimo, what a name. Could he be my next guardian? Much will depend on the amount of funds he redirects toward me. I suppose I should thank you for your church donations – or your friends for theirs -- but I won't. You never knew where that money was going anyway. I'll just be another of those "mysteries" attributed to the Lord's work. Nevertheless, it is satisfying to share news that a female is finally pulling the strings.

If you'd like to continue our association, I'll look at your résumé. I'm sure you'll have few questions about the job, and me. But first, I must sleep.

Ciao,

F.

~ The End ~

Bonus Content Exclusive to Hardback Version:

AGRIPINA

Look at his perfectly shaped fingers dimpling her naked thigh near her buttock. His other hand corrals her waist which is also bare as her robes fall away. I've never seen a sculptor capture the pliability, the vulnerability of human flesh like this. Damn you, Gian Lorenzo Bernini, you were a master manipulator – and not just of pure white marble. With her hair flying, Proserpina looks like she's being lifted to heaven but then you remember she's with Pluto and her destiny is to spend six months in the underworld as his slave, every year, because she ate his pomegranate seeds. Another metaphor twisted to blame the victim? For those who casually digest Greco-Roman myths, this is the origin story of winter. When you first heard it, did you wonder if she'd miss the sound of birds, a lover's embrace, or just being by herself? Six months a year may not seem horrendous until you realize her cycle of captivity lasts forever.

This statue was finished in 1622, but I recall Proserpina (aka Persephone) being raped at least a dozen times, each artist or poet reducing her life to a single violent event. Same for Daphne, taken by Apollo. Her assault, also rendered by Bernini, is nearby. How do these depictions seem perfectly at home with other, less intense works -- such as that semi-nude reclining on a couch? Having lived for centuries, I've found it easier to assimilate this juxtaposition of brute force and easy dignity. But every time it snows, I remember Proserpina and my brazen decision to compel Bernini to sculpt me, or rather my origin. Not that I couldn't afford to hire him. I just wanted him to experience doing something he didn't want to do. Whatever the case, he died two weeks after a health scare that happened to coincide with my visit to Rome. I'll admit nothing other than I can personally attest he did not have the eyesight or stamina to match his previous work. Of course, this is the tragedy about being human. You're at your best for two decades, maybe three. As for me, I never reached my human potential. I would've loved to learn to use a chisel or paintbrush, maybe play the lute. I still hope to have time for such pursuits, but I have a mouth to feed – namely, mine.

How ironic that a creature like me, who keeps on living, can't find the time to study anything but survival. Such is my lot and that of all predators. Yours is to read about it or be my breakfast. Yes, we've come to the point where I remind you that your main purpose is prey, and you call me a hypocrite for pitying some statue and not you. Just remember: You have a choice. How you choose matters little to me -- but decide now because all this talk about Bernini reminds me of how delicious he was. And I am starving.

What's that? Smart choice. Now before you read, give me the name of a neighbor who's earned your weariness or animosity and I'll leave you with my story. By the way, don't bother looking for a summary on the internet. I don't exist there.

***

"More hot water? "

Mother lifts a kettle off the fire, swings it toward the tub, and pours near my submerged feet. "How's that?"

"Better, thanks." I begin scrubbing my arms but then pause. "Did you hear that?"

"Just the wind, darling." She glances at my breasts as she returns the kettle to its holder. "Goodness, Dear, when did your boobs get so big? I'll have to add more material to that dress I'm making."

"Shh, there it is again." I lean toward the edge, staring at the drawn curtains. "It's a man's voice." My eyes go wide. "He keeps calling a name – a woman's, I think – but it feels like he's calling me."

"What name?"

"Agripina."

"He's mixed you up with some foreigner."

"Someone Greek. From one of those myths perhaps."

209

"Oh, enough with your fantasies." Mother walks to the window, lifts the curtain, and stares into the night. "I can't see anyone." She lets it go. "Could be a boy from the village. You been flirtin' at the shops?"

"They're all wet behind the ears." I nod toward the mantle. "That musket still work?"

"That thing?" She scoffs. "It's as rusty as your dad. You're better off with your slingshot. 'Course, I packed that up with your tomboy things. You're a woman now. We should do your hair up fancy and start showing you around."

I shiver. "I swear I felt someone's eyes on me last night. And the night before."

"Why didn't you say anything?" Mother holds up a towel as I stand. I wrap it tight before stepping out, water dripping around my toes.

"I don't know." I sigh. "Didn't want you to think I was crazy."

"Boy crazy is what you are." She uses another towel to dry my hair. "Go on, get your bed clothes."

Minutes later, alone in my room, candle smoke lingering, I hear that voice again, riding the wind: "Aaa...griiiii....piiiiii...naah."

***

I have no idea if my human life ended like this. I want to believe with all my heart that Mother and I loved each other; That our home was clean and well-kept despite being modest; That Father worked hard every day on a farm he aspired to own. This is the worst part of dealing with who I am: the theft of any memory of who I was. I don't even recall my former name. What I do remember is one man and one woman called for me after I was... transformed... and they didn't run away. I know what you're thinking, and yes, it is awful. Few rules are more vital than the one that says you shouldn't eat your parents. But how could I have known?

Now that you know my original sin, you have some idea of the debt I owe Nature. I have attempted to appease Her by embracing a philosophy that allows both of us to live in harmony. Still, I'm aware She may, at any moment, lift me from my familiar dark netherworld to your land of green grass, blue skies, and a sun that longs to set me ablaze. This divine act of arson will be Judgement Day for my second sin which is beyond exoneration. For reasons I can't explain, I relived the circumstances of my transformation – only this time *I* was the attacker. Truth be told, I probably inflicted even more damage, such was my rage. This is no excuse, but I was abandoned, afraid, and needed to strike back at the world. There is no way to forgive what I did to her, and I will accept my punishment when it comes. But she'll need to catch me first. The fact that she pursues me is my concern. That she continues to gather power, wealth, and influence should worry everyone. What's more, her lack of a name keeps her hidden. In human life, she was Delilah, something she wouldn't remember. The moment we're reborn, a new identity gives us a smidge of certainty when we're figuring out how to survive. For me, in the absence of everything else, I knew who I was.

Having confessed my sins, I accept that "vampire heaven," or whatever it's called, is permanently closed to me. It might amuse you to know that place is also nameless. For what it's worth, I had nothing to do with that.

***

At least *he* granted me a name. This is the only positive thing I'll ever say about Miklós. With one eye missing and the other colored blood orange, seduction could never be an option. It was always a full-on attack led by teeth and nails. And he's impossible to satisfy. Never once did I see him pause to savor a victim -- something I always make a point of doing. Miklós was terribly cruel, often playing with a victim's mind as they slowly suffocated. When his prize was near death, his gaze probed every corner of their psyche, ransacking their most private thoughts. That's how he discovered my yearning to soar high above the earth, gliding like a hawk through branches and clouds. Oh, how he grinned when realizing my jealousy at how he could drink me dry whilst hovering mid-air.

"You want to fly, eh?" His glowing orb stared into my fading irises.

"I want...what you do...without being you."

"You can't have one without the other."

"Then..." A rattle escaped my bluing lips.

Hold on. Those last words must have come from her because I wouldn't remember Miklós attacking me. What I do remember is his blood dripping on my face from a gash in his wrist. My tongue lapped it up and suddenly I felt more alive than when I was living. All the world's colors and sounds seemed amplified. He actually looked frightened as my face shot forward, demanding more. It was my first strike and I missed, my elongated canines piercing my lower lip. Wresting away his wound, he threw me to the ground. Strangely, I felt no pain as I got up on all fours, only an empty stomach. Slowly, he floated lower as he stared at his wrist, willing it to heal. My lips curled, then I leapt – catching him by surprise. "You've never seen your wrist heal before. That means I'm your first. WHAT AM I?"

Fuck. My mind keeps playing tricks on me. It had to have been Delilah who yelled that – but it wasn't Delilah anymore. It was *my monster* staring up at me, crouching, growling, ready to pounce. They say trauma has a way of scrambling memories, but my face can still feel her nails which slashed when I refused to give up more blood. She snarled, then sniffed as she turned toward town. Before she took off, I repeated the last thing Miklós said before abandoning me:

"Stay out of the sun."

***

It's been fifty years, maybe seventy, since I last saw her. I was still in Rome thinking of *signore* Bernini when I learned of yet another atrocity committed in a far-flung land that defied reason. Something about the brutal nature of these slayings, plus the senseless waste of blood, reminded me of similar events through the decades. An enraged spirit was walking the Earth, sparing no one in its path. I was sure it was her but felt ill-prepared for a confrontation. Coward? I'll admit, self-preservation is my first principle. Still, that moment in the Pantheon, beneath the hole where the stars shine through, I resolved to create something better than myself, someone who could -- at some future date -- mend the tear I made to the cosmic fabric.

As I stared upward, the wind quieted, then shifted. Slowly I became aware of a melody piercing the human din: a song born of loneliness, sung by a girl on the verge of womanhood. This voice was more than just beautiful. It conveyed her honesty, her trustworthiness, her…purity of heart. But also, sadness. Could she be the antidote to the evil I let loose? Yes, I was being foolish and tremendously unfair to Fiona (thus I named her) but I was in love. Judge me if you can. Convinced of my duty to preserve her like a bee in amber, I left Italy to find Fiona and protect her from the ravages of time, from everything bad in the world... plus something acrid burning nearby. This smell, which I hated, led me like a beacon to her family's farm in Ireland. She lived about a mile from Waterford Castle, which was a ruin then. Later I learned the smell came from a fuel called peat. To this day it reminds me of something Satan would suck through a pipe while deciding which soul to buy next. Not that he could ever buy Fiona, who defined all that is gentle and good; you could tell by how much animals loved her. As I neared, her horse seemed alert to my presence. I kept my distance while she brushed him, that lovely voice trying to calm his twitching ears. My fingers ached to stroke her pale shoulders and pluck the straw from her long black hair. Had she been sleeping in the barn? Her father turned into a beast while drinking, night after night, and I could tell his hands left those marks on her neck and wrists. The world would never miss him. But his blood I didn't want.

Nor did I desire the woman I assumed was Fiona's mother. She stayed indoors mostly, only emerging at night to place a basket by the rear door. She hid it behind a bush, then went back inside. Long after the drunkard passed out, a young woman silently approached. When I first spied her, it was a moonless night, but she knew exactly where to look. She took the basket and left, returning it empty the following night. The night after, she returned to find a refilled basket which I saw contained dry linens and occasionally a tiny gown or knitted cap with chin strings. How nice, I thought. Fiona's mom was helping another mother who was obviously in need.

After a few nights the young woman stopped coming but I lost interest in her; Fiona was my sole focus. The life that flowed through her veins was special, I could smell it. When I slept, I thought of no one else. Over and over my lips replayed the name "Fiona." I dreamed of her body going limp in my hands, her whispers urging me to take more and more, making me stronger while she edged toward death. I felt blessed knowing this gorgeous mortal would be in her prime when I finally had her. But would she want my life blood? And would she agree to live forever by my side?

I won't keep you guessing but I will not divulge details of our consummation. For the record, this is something I remember in minute detail, especially her smooth, pale skin which smelled of roses and horse sweat – a surprisingly seductive combination! Her body also revealed hints of a certain history that I ignored then but would soon be forced to confront. I'll save that for as long as I can. For the moment, I'll just bask in the knowledge that I alone shared Fiona's last human hour, a memory I will not spoil with added exposition.

As she came back to life, my blood still on her lips, I too was transformed. Fiona, if you're reading this, please know I always wanted to take you back to where we became one. Of course, if you're reading this, Nature has likely returned me to dust. Please don't be sad. Just remember our time together as you gather whatever ashes you can find. It would be wonderful if you spread them around Waterford Castle, the place of your rebirth. I hear it's a hotel now but I'm sure you'll find somewhere discrete. You'll do this for me -- won't you, my love?

***

"Does this mean I'll live forever?"

Such innocence, even after devouring me. My bloodied wrist starts healing after Fiona's first bite. "Well, you'll go on living. Until you don't."

"No need to be coy with me." So beautiful, even when scolding.

"For your chin." I hand her a silk kerchief. "The important thing to know is this: So long as I'm alive, you'll be safe. But I can't

214

promise anything after I'm gone."

"After you're gone? You might as well have said `when'. Why so pessimistic?"

"So... You already know about the sun. But there are other ways to kill us." I pause. "Shall we discuss them now?"

"Maybe not. I'm hungry."

"Of course you are." Leaning forward, I grin. "I know a man about a mile from this castle, on a farm. A real bastard who gets violent when he drinks. We could lure him to the barn, share him, then continue hunting in town."

"But no women or children."

"That's right. You're learning."

"But why?"

"Women make tiny humans. And those little ones grow up to be adults with lots of blood. A fully grown man has just about what we need to survive."

"For how long?"

I shrug. "A night. Maybe two. I've never tried to find out. But we must hunt every night."

"So, we're wolves."

"And they're sheep." I rise and take her hand. "Time to look after our flock."

***

Yelling greets us as we approach the house. Him, drunk again, but this time his wife yells back. She utters the name "Fionnuala" and then a baby starts crying. I stand in front of Fiona. "I need you to go to the barn and wait for me. Whatever you hear, please remain there until I come for you."

She looks cross. "For how long? I'm starving."

Both my hands gently land on her shoulders. "I promise you'll have what you need. Just wait a little longer, okay?"

Fiona pulls away but nods reluctantly. As she runs to the barn, I quietly enter the house. The crisis I only half-expected has finally emerged. Fiona's mom holds the infant and tries to get it to eat bread soaked in milk. Standing over them, voice slurred but getting louder, is the father – and I mean "father" in more than one sense.

The woman's eyes narrow as she hisses at him.

"Defiling our daughter was bad enough. After Kieran was born, I decided to let God decide your fate – so long as you never touched her again. But now Fionnuala's gone, and Kieran's new mother is sick, and I don't know who to trust anymore. If you don't tell the truth, I will insist you leave this house."

"This is my house -- I decide who stays and who goes!"

"Is that what you decided – to make your daughter disappear? What did you do, take her to Dublin and sell her off?"

His hand goes up, but I grab it. He's confused because I'm still invisible. When I appear, his free hand grabs an iron from the fireplace. I actually let him hit me a few times in the head. I don't know why; I guess I wanted his wife to understand the threat this man posed to everyone around him. As I stare back, head bleeding, he swings a fourth time, but I grab the weapon mid-swing and yank it away. Now I aim it at him. "Come with me."

"Fuck off."

"I found your daughter's body. You'll need to identify her for the authorities."

"Fionnuala?" Her mom's eyes go wide. "What happened -- where is she?"

"Madam, I am very sorry to bring this news." I lower the poker. "But I think it best to let your husband prove he's useful, just once in his life."

"You big fucking cunt." He advances again but stops when I again raise the iron. "Where is my little girl?"

My eyes remain on her. "The woman who was raising Kieran. Will she make it?"

"Scarlet fever." She crosses herself. "Her family expects the worst."

I lean toward her. "Fionnuala is in a better place now. And you have her son. I will make sure you can afford to care for him." My voice drops to a whisper. "But no one can know I was here."

"My husband can provide for us."

I slowly shake my head. She seems to get the message. Little Kieran fusses again but she manages to calm him for a moment.

Without looking at me, her teeth grind out the words: "Do what you have to."

***

A light snow is falling as we leave the house. "Your daughter is over here."

"The bloody barn? I searched that already."

"You should've looked harder." I swing open the door and there stands Fiona with her back to us, hand out, trying to calm her old horse. It raises its head, snorts, and stamps its feet before moving to the back of the stall.

"Fionnuala!" her father steps forward. Then he stops and gasps as she turns to face us. Tears of blood flow down her cheeks, and she shakes with anger and confusion. "This place... It feels familiar but I don't know why. Where am I, Agripina? And YOU," she glares at her father. "Keep away from me."

"My God." He breathes heavily. "This is the work of the Devil." Now he looks at me. "You're a witch, aren't you? You cursed her so she'll walk among us like an evil spirit." Both his hands reach for my neck, but I'm already next to Fiona.

My gaze remains fixed on him while I whisper: "He may sound like he's protecting you. He just wants you for himself. Are you ready to hear what he did to you?"

Fiona's hands cover her stomach as it growls. Wincing, she moans. "There's no time. Just give him to me."

My fingers brush her hair, revealing her shoulder. "He's all yours. I'll be back in a bit."

"You're leaving again?"

"I'm going to a house nearby. Heaven is about to get another angel and I want to be there to say farewell."

"Make that two angels."

"No Fiona. This one goes straight to hell." Walking by, I whack the iron against his knee. He collapses into a quivering ball. "Make him suffer."

***

My beloved Fiona, I hope you can forgive me for not revealing what I knew

217

about your former life. The right moment never seemed to come up and frankly I wondered if the details you just read could still be relevant. The only part I truly regret is not revealing Kieran, but what would knowing about him accomplish? I truly believe some things should remain in the past. Having said that, I'll assure you I kept supporting your mother until she died. Kieran had long left for America and served in the Continental Army. Last I heard, he died of wounds suffered in the next war, in 1812. He had five children. I promise you, that's all I know.

Speaking of war, another one seems to be coming for us. A little bird informed me that our old rivals, who we vanquished in 1900, have regrouped into a new outfit with new technology. Not to sound paranoid, but I have felt my house being watched lately. I raised this with the Council leaders but Miklós, Konstantin and Feckless Ferdinand jeered at me. I guess they'll just keep living as they have until it's too late. Of course, they ordered me to keep quiet so as not to scare the others. I will, however, inform you at the next Solstice Ball. Save a dance for me, will you? God, Fiona, I am so excited at the prospect of seeing you again. It's been way too long.

Your ever-loving Agripina.

Stay Dead

A short story by Dan Klefstad

"I was starving, I couldn't help it." Camilla wipes blood from her chin and points. "He's in the car."

"You had ten pints before you left the house." My stump finds one jacket sleeve while my left arm fumbles for the other. "How could you be starving?"

"Okay then, he was delicious. What's wrong with enjoying a snack?"

A Corvette convertible sits at the edge of the park, red finish partially lit by a perfect half-moon. I lower my voice. "Front or back seat?"

"There is no back seat."

"Where is he then?"

"The boot, or whatever you Yanks call it."

"Please say the interior isn't white."

"Okay. It's some other color."

"Don't play with me."

"You're the one who's playing." Her bare feet are silent on the grass. In contrast, my loafers seem to find every leaf that gave up the ghost during the drought. I shine a light inside. "It's like a Jackson Pollack. Fiona was never this messy."

"You don't work for her anymore." She folds her arms. "And I like Jackson Pollack."

"Did you forget our agreement? I raise money to buy blood and you don't kill anyone. We don't need police sniffing around." I open the trunk and see a man in a polo shirt and plaid shorts. He looks 35, maybe 40.

Camilla leans her torso against the fiberglass and runs her hands over it. "I want this car."

"This car is a crime scene, and we have to ditch it."

"Not we."

I swallow the bitter truth and take out the man's wallet.

"Oooh." She sidles up. "Make it look like we robbed him. Clever."

The wallet opens and my thumb lands on metal. Oh God. Please, no. I inhale sharply, preparing myself for the worst-case scenario. Flashlight in my teeth, I look down. "Fuck me."

"That's not in our agreement," Camilla snaps back. Then she groans as her hands encircle her belly. "I'm too full anyway."

"You killed a cop."

"Okay."

I stare at her, flashlight dangling like a cigarette. Finally, I remove it. "Cops never stop looking when one of their own...OH JESUS CHRIST." I slam the trunk and turn away, gathering my thoughts. Camilla is only six months old, but Fiona warned me she'd always be reckless. I can't believe I signed up for four years of this.

"Is that what I think it is? Cool."

It's best if I hide the body several miles from the car, but I haven't used a shovel since losing my arm. And Camilla? She's allergic to work. Just now, though, I remember a secluded lake half an hour from here. Perhaps we could find weights to keep him down...

BANG

"The fuck?" I whip around to see smoke curling up from a pistol. Camilla can't stop laughing at the hole in her left hand. "I shot myself." Her excited eyes meet mine. "Coppers back home don't carry these."

"Give it to me."

"No, I'm gonna keep it."

"You have no need for a gun."

"We're in America now." She waves it in front of me. "Everyone needs a gun."

"Camilla, I need you to give that to me."

Her face moves right up to mine. "You're not the boss." I feel the barrel against my ribs. "I am, remember?"

"If you kill me, you're on your own." I stare back. "Think you can survive?"

Our standoff lasts several seconds. Finally, she grins, exposing sharp canines. "You're right." She turns and walks away. "You're always right." She tosses the gun in the bushes. "Have fun with this mess."

***

It's after seven when I get home. Camilla went to bed an hour ago. Everyone else on our street is scurrying to work, or wherever normal people go when the sun comes up. In the kitchen, I pour myself a scotch, noting I have two hours before my alarm goes off. That's when I place my orders with hospital workers who steal blood for us. Before my nap, I walk down the corridor and turn the handle to Camilla's room to make sure it's secure. I always have the bolt installed on the inside to protect my employer when they're most vulnerable. To her credit, Camilla always locks it. So maybe there's hope. When I return to the kitchen, I see a letter from Rome on thick, faded stationery:

Dear Daniel,

How's life in the New World? Is Camilla behaving herself? Despite her wild ways, I remain confident that you'll guide and protect my progeny during these difficult early years. I just hope she's paying you enough. Speaking of money, I'm enclosing a check which should help with surprise expenses. I do hope you can return to me someday. My current guardian possesses only a fraction of your expertise.

All my best,
Fiona

The check is for $10,000, not much in our world. Still, it might be enough if I were to abandon my duties and fly to the Equator where the sun shines twelve hours every day. No doubt, a spurned Camilla would risk everything to retaliate. Fiona, ever more cautious, would send human assassins, though she knows most lack my experience. I reckon I could hide for months thanks to secret deposit boxes filled with cash, false passports, and gold. I'm still calculating my chances when I hear Camilla:

"Hey."

I turn and see her door slightly open. My eyes immediately go to the window shades to make sure they're down. "Yeah?"

"Can we talk?"

I walk to her room and see a teary eye staring out. "What's wrong?"

"I'm sorry."

"For what?"

"For being... difficult."

"I'll forgive you. Eventually."

She sniffles. "It's just that I'm so unprepared." Her eyes roll. "That's probably obvious to you, but I'm finding it hard to adjust to... this."

"I understand. Fiona said it took her a couple decades. Try to get some sleep."

"I can't."

This is new; Fiona always slept through the day. "Want some B positive?"

"No. What are you drinking?"

"Whiskey. You wouldn't like it."

"Can you sleep with me – just for a little while?"

"Umm..."

"I know it's not part of our agreement."

"I've never slept with..."

"A monster like me?"

I sigh. "You're not a monster."

"You sure?"

"Yeah."

"I just need someone to hold me." An icy hand takes mine. "Please?"

I let her lead me in. We face each other for a few seconds -- she in silk pajamas, me in slacks and a button-down shirt – before she lifts the covers and slides in. I remove my shoes and lay down next to her.

"Spoon me?"

The last time I did this, decades ago, I had two arms and one grew numb. Now I see how one arm can be a benefit. I press my chest against her back and feel her relax.

"Please don't leave."

"You want me to stay all day with you?"

"You can go once I'm asleep. Just don't take off permanently. I don't know what I'd do on my own." Both her hands press mine against her chest. "God, I hate being so dependent."

"Everyone depends on someone."

"Oh yeah? Who do you depend on?"

"I... *Touché*."

She turns her body, eyes searching mine. "I'm here for you. I just need to know what you need."

***

The next evening, I'm reading the news, swiping at my tablet, when something catches my eye: a story about a body, drained of blood, in an alley. Enraged, I push open her door and hold up the tablet. "You did it again."

She's in her closet, topless, sifting through dresses. "Hello, that door still means something. What do you want?"

I step in. "Someone sucked a body dry last night. It's all over the news – we're exposed."

"I didn't do that."

"Then who did?"

She's smiling when she faces me. "Congratulations!" She kisses my cheek. "We're parents."

"What?"

"It's a miracle." Still smiling, both of her hands take mine. "Remember that copper in the sports car?"

"The one you killed, and I dumped in the lake?"

"I'm calling him Austin – hope you like the name. He's alive and living nearby."

My breathing becomes shallow as I extract my hand and grab her upper right arm. "Are you saying you sired that cop?"

"We sired him. We had sex and I drank his blood..."

"His name was Officer Jared Brown and we had sex after you killed him."

"I don't remember the order -- I don't know how this works -- but aren't you happy? We have a son." She tries to move, looks at my hand gripping her arm, and locks eyes with me. "Let go."

"Walk me through it. You were alone with him in the car, and you drained him. When did you give him your blood?"

"I can't REMEMBER." Her breasts sway as she yanks herself free. "Really, I thought you'd be happy – at least for me. I didn't think I could sire someone."

"Camilla, listen: You brought a being into this world that we can't protect..."

"*We* brought him into this world."

"...and once the police catch him, they'll start looking for others..."

"But you can teach him to survive – like you're teaching me."

"I can't protect you and him."

"It'll be easy once you get to know him."

"Know him? STOP ACTING LIKE I'M HIS FATHER."

Blood pools in her eyes as her body shakes. She points toward the door. "Get. Out."

I point at her before I leave. "We will talk about this tonight."

"GET OUT OF THIS HOUSE."

***

Finally, something I agree with. Fiona's check is still in the kitchen. I pocket that and grab my tablet. My Go Bag is under my bed. I open that and feel for the pistol at the bottom, a trophy from a battle that seems ages ago. I pull that out, release the magazine, and dump it on the table. Regular bullets. Reaching back inside the bag, I find the other mag containing wood-tipped rounds. One through the heart is all that's needed. My lone hand places the empty pistol over the magazine. With one push, I secure it in the grip.

Moments later, I'm driving to the neighborhood where the latest body was found. I'm testing that TV trope that says a criminal always returns to the scene of the crime. The alley is easy to spot with yellow police tape littering the ground. I get out, stuff the gun behind my belt, and begin walking, occasionally looking through a thermal imager. It takes five minutes to find him. He's still wearing the polo and plaid shorts, although this time he's 28 degrees and walking several paces behind a woman registering 98.6. He glances back, making eye contact, and I see him struggle. He knows I'm there for him, but senses the woman is an easier target. Consumed by hunger, the two-day-old continues his pursuit.

I quicken my pace, determined to render mortal this thing Camilla hoped would live forever. No doubt, she'll come after me for killing "our" child – for shattering the illusion that it could bind us forever. Reckless as usual, she'll disregard her safety and the universe will respond; there's a reason most vampires die before their first year. What a shame she won't last. I can't believe I'm saying this, but I'll miss those emerald eyes that flash from commanding to questioning within a second. And if this morning never happened, I wouldn't know how easy it is to forget her annoying behavior. All I'll remember now is the curve of her slender figure, the weight of each breast, and the smell and feel of her hair. The way she tasted…

This is all my fault. I broke the first rule of guardianship and am about to commit the undead equivalent of infanticide. Nevertheless, I hope Fiona and Camilla decide it's easier to let me go as long as I keep quiet. After all, I made a career out of helping them cheat death. Don't I deserve to spend my remaining years in peace? Yeah, like that would ever happen. As dawn approaches, the rational part of my brain knows I'll be dead in a week. So it really is a question of who gets to end my life. For the first time, I see mortality as a gift, one that releases you from the burden of facing consequences. Of being judged and found unworthy. And, of course, all those haunting memories could finally disappear. But if I must die, so too will this creature who'd keep on killing night after night because no one is left to civilize him.

My pace quickens as I free the pistol, ready to end a life that can only be described as a mistake, born of ignorance, with no chance of success. Well, you poor bastard, I can't promise much right now. But I can guarantee your return to inert matter will be as quick and painless as possible.

For this, Officer Jared or Austin or whatever you call yourself, you are welcome. Just stay dead.

###

ABOUT THE AUTHOR

Dan Klefstad is a longtime radio host and newscaster at NPR station WNIJ. His latest novel, *Fiona's Guardians,* is about humans who work for a beautiful manipulative vampire named Fiona. The book was adapted by Artists' Ensemble Theater for their Mysterious Journey podcast. Dan is currently working on a sequel. He writes in DeKalb, Illinois. (Photo by Jesse Kuntz).

If you enjoyed reading the book, why not listen to the theatrical adaptation of the novel on this cool podcast, produced by Chicago's Artists' Ensemble Theatre

Casiena Raether (top left) as Fiona; Andrew Harth (left) as Wolf; David A. Gingerich (top right) as Daniel; John Chase as Elevens. Photos by Margaret Raether.

https://artistsensemble.org/podcast

More books by Burton Mayers Books

Renata Wakefield, a
traumatised novelist
on the brink of
suicide, is drawn
back to her childhood
hometown following
her mother's ritualistic
murder.

£7.99 UK

A fast-paced blend
of science fiction
and historical fiction
interwoven into an
ancestral, time-travel
mystery.

£7.99 UK